Tabula Rasa

Travis Lane

i

ISBN: 9781961804432

Dedicated to my family.

Contents

Preface

If you're reading this, then you've undoubtedly experienced the same stimulating desire that often consumes me. This feeling arises from either a sudden spark or a persistent surge of dynamic energy, both of which prompt you to ask yourself, "what if?" Moments when a swarm of thoughts coalesce with unpredictable elegance, resulting in a perfect blend of conscious randomness that ignites a spark of inspiration. Not just a *new* idea. No, this sensation is far more exciting. Whatever your mind absorbs throughout life creates the necessary ingredients to forge the basic blueprints of a *story*.

Whether universally fresh, this specific sensation excites us to a certain degree because humans are inherently designed to be storytellers. You can lazily label it as creativity, but I desire to go beyond that vague description and playfully ponder the genesis of a *thought,* without going beyond my boundaries of philosophical and literary understandings, of course. To me, there is something truly captivating about the moment when a single idea arrives so passionately, and despite everything you know about yourself, you are left in awe by your own mind's boundless capabilities as it conjures up thoughts that seem to come from beyond the limits of your consciousness. This book is the exact product of an infinitesimal spark igniting into an unforeseen blaze, and I desired to take that small idea and build upon it.

Despite my lack of experience and skill in creative writing, I dove headfirst into this project. And shortly after I sketched a rough outline and the first few words hit the paper, I began to love the work but simultaneously started to loathe nearly every aspect of it. Every sentence seemed like a mistake. I would read countless other authors' works, and by comparison, I would become overwhelmed by my incompetence. But I had set a goal for myself, and no matter the absurdity and mediocrity, I was determined to follow through.

I must admit, during the infant stages of this project, my vision was unclear, and I wasn't quite sure what would become of it. My underlying intention was to complete this literary endeavor that I had started to the best of my ability. But, as the book evolved into a substantial undertaking, I realized that one of the main reasons I was able to ignore the apparent constraints of writing a book, such as my utter lack of experience (my apologies), is similar to one of the major themes of this story. The intimate relationships in my life were a constant source of inspiration, driving me to improve my abilities and tell a meaningful story. My motivation seemed to be catalyzed by the people I love and my willingness to be better for them.

Moreover, this story is *not* just about close bonds with people that assist in one's progress; it is also about the certainty of how antagonists play a significant role in the growth of an individual. So, just as a blacksmith hammers and shapes raw metal into useful tools, we, too, have the power to forge our struggles into sources of strength by recognizing their value and molding them into something positive.

So, suppose you continue past this section. Even if the content fails to captivate you, I sincerely hope that you realize the significant influence that the people in your life exert over you and, undoubtedly, the impact you have on them. Whether or not you are reinforced with this idea, taking time to consider the impact others have on your beliefs and actions can lead to a greater sense of self-awareness. Consider and evaluate what characteristics are important to you and recognize who motivates you to demonstrate those qualities naturally. An unintended consequence of writing this book led me to reflect on my life and the people I share it with, and I believe I am better off for it.

It is our interactions with others that shape us, define us, and leave an indelible mark on our lives. I owe much of who I am and what I've accomplished to the people in my life, and luckily, I have been cosmically intertwined with some amazing people; some, from the very beginning. I am fortunate to have much authority over whom I decide to spend my time with, and I choose the ones who make me, what I believe, to be a better man. I am blessed to have some of the most remarkable people imaginable in my life, and I make it a priority to cherish each moment I get to spend with them.

Throughout this story, the protagonist confronts a range of obstacles that span eras and altered realities. With only their personal insight and guidance of those around them, they must navigate these challenges while making critical decisions that will ultimately set the course of their fate. Amidst the tempestuous whirlwinds of fanatical scenarios, I wonder whether the intrinsic essence of a soul would prove potent enough to surmount adversities and uncertainties, sculpting a being of unmatched fortitude and grace.

In my attempt, utilizing whatever control I have over my fate, I aim to be a better version of myself than the day prior. I surround myself with the individuals that have the *most* positive influence on me; they know that they do because I express my gratitude to them frequently. You know who you are; if I don't say it enough, let me know. I can be better—because without you, I am nothing.

Prologue

I think... therefore... I am?

Is that true?

Why am I thinking this?

Where am I, by the way?

*I did have **that** thought... so... it must be true?*

Another region of the Sentient's mind intruded upon the idea.

Do not be too sure! You do not even know where you are.

*But I don't think I am allowed to have doubt **now**... and where am I?*

All five senses were completely absent, yet cognitive perception remained. Enveloped in an endless expanse of nothingness and unencumbered by any physical anchor, thoughts and emotions were like a surging current, relentlessly pounding against the banks of his consciousness. There was a pause in the transfer of sensory data en route to the dedicated areas of the cortex, and multisensory integration was superfluous as spatial awareness was also non-existent. Not black, not white. Oblivion.

The emptiness of the void now seemed to press down on the Sentient's mind, stifling perception like a slowly deflating balloon, causing a perpetual stream of thoughts to slip from his grasp. Eventually, his minimal control fully dissipated as an authoritative presence materialized, producing a calming murmur that reverberated through his consciousness, directing his focus.

You think, therefore, you exist, but such a notion is not absolute. Within the bounds of your consciousness, a ceaseless array of thoughts and reactions manifest, yet at times, their genesis eludes most.

The Sentient regained cerebral control momentarily, identifying a flicker of familiarity amidst the unusual sensation.

The Rhetorician continued.

Your time on Earth has expired. This condition is created to produce ease during the transition.

Avenues of his mind struggled to perceive the intentions of the imperious "Being," though simultaneously, an embracing calm pervaded within.

Condition? Transition?

Manifested as the last cursory thoughts before the Rhetorician resumed.

To prevent mental dysfunctions, an unwavering calming presence is generated within your state of mind. In the purest sense, only your character remains. Basic cognition persists but is *driven primarily by the essence of your person. While personal memories and feelings are currently absent, the experiences and influences encountered in life coalesce to construct one's disposition. These factors **almost** exclusively shape one's character. Others though, there is a bit more.*

Your presence on Earth was merely precursory. The motions of progression that took you from worldly life to the ultimate exiting of your body are a form of observance, preparation of the mind through a physical plane of experience. The next phase is a journey guided by your all-embracing intrinsic nature. You will be thrust into experiences specific to the complexities you faced on Earth, compounded with intimate imagination. Unburdened by personal realities, relying solely on intuition and the growth from experiences endured on Earth.

*An amalgamation of all that comprises you—your authentic experiences during **any** existence precisely intertwined with your cognitive framework. An expedition to uncover the depths of your character. A journey where details are negligible, but the path is paramount.*

You will be appraised with only your moral compass regulating your decisions, the very choices you made in conjunction with personal beliefs and opinions serving as the designer of guidance. Your comprehension of virtues will be put to the test as you navigate the boundaries of decisions, both profound and mundane. What knowledge have you gained from your existence? Evince the truth of who you are at the very foundation of your morality. Will you be able to know yourself and proceed with an unwavering perception of integrity?

A brief silence prevailed before the Rhetorician's last words.

The culmination—a judgment for the salvation of the soul.

Part I

"To do great things is difficult; but to command great things is
more difficult."

- Friedrich Nietzsche

Chapter One

His angered paces required a much shorter gait and constant about-faces as he had little room behind the table. His broad shoulders strained against the confines of his uniform, emphasizing his imposing stature. After a few more manic steps, the Colonel perched onto the only functional stool available in the structure, slouching his head forward as he rested his fists and forearms onto the surface. His weathered hands, etched with scars and calluses, held a preemptive posture as he felt the urge to slam his fists onto the collage of military resources necessary to execute the crucial plan.

The Colonel's mounting frustration conveyed the urgency of the situation to his men, as the constant reminders were growing irritant.

"Gentlemen, I understand that we need to execute before it's too late, but we must remain patient."

His men received the message as muffled and eventually trailed off to a whisper as he finished the statement in his lap, his fists pumping above the table as he cracked his knuckles. He was *not* impatient. His frustrations stemmed from his inability to explain the necessity of forbearance at that moment.

The Colonel and his men stood quietly for a while, silently gathering their thoughts on the task at hand. The damp and diminutive chamber was illuminated only by flickering candlelight, casting long shadows across the men's faces as they contemplated.

The Colonel stood tall with an air of authority, his military bearing undiminished by the confined space. Alongside him, the men's expressions varied—some wore furrowed brows, deep in concentration, while others revealed a mix of determination and resolve.

While silently perusing the display of intelligence atop the map of the enemy encampment, the four men were acutely aware that time was of the essence. The last crucial and elusive element that remained astray was covertly in transit, presumably already in the adversaries' hands.

Although Fort Locke had undoubtedly dispatched their fastest rider to the Colonel and his men's hideout, fashioning oneself deep within enemy territory presented its own set of challenges.

The Colonel and his men had established themselves deep within enemy lines weeks prior. Concealed deep within the wilderness in a modest cabin, the four men conducted ongoing reconnaissance missions on the enemy while living discreetly off the land. Each man's unique aroma had quickly dissipated, now replaced by an amalgamated scent of *beast,* which remained pungent within the walls, only partially masked by the white pine and the fragrance of that evening's supper radiating from the cast iron stove.

Despite the rugged bivouacking, complete tidiness was obligatory. Clothes and gear were stacked serviceably to be ready at a moment's notice. Outside the door, wild animals hung, and enzymes acted on the collagen and connecting tissues, tenderizing the meat. The brutish living conditions had even prompted most moments of leisure to be conducted in absolute silence.

Amidst the sounds of the bustling natural environment, the wind stood out as the most constant and overwhelming, leaving the men feeling vulnerable and diminutive—inconsequential creatures merely sharing the ecosystem.

Profound depths within the forest revealed nature's emphatic pulsation, giving awareness to the molecular level an individual possesses as one flows haphazardly through the vast self-regulating organism of Earth.

Living as miscreants of the wild had hardened their exterior, while the traumas of war had tempered their spirits.

Notwithstanding their remoteness, a modest port town was accessible through the woods and was their main point of interest. A substantial inlet of water stretched within, creating an advantageous connection to the coast while penetrating crucial territory. As the majority of the inhabitants sympathized with the invaders, occupancy was quickly established by the enemy.

Vessels shuttled supplies and bodies, dead and alive, on a consistent basis, and understanding the inventory of the imports was paramount. Luckily, for the Colonel and his men, the vibrant activity and size of the city provided ample cover to infiltrate the town undetected.

Commuting between the camp and the port, they would often disguise themselves as locals, donning rough-spun threads and dusty boots or, sometimes, clean-pressed military uniforms of the enemy, as the situation required. Gaining rapport with the locals was essential as the bulk of their information derived from friendly gossip with the citizens.

Obtaining intelligence on vital enemy activity developing at the port necessitated persistent surveillance. Overwhelming evidence concluded that something was causing a commotion with the enemy's collective composure. Examining the leadership, the Colonel and his men noticed they were increasingly secretive and cautious in their daily activities. Years of experience had honed the men's instincts to a razor-sharp edge. They could read a person's intentions from the slightest of movements or expressions and had ascertained that the invading troops *were* shielding something from potentially unsolicited eyes. With an intimate bond forged through tours in hell, the warriors could recognize even the most minor idiosyncrasies within their enemy. Unanimously, the men believed their adversary was anxiously attempting to enshroud activities, and they were determined to confirm their presumptions.

With consistent liaisons, they identified an eternally inebriated specimen residing in the area. Like all drunks, the man was infuriatingly communicative. After careful consideration, one of the Colonel's men recognized the potential usefulness of the drunkard's talkative nature. Possessing an astute ability to impersonate the enemy, he intended to use this skill to deceive the mark into revealing secret information.

Under the cover of darkness, and disguised as an enemy officer, he encountered the souse outside a saloon. The air was thick with the sour smell of stale beer and burnt tobacco. His disheveled clothing hung off his frame in a haphazard manner, giving the impression of neglect and wear.

Already lushed from a night of consumption, the man's faculties were diminished, and he swayed on unsteady legs. Seizing the opportunity, the imposter offered an invite to share a bottle of fine imported spirits with a "diligent officer." After some customary gab, they eventually relaxed in an area of comfort for a proper round of drinks—dark and lonely.

Drowning themselves in the social lubricant formed the intended union. Once the soldier and the drunk established a trusting rapport, he delicately probed the local's knowledge of essential actions developing around the harbor.

Secrets acquired through his perpetual socializing poured out of him most ostentatiously; a man desperate to be heard and mindful of the power of information. He divulged details about a vital "package" arriving shortly—apparently a formative addition to the enemy forces. He was spewing information to impress upon his intellect while veritably displaying his ignorance.

The Colonel's man proceeded until he gathered all that he believed useful from the nefarious individual. He then quickly made his excuses in order to slip away into the night, retreat to camp, and leave the drunk to continue his revelry.

As the Colonel's man wrapped up their conversation, the drunk posed a seemingly innocent question regarding the officer's living quarters in town. Partially ignoring the query as he gathered his belongings, he briefly mentioned living on the third floor above the post office. Despite his drunken demeanor, the local noticed a slight irregularity. It was customary for the enemy to regard the second story of a building as the first floor, eschewing the ground level from such labels. However, since the post office only contained three levels, it would be impossible for the officer to live where he claimed.

The unusual silence from the loquacious man sent a chill down the imposter's spine as he realized his error. As they locked eyes, deceit and fear washed over the drunken man's face; his eyes widened in panic, and he stumbled back as if preparing to retreat. Each man's movements were barely perceptible as they clung to the delusion that they could simply tiptoe away from the tense situation.

In a split second, the local turned to sprint away and alert the enemy he sympathized with. But before the stumbling drunk could make his escape, the impersonating officer responded with force. He theatrically unfurled his jacket and swiftly drew his broadax, cocking the deadly instrument behind his head.

An acute awareness of the environment flooded his mind, but the darkness obscured his fleeing target as the alcohol stymied his focus. His senses were near their meridian as his accelerated breathing was deafening. He absorbed the acrid tang of sweat cascading over his lips, coupled with a pervasive sense of dread. His grip held firm on the weapon, taut in his backswing; he then transferred his weight and lunged toward his target. Shifting his powerful body forward, he released the sharpened tool at the vagrant. The ax sliced through the stillness of the evening air, generating a brief *whoosh* before the thud of the blade struck the man's spinal column, collapsing his languid form face-first onto the earth.

Admiring his bullseye lodged in the recently departed, he could not help but wonder how such a skill would be useful proceeding the current campaign. The lifeless man lay face-down on the cold dirt, and the soldier walked over and firmly positioned his boot on the nape of the departed to remove the lethal device. As he gripped the handle and yanked backward, a nauseating suction sound resonated as the steel blade separated from the flesh and bone. Removal of the body would require further drudgery. Regardless, the men now had the intelligence they needed to formulate a strategy.

***

The original plan was relatively simple—expedited ambush promptly upon the arrival of the package. The package was a man of *Herculean* military prowess. Trained by the Irish Rapparees and Finnish Sissi, he had been delivered across the ocean to thwart their military's Fabian strategy.

The occupying force's current approach was derived from the Roman General who defeated the rebellious Hannibal through a war of attrition and continuous maneuvering. By avoiding large outfits of enemy soldiers and disrupting smaller movements, they had successfully undermined the enemy and seemed to destructively affect morale. Their hope was that this foreign invader would grow tired of deploying supplies and human life to a distant land and eventually withdraw due to communal fatigue.

After several successfully orchestrated schemes, it *did* appear that the enemy's traditional military tactics were growing vulnerable to the onslaught of their guerilla warfare methods. Once word of this well-trained soldier with vast expertise was known to be joining forces with the enemy, he quickly became their most critical target.

The men were apprised of this newcomer's military proficiency but were more concerned about the potential morale boost he could provide the enemy. An accelerated shift in momentum at this juncture of the war may prove fatal, and the men grew thirsty with thoughts of eliminating this impetus.

Although, the four military gentlemen were *not* yet aware of the critical information that had been discovered—intelligence intercepted by the Colonel's Spy.

As a small unit of seasoned warriors, they traversed across enemy territory and conducted multiple operations to devise a plan. Initially, they agreed to set out at sunset, giving them just enough time to establish a position to conduct a surprise attack.

They would situate themselves on high-ground, favorably positioned above and on both sides of the only trail leading out of the port. There, they would create a crossfire of inescapable hot lead, as each man was trained to fire deadly accurate shots and reload at twice the speed of an average soldier. Shooting would not cease until they eliminated the package and anyone that stood to impede.

Despite the devotion rendered to the newly appointed Colonel, the anxiousness was intensifying in the cramped cabin as the men struggled with the implications of a delayed departure.

Each man had spent a considerable duration of the war alongside the Colonel, observing the highs and lows of the human condition—an unavoidable component within the brotherhood forged during a long and arduous war. Confronting scenarios that inevitably force one to cross boundaries of moral ambiguity, stressing the thread of right and wrong. Who judges?

A natural impulse to guard against inner turmoil through self-justification occasionally precedes. However, one must be wary of the effects of personal vindication, as one's moral compass can frantically deviate from true north once thrown into slight disorder.

All the men standing alongside the Colonel had been present during multiple occasions of moral discord. In every situation, they believed they had witnessed the illustration of pure virtue, with the Colonel seeming to know the "best" course of action. The "right" decision. Although, such a disputable word and no other time is the argument over right and wrong so measurable than during war.

Without question, the men had disagreed and argued with the Colonel's actions, which sometimes seemed unfavorable to their military operations. But, after long introspection, the decisions settled, and they could see his judgments were of an unblighted disposition, as if prognosticating the conditions of posterity.

Scrupulously questioning his perception of reality broadened his orientation of the world, but such a doctrine requires pragmatic reinforcement—indeed an arduous task to conduct during a lifetime of battle.

***

Granted, the plan was set forth days prior, but recent remarks from the Colonel's Spy indicated that crucial information was forthcoming. As the Colonel stared at the map unfurled on the table, he was highly aware that his men were growing impatient. He sensed their blood was running hot for delaying an ambush on an individual of such importance, undeniably experiencing the gravity of the situation.

But more importantly, he knew to listen to *her*—his Spy; this awareness was more intuition than knowledge, and that intuition triumphed over the logical military planning approach. This instinct was established through a relationship spanning nearly the entire length of the war.

Although the Colonel and his Spy never officially met, he felt a deep connection with her and was confident the feeling was mutual. She sympathized with their cause but faced extreme emotional and physical uncertainties as she was also a married woman—the spouse of an enemy officer. A formidable woman hindered by a structured existence of her realities, she quickly and secretly tendered herself to the local forces in any form she could. This offer of defiance against her heritage was equally attributed to the hatred of oppressive rule she witnessed, as well as a rebelliousness she could no longer withhold toward her domineering husband.

Both the Colonel and the Spy were appalled by how a nation maintained such governing control over people so far away, taking advantage of the inhabitants and resources without allowing a respectable representation of their circumstances. War was an inevitable reality that they despised, and they were equally repulsed to witness the atrocious elements that accompany it. These shared sentiments eventually revealed themselves to the Colonel, and a bond initially seeded in espionage sprouted over the years and eventually grew into an intense admiration for each other.

As the war progressed, the Colonel and his scout found themselves communicating more frequently, and over time, a relationship beyond professionalism blossomed. They transmitted their messages with invisible ink using ferrous sulfate and water, which was then shrouded in otherwise innocuous letters. The work was tedious enough to create the most diminutive narratives. Still, as their relationship grew, they exerted the time and effort to transcribe thoughtful dialog, both eager to deepen their connection.

The Colonel stood within the hideout, noticing his thoughts drifting toward their written conversations. Feelings of extreme comfort regularly washed over him when she captured his focus. Even the occasional difficulties of sincerity relinquished as his reticence toward the truth seemed to diffuse when imagining intimate conversations upon their impending encounters. While these admissions of guilt and insecurities seemed impossible, even within the confines of his inner monologue, he awaited with enthusiasm at the chance to expose his authenticity.

This novel impulse toward brutal honesty with his Spy also served as a catalyst to remain focused while traversing the ever-narrowing trail of moral ambiguity in which this war had placed him.

Despite his eagerness, a prophecy of the most heartbreaking reaction after exposing his negligence toward the harmony of life uneased his thoughts. Could the depth of her disgust toward him prove fatal, lingering in perpetuity? Might it manifest as an enduring disdain, which eventually leads to his emotional demise?

No, he knew the worst thing would be her pity, the kind that conveyed disappointment and sorrow but without a hint of compassion. She would pity him if he strayed beyond the primeval moral boundaries, and the remorseful look in her eyes would vociferate his fate—*you are lost and beyond saving!*

But this fear also served as a powerful stimulus that cleared the path and lifted the fog that surrounded him.

He often fantasized about a day in the future when the war was over, and he could locate his illicit but intense infatuation. Seeing her for the first time, looking into her eyes, and feeling what he already believed in his heart—if all this fighting and agony gets him to her, it may have been worth the sacrifices.

At that moment, all the men's thoughts were interrupted when they simultaneously heard the unmistakable sound of hooves of a single horse approaching in the distance. Ample time had passed since they placed themselves behind enemy lines, and the tension was at its apex. Although, the mental and emotional strain only heightened their awareness, and they each reached for either a musket, revolver, or a broadax—prepared to deliver violence upon anyone who might expose them.

Their weapons were held steady as the battleax still bore an inadvertent aesthetic stain of darkened coagulated blood; a grim reminder of the violence already endured. The thud of two feet struck the ground after a dismount, preceded by light footsteps that converged on the poised warrior's hideout.

Advancing closer, the strides slowly ceased their pace, leaving only stillness in their wake. As the room fell further into a state of palpable tension, all were breathless, waiting for the crucial cue that would determine their next move. Seconds stretched as if time itself had paused to catch its breath, until, at last, a lone voice pierced the silence with a sharp ring.

"The funeral is at dawn for all those who shall attend!"

"But the wake will commence in the evening!" Retorted the Colonel through the walls of the shack.

Before departure to their secret shelter, they established bona fides to develop credentials of any men sent from Fort Locke to verify contact with the four warriors, and the lone rider outside was most assuredly the one delivering the secret message.

They opened the door and entered a young man of about fourteen years. His stature hinted at youth, his frame still slender and undeveloped. The mud-stained boots and tattered shirt, adorned with hints of hay and soil, attested to his familiarity with the land and the invaluable skills he possessed.

Though too young to be a soldier in their army, boys his age proved their worth as valuable carriers through treacherous territory. Most were ignored if discovered by the enemy as they were deemed non-combative. Although, this young man may have

15

executed one of the most crucial tasks in the entire campaign—delivering information necessary to cripple the enemy beyond repair.

As the Colonel looked around the room at the older men's faces, he remembered the once boyish looks and behavior emanating from the hardened souls before him now. He hoped that the young man before them would be spared from the same accelerated maturation they had all been subject to. The innocence of a young soul must be retired early during such turmoil; despite appearances, no children are present during war.

The Colonel quickly demanded the information the Carrier was sent to deliver. The Carrier then removed an innocent-looking letter from his satchel and handed it to the imposing man. Anonymity was essential to maintain on the boy's behalf in order to protect him from any form of retaliation, so the letter was supposed to be interpreted as personal information being delivered to a fellow family member. All necessary measures needed to be taken to ensure the enemy stayed oblivious to their motives.

Once the Colonel removed the letter, he wasted no time reading the fabricated story written on the paper. Instead, he immediately placed the note on the table and brushed sodium bicarbonate solution over it to reveal the hidden contents. He was expecting a long, detailed narrative of yet unknown pertinent details necessary to execute the attack. But after soaking the entire letter in the solution, only four words appeared...

Nephew of the King

***

At first thought, the Colonel was dumbfounded. There had to be more! He quickly perused over the actual contents of the letter to see if something else alluded to the secret inscription. Flipping it over and shifting it in all directions, nothing else was visible on the paper. Nothing!

The three other soldiers and the boy could also see what was written and were equally confused. The Colonel's men all grew increasingly angry that they had delayed their departure for this ostensibly useless encrypted message, fearing that it may have already cost them dearly.

The once silent atmosphere of the room now erupted into incoherent discord. As they bellowed back and forth, demanding to depart immediately, only the Carrier and the Colonel remained silent.

The Colonel needed to gather his thoughts. He was *not* frustrated with the brevity of the text. He trusted his Spy and knew she would only include what was necessary for him to understand the next steps. Conscious reasoning was unnecessary, as he might not have been able to do so even if he tried. Faith came naturally when considering her.

As he deliberated over the message, he could almost feel her communicating with him. He closed his eyes and *imagined* her soft breath falling on him as she spoke. Her voice was peaceful and enduring enough to calm him at his most egregious moments. She was his guide, his liberator, freeing him from misguided judgments tormented by reality.

"We must not execute this man!"

The Colonel announced finally, interrupting the commotion. The room fell silent, and then confusion morphed onto the faces of his men.

One of the Colonel's men spoke up heatedly.

"By what measures do you arrive at this conclusion, Sir?"

The Colonel took a moment to gather his thoughts. She had revealed the path, and it was now his turn to lead the way.

"We have been instructed to take detrimental steps to implement the execution of a man of great danger to our military operations and our freedom. I oversee this complement and all commands we have received. A task I do not seek lightly. But our overarching goal is to win this war, banish the enemy and do it with as minimal casualties as possible."

"Now, may I protest?" His Lieutenant interrupted. Since their arrival at the encampment, he had consistently challenged the Colonel, voicing opinions in a candid and often confrontational manner. While contesting the Colonel on many occasions, he continuously frustrated his leader but forced him to consider alternative approaches and abstain from complacency—a necessary antagonist.

"Let me finish, Lieutenant!" The Colonel shot back as his stare spoke more forcefully than his words.

"As I mentioned, and as we all know, our purpose is to end this war. I believe an assassination of the King's nephew will not weigh positively in our favor, gentlemen. The King's behavior has been increasingly erratic, and he undoubtedly had reservations about sending his well-experienced and crucial asset of a nephew to engage in this campaign. We must consider why."

The men now gave their commander their full attention. While they sometimes disagreed with his approaches, each man had the utmost respect for the Colonel and trusted his judgment without demur.

"If this King withheld from sending in a military strategist of such prowess for so many years, he must have done so for personal reasons. I believe he would not delay this man's contribution to the war out of spite or attempting to suppress his personal glory. This King has gone to insurmountable and deplorable measures to try to gain every advantage during this war. He kept this man from coming here either by his personal worriedness or possibly on behalf of the Queen's request. Either way, deliberately guarded for many years."

An inundation of ideas materialized as the Colonel felt a surge of inspiration. Beyond the titillation of a close whisper, he sensed a more intimate communion with her, revealing to him that there is always another way—an alternative course of action.

How could those four encrypted words reveal so much? How could an individual he has never met hold this much influence? How was communication between them so discernable when others simply could not connect? He wondered how this new and informal relationship was so capable of consuming his thoughts; even in his darkest moments, serving as a source of illumination.

"We will capture him instead."

The Colonel's proposal prompted an abundance of opposition.

"Impossible," retorted the Lieutenant. "We do not have the men or the resources to execute something that unwieldy."

"Let alone the time to plan." Another soldier added.

As they spoke out against this new proposal, the Colonel started planning how these fighters would execute such an outlandish but necessary plot. They knew from reconnaissance that twelve dragoons had recently arrived at the enemy port to retrieve the package and transport him to a more extensive fortification. The dragoons had brought with them four extra horses, insinuating to the men that the package had three personal aides with him. Sixteen men in total would be their target.

The main concern was devising an approach capable of eliminating the other fifteen men without harming the package.

"Colonel." His most trusted ally, the Captain and second in command, uttered mildly to his senior officer. "Why do you believe capturing him is more advantageous than eliminating the entire unit?"

"This man is arriving on our land and in this war on the eleventh hour. If he is executed as planned, that will only infuriate the King. Dying in battle is glorious and acceptable within our affairs. I believe an assassination will embolden this overlord to actions we have yet to imagine, prolonging this war and furthering the carnage. The faces on some of these enemy soldiers seem to be getting younger and younger, and I will not stand by and decimate children, for country or not. Kidnapping his nephew gives us extreme leverage and could arguably end this war." The Colonel expounded, trying to be as persuasive as possible.

"What do you propose, Sir?" The Sergeant and only enlisted man in their complement inquired. There was little time for deliberation, so the Colonel had to think fast and garner support and opinions from his men quickly.

"We still conduct our assassination attempt as earlier prepared, situating ourselves upon the declivity and ambushing the unit, but this time, preserving the package. He should be distinguishable by his uniform. Soldiers who trained alongside the Finish Sissi do not typically wear traditional military dress, similar to our militia fighters. He will also most certainly be carrying a longer-range rifle than the standard musket carried by the enemy." The Colonel pronounced, now pacing the premises.

"That will never work! Our ambush has been designed to obliterate each member of the envoy. Even if we succeed at executing accurate shots while preserving his well-being, this man is a war-hardened fighter who will most certainly perish before being captured. Our position upon the declivity is *not* within limits to perform a precision shot to wound him accordingly. There is absolutely no way we can capture him alive!" The brash Lieutenant shot back in defiance.

The Sergeant spoke up firmly.

"We need to create a distraction that will cause them to halt their advancement—and then strike!"

"What do you propose?" the Lieutenant was not amused.

"Since they will be taking the package and his aides through the single passage to their main encampment, we can plant an obstruction on the trail. A fallen tree, perhaps."

"Possibly. This may work, gentlemen. We still situate ourselves as planned but knock down a few trees, forcing them to dismount and clear the obstruction. At this point, we will be able to take more precision shots while they are distracted." The Colonel scrutinized.

He paused briefly and then aimed his gaze toward his enlisted man.

"Sergeant, you are a part of this complement because you happen to be the best shot in the regiment—time to prove that, boy. You will be designated to shoot the King's nephew in the leg, rendering him ineffective. Your job will be to keep aim on him, impeding him from continuing the fight but keeping him alive. The other men and I—"

"Colonel, I must protest again. Not only will that not be successful, but it will also make matters worse. These men are savvy and will most assuredly see right through this plan. We will lose our element of surprise and arguably lose even the possibility of executing the nephew."

"This is the plan, Lieutenant! I am your commanding officer, and I suggest you refrain from opening your mouth one more time unless you have something useful to contribute to the specific strategy at hand!" The Colonel was now on the edge.

But the Lieutenant interjected again, this time more cautiously.

"Colonel, I believe we can approach this more cleverly. If you allow me, Sir, I have an idea that would eliminate the cause for suspicion and will enable us to capture the nephew more effectively."

As he ground his teeth at the perceived insubordination, the Colonel knew his Lieutenant was an intelligent and capable man, and ignoring his input could create tension and discord among the group. It took many occasions for the Colonel to learn the hard truth, a truth which clarified his lack of omniscience. He understood that a true leader values the wisdom of those around him.

"What do you propose, Lieutenant?"

"We can all agree that setting up some sort of blockade will draw too much suspicion and cause detrimental impediments to our attack. The only way to genuinely surprise them is to create a situation that *appears* completely random."

The Lieutenant waited momentarily to receive nonverbal affirmation from his commander and to ensure he had everyone's attention before continuing.

"In our medical bag, we have several ounces of camphor oil, which is an extract from the camphor tree. We use it for inflammatory fever and chills. This ointment is indeed also poisonous if ingested."

A collective demeanor of curiosity surfaced over all the other members in the secret chamber. The Lieutenant was masterly at his crafts of a field doctor who constantly influenced the other men with fascinating observations.

He continued with his narrative.

"Only a few ounces of this will cause burning of the mouth and throat, nausea, and vomiting. I suggest we disguise this oil in some carrots or berries and feed it to one of the dragoon's horses before they depart. Our original point of attack is close enough to the port for this to work somewhere in that range. We would spread further out in the same vicinity, prepared for a hasty ambush, and the poison should take effect by the time they reach somewhere in that section of the trail. One of their horses succumbing to sickness should arouse no suspicion. There is one problem, though."

The Lieutenant now focused his gaze upon the Carrier.

"Your services will further be required, young man."

As the hardened warriors discussed their battle plan, the boy had been a passive listener. But at the sudden inclusion of their scheme, a surge of adrenaline flooded his body, doubling his heart rate in an instant. With newfound alertness, he sprang to attention, his eyes fixed on the warriors as they continued to plot.

"Pay close attention."

The Lieutenant advised the Carrier, then continued. "Ingestion of camphor can cause these severe side effects within five to ninety minutes. If we wrap all the oil we have around some food, that will quicken the reaction time—assuming a horse will succumb to the sickness not *much* longer than a human would. Young man, you will be required to ride to the port and administer this poison to any of the horses *immediately* before they depart."

"Absolutely not!" The Colonel decisively exclaimed. "We must not put this boy in any more danger than we already have."

"Colonel, there would be nothing sinister looking of a child feeding a horse. The dragoons will not suspect foul play even if he is caught. Colonel… this is the only way."

***

As the Colonel's beliefs contrasted with the Lieutenant's ideas, he could also sense a conflict of introspection. Instinctively, he knew this was objectionable, but upon further reflection, the Colonel sensed that this was arguably the most reasonable course of action. Acclimatizing to pressure hardly assisted in these fierce *internal* struggles.

Burdened by the decision to put an innocent boy at risk, the Colonel pulled all his emotional resources to the front lines of his mind. As the power to trust the encrypted message produced clarity, his deductive reasoning exposed solutions. Aggregating thoughts, ideas, and experiences, the Colonel calculated possible scenarios and scrutinized every detail to avoid any potential oversights that could result in needless problems or even death. Had he considered all the available data points to make this decision confidently, and hopefully, remorseless?

"I can do this, Colonel." The Carrier softly offered.

The Colonel glanced at the boy, and as he made eye contact, he noticed they were glossy with tears but still exhibiting a definitive toughness. He sensed the tears were derived more from pride than fear. This young man was no different from the hardened warriors that occupied the room, in the respect that he wanted to prove his worth and service to the cherished land.

Was the encrypted message sent as a stark reminder of the personal impact caused by war? The sacrificed pawns on the battlefield are diminutive in the campaign, but they are princes and emperors in *their* microcosmic kingdoms.

Maybe he was to reflect on his intimate feelings about sending a loved one away and into danger? Maybe he was intended to show compassion to the enemy? Either way, everything seemed to be converging within the Colonel's thoughts.

A vital choice needed to be made. He felt the mental dichotomy resolve itself. He sensed the voice from his Spy had reached him thoroughly. He trusted the plan, and he trusted his men.

"I have confidence in you, young man, as much as I have with you other fine gentlemen. We are entrusted by our leaders to perform actions of insurmountable importance. However, these situations are often accompanied with immense danger, conditions I recognize we *all* rejoice in. I believe capturing this man is necessary and doable, but if things begin to go wrong at any moment, make sure neither of you hesitates to introduce him to the business end of your bayonets!"

The atmosphere was now buzzing with anticipation as the men began to gather their supplies and prep themselves mentally. The Colonel's words had a profound impact on them, and they believed what he said—*this operation could end the war.*

Ambiguity lay ahead, but so was the possibility of freedom and salvation. Excitement and eagerness overwhelmed each of these warriors as they were mindful of the implications. And who would not want to be part of such a pivotal historical moment?

As the Colonel gathered his supplies, he met the Carrier's determined gaze once again. The child with tears welled in his sockets earlier was now a vital part of the team, and exuded an air of readiness and determination. Instantly within that room, the Carrier shed his identity as a boy as he was forced to mature by the atmosphere of his existence. These obligatory duties bequeathed upon these countrymen had transformed him into a man. The Colonel merely nodded, and the gesture was returned. A reassurance that the boy would accomplish his mission.

Their fearless leader addressed his men briefly one last time before commencing the orchestration of their vital objective.

"Men, as you value your own sacred honor and the love of which you hold deep in your hearts for your families, I request of you now to express the utmost devotion to your country. There is no truth more thoroughly recognized than an unbreakable unification between virtue and pride, and within the factions of our nation, we choose to unite and liberate our restraints, emboldening us to envision a better future—for all."

Chapter Two

As he pulled his ground panoramic night vision goggles down over his eyes, the low-level incoming light converted the photons into an electrical signal that amplified and displayed the landscape before him on a green phosphor screen. He marveled once again at the stunning beauty of the foreign terrain he was navigating.

This territory was never meant to be developed, he thought. It was never intended to see the twenty-first-century technology that his combat kit was made up of. No, this land was forever to remain in the antiquities of modernization, a never-ending loop of ancient barbarism that only hardened souls could endure.

As he adjusted the straps of his vest, he could not help but feel the weight of history pressing upon him. The cutting-edge weaponry and advanced gadgets in his possession were incongruous with the land's untouched realm.

This region persistently proved itself treacherous to all foreign intruders—a perfect haven for the evils of the world to hide.

As the Chief, he commanded a small unit of elite warriors who had departed their camp only moments earlier to conduct their mission. Like many operations before, he felt propelled into the situation, constantly aware of the intricate details, but *now* more focused on momentum, energy, and reason.

After internal deliberation, he concluded that the focus was *not* supposed to be on the details of the event; instead, the emphasis was on the precise *emotions* he was experiencing. Time is the only witness, jury, and judge to all trials and tribulations; journeys with different faces and details, but undoubtedly similar—the path remains.

This was merely another stage in a grander quest. His resolve was simple: *Just get the job done right.*

His thoughts returned to his team and the plan of attack. Accompanying him through this unstable landscape were his Medic, Sniper, and Communications Operator. They were navigating an unforgiving terrain of steep inclines, sharp rocks, and numerous other obstacles where a single misstep could easily lead a man to his painful and certain death.

The mountains' geographical location subjected the terrain to extreme conditions: chaotic collections of snow and ice buried the terra firma, while the scorching sun paralyzed the same landscape in a single rotation of the sun. These polarizing conditions scarred and defined the topography, showcasing the geological suffering endured since inception.

Land created to repel the human species, with tempestuous passages over the treacherous terrain being the only arteries supplying life to the resilient natives. Frivolous indulgences once conditioned to enjoy were now rendered obsolete in the men's minds. A sense of admiration overtook them as they understood what the local inhabitants endured merely to survive.

Despite residing in such a harsh environment on Earth, this place has borne witness to countless wars.

The four combat operators were an advance team dispatched to reconnoiter a bridge located deep within enemy territory. Control of the landmark was imperative for the advancement of coalition forces, but was also heavily guarded by the enemy. Therefore, crossing the bridge was critical to gaining a strong foothold within the opposition's refuge.

Negotiating unforeseeable hurdles amidst the treacherous terrain was as much of a challenge as evading enemy fire. However, establishing such a position was imperative.

During their patrol, the main form of communication was via hand signals as they navigated the territory—advancing steadily, smoothly, but swiftly. Each step required sheer precision, while the three-hundred-and-sixty-degree environment also necessitated maintaining their senses at heightened operations.

Their unblinking eyes scanned the surroundings for objects unusual in nature, while alert ears and active noses noted possible irregularities. The operators had only minimal areas of exposed skin: Faces, blackened, allowing them to conform to the shadows of the night; lips, to detect the lack of oxygen with each breath at this elevation; and, of course, their trigger fingers to maintain that unobstructed connection with the essential elements of steel.

Their arduous lifestyle even granted them the ability to disregard physical fatigue, even as nearly one hundred pounds of gear weighed them down as they hiked.

While their physical capabilities allowed them to endure hardships, it was their mental fortitude that enabled them to conduct such rigorous assignments. Every step they took through the untamed territory pumped their blood faster and faster to each extremity.

The depleted air at these altitudes required deep, continuous inhalations to propel them forward; nevertheless, these men were even disciplined to keep their breathing under a whisper.

***

Danger lurked throughout. Penetrating deep into enemy territory in the dead of night demanded unwavering focus and diligence. Despite the high stakes of their mission, his thoughts drifted to details of his life thousands of miles away.

Shortly before departing for this unforgiving foreign land, something happened that changed him irrevocably.

He had met someone who ignited a passion in him. This was not just a fleeting infatuation or lustful desire, but a connection undoubtedly once-in-a-generation. He was sure of it.

Standing there in the midst of the enemy, the Chief could not help but wonder what she was doing at that moment. Their relationship was still very fresh, but he knew it was unique and that the feelings were mutual. While her presence remained a constant thread in his consciousness, each time she fully infiltrated his thoughts, it was as though the world had shifted into perfect alignment, with every piece of his scattered existence falling seamlessly into place.

To evoke an image of her face, he would often envision one of her enduring quirks, such as prancing around the kitchen wearing only one of his shirts while making him breakfast or tilting her head and resting her chin on her hands, her infectious smile illuminating an already perfect face. Well-practiced mannerisms that he cherished. Those moments and similar ones were etched in his chamber of memories.

Previously, he had purposefully refrained from nostalgic exercises, as little in his life deemed worthy of recalling. That is, until her. Even on his worst days, his thoughts always centered around her, with an unwavering desire for her happiness and well-being. His intrinsic pain seemed redundant as he only felt for her.

He often wondered why this spirited encounter transpired right before shipping off to this land that all gods appeared to have neglected?

Focus! a voice within reprimanded. He forced his thoughts back to the situation at hand. With his night vision goggles firmly in place, the Chief resumed his watchful vigil, lifting the optics above his head occasionally to peer through his thermal scope mounted atop his M4 rifle for any heat signatures he might miss through the green hue of his goggles.

Abruptly raising his fist, the Sniper halted their patrol, prompting the Chief to move up and discuss the reason for the stoppage.

"What's the situation?"

"Encampment and movement about two clicks ahead."

Via helicopter, the four men were inserted on the enemy side of the river. They were instructed to patrol within a visual distance of the bridge while maintaining a high-ground position. Due to the fast-moving waters of the river on their right and a daunting cliff face to their left, they were currently at a chokepoint.

If the sight of the rushing waters was not intimidating enough, the current produced a thunderous cacophony, effortlessly slicing through the mountain as years of force and inertia created a rhythmic highway. A boastful river, as if aware it was the only

35

entity to traverse the hills so easily, carving a disorderly path through the immovable object.

The towering adjacent cliff-face exhibited an imprint crafted by eons of erosion and movement. A precipice so colossal that it may possibly reach the heavens; from their view, they could not deny it. In the darkness, the full measure of the obstacle was hidden. Visibly exposed was merely the tip of the iceberg, leaving further challenges concealed. A lonely slice of the earth ascending from the surface, prohibiting any permanent inhabitants.

Climbing the rock would require constant focus and skill. Each upward movement would increase the force pulling on the climbers, ominously drawing them toward the unforgiving terrain below.

This encampment appeared to be a strategic placement intended to impede such a unit as themselves. The last satellite imaging indicated no structures along their path. These facilities were strategically constructed within the natural environment, rendering them nearly undetectable with any satellite feed. If operations went as they intended, only then would something truly be amiss.

***

The Chief signaled to the other two men holding security to gather around him and his Sniper.

"Look, gents. There is a possible enemy encampment about two kilometers ahead. From first inspection, it seems to be a strategic military position. One of you will come with me to conduct a little recon on the situation while the other two hold our six."

He then looked at his Comm. Operator. "Drop any unnecessary gear and get ready to step off."

The unit's Comm. Operator was arguably one of the most proficient operatives in the team but was also one of the most bullheaded. Small, yet powerful in his stature, he embodied a potent force, his presence commanded respect while his actions spoke volumes. The success of their assignments hinged primarily on effective teamwork and communication. However, despite the tendency for confident personalities to rise to the highest echelons of their military position, this particular individual's recurring selfishness and arrogance consistently hindered both training and actual operations.

Personal growth and well-being seemed to be his Comm. man's sole desire, which was a cause for alarm, and the Chief often wondered if his team was truly united.

The Chief looked over at him for confirmation of readiness, and when he received the required signal, they surreptitiously proceeded toward undeniable danger.

Complete silence was imperative at this juncture. They slung their rifles to their sides and wielded combat knives, positioned at the hip and ready to strike as they stalked. A black matte shade covered the seven-inch blades to reduce any shimmer from ambient light. Handling these blades, they were certifiably more dangerous than most humans are with any other weapon.

Every precaution was taken to remain lethal stalkers lurking in the shadows. If they came across an enemy sentry, they would sever him from existence as swiftly and quietly as the perceptible organic movements of air.

As they approached the small enemy encampment, the scent of the evening's meal and the crackling embers of the fire which produced it grew stronger. As the smell of grilled meats and spices overtook the Chief's olfactory system, he felt powerless to resist a growing bond with his foe.

With more intimate engagements with his adversaries, the Chief observed a shift in mentality. He came to the realization that they were *not* fighting against people, but rather an *identity*. This revelation highlighted how humans tend to prioritize personal identifiers, driving wedges between the universal similarities shared by all. It led him to wonder if conflict truly was easier to accept than harmony and if the mind instinctively dismisses the possibility of overlap—I am *this*, so I cannot be *that*.

Within earshot of the enemy now, they could no longer lurk quietly on foot. It was now necessary to mimic the natural rustling of the environment, so the stalkers lowered into the vegetation. Shifting into the prone position, the two warriors clenched the seven-inch blades between their teeth and began to crawl. To ease the discomfort, the Chief tucked his bottom lip under the sharpened edge while clenching down with his upper incisors. With each breath, his moist upper lip gently massaged the steel.

Face down in the dirt, they extended their forearms out in front of them as the opposite knee's abduction pushed their bodies forward. Slowly and methodically, they advanced across the inhospitable wilderness, inch by agonizing inch, waiting for the wind to prompt their movements and keep them concealed under nature's unpredictable veil. The situation dictated a fine line between patience and promptness. They edged closer, moving over the cold hard ground like a serpent approaching its unsuspecting and inescapable prey.

Biting down on the cold steel helped mask the sharp discomfort of dragging one's body across the jagged rocks, splintered wood, and cold-packed earth. Occasionally lifting their heads to probe their orientation, they kept their faces inches from the ground, inhaling specks of Earth with each motion.

In a moment of instinctual reflex, the Chief halted his advance and trained his focus upon certain death. Schooled to identify objects uncommon in nature, he recognized the thin straight-line directly in front of his face—tripwire. After signaling his operator, they each pursued the wire to identify the location of the explosive device.

Moments later, the Chief located a grenade several meters away affixed to a tree. The safety clip had been removed, and the wire was fastened to the pin, awaiting a trigger to release the strike lever, light the fuse, and sabotage the mission.

Fortunately, since nothing appeared to be ancillary to trip the defense mechanism, cutting the wire was the imminent course of action. But upon misfortune, his proximity to the incendiary certified a ghastly outcome. Identification tags around his neck and boot were indispensable, given that his remains would be too scattered to recover.

Though he was aware of this, his focus stayed on the welfare of his men and the mission's objective.

Remaining in the prone position, the Chief slid his gloves off, removed the scissors from his medical kit, and slowly guided the shears. He positioned the scissors with diligence, carefully aligning them with the cable—only fractions of an inch away now.

With a furrowed brow, he contemplated just how delicate of a touch would set off the deadly device. Were the blades sharp enough to generate a quick clean cut? Anticipating that the fuse granted him only a split second before detonation, he was well aware of his limited options.

As he exposed his hands to the cold air for the first time that evening, his dexterity significantly diminished, but his eyes maintained focus on the two trembling blades of the scissors adjacent to the wire. Moving his other hand slowly, he gently grabbed the grenade. He placed his thumb over the lever and proceeded to cut the wire with meticulous care.

His teeth chattered against the cold blade with beads of sweat thick on his face. With his eyes tightly shut, he squeezed the scissors' sharpened edges together. Snip!

As he warily peeked one eye open, relief flooded him, and his heart rate resumed its steady rhythm.

***

The two warriors reconvened and remained hidden in the bushes, while faces painted black, only the white of their eyes visible. Drawing nearer to their target, the wakeful occupants' foreign tongue grew clearer, and the details of the site started to come into focus.

The tripwire confirmed what they had suspected—sophisticated enemy fortification. The encampment was significantly larger than previously presumed, and with this realization came a renewed sense of urgency. They knew they needed to meticulously identify every detail of what stood between them and the objective.

Impromptu structures were erected to house at least fifty inhabitants with machine-gun bunkers and mortar pits. Even as advanced warriors, the Chief, and his team could not successfully eradicate this establishment without casualties. It was a sobering realization—that in order to succeed, they would have to employ drastic measures. Calling for fire from headquarters and turning this section of Earth into a smoldering crater was their sole recourse.

An M777 howitzer would fire a 155-millimeter artillery rocket approximately thirty kilometers away. The missile would approach speeds of eight hundred and twenty meters per second. Streaking through the sky like a fiery comet and fiercely determined, the propellant would soar above the clouds, remaining hidden within, waiting to be unleashed upon its unsuspecting target below. Upon detonation, the rapid expansion of gas and heat would produce a shock wave blasting outward from its core at supersonic speeds. This generates a tremendous surge of force affecting an area spanning several hundred square meters. The air molecules will then rush back toward the low-pressure area, causing a sudden drop in air pressure, which effectively annihilates any element in the surrounding area. If the effects of the pressure do not decimate all living creatures, the fiery fragmentation ripping through the air surely would. Essentially, when the operators fire for effect on the encampment—nothing survives.

The Chief's initial inclination to launch rockets into the encampment was quickly replaced with hesitation when he noticed the soccer ball lying on the ground. Despite similar distractions at their base, something in his gut, mind, or heart told him to take a closer look.

He scanned the grounds again, this time even more carefully, searching for any signs of non-military-aged males. Through his goggles, a sickly two-dimensional green portrait rendered a vague layout of the camp, and the countless shades of green coerced his mind into concocting narratives. Yet he fought to remain objective, mindful of the implications of *any* decision moving forward this evening.

As he surveyed the area, his attention was drawn to a clothesline that gave him pause. An *almost* unmistakable exhibit of women's and perhaps even children's clothing appeared to be draped over the line, and while lacking certainty, the display suggested the presence of civilians.

He gestured to his Comm. man to share his discovery, but his eyes returned a look of indifference and dismissiveness. To him, it was merely data to input and process—mechanistic and absolutely devoid of sensibilities. The Chief certainly understood the man's perceived position, though. This was war. Sometimes, there were unnecessary casualties. When stripped of its defining characteristics, war is achingly illogical; unraveling the particulars, though, will erode the soul.

With the decision on whether potential women and children would wake to the chill of the morning's air, the Chief questioned his authority. From mere fate—randomness of the universe, these poor souls inherited this unfortunate reality. The children at this base camp had no profound political or religious beliefs, no personal ideals that perpetuated a divide between us and them; the absurdity that effectuates these conflicts. Their only agenda required kicking a ball around while discovering the world they fell into.

The Chief was never naïve to the polarity in his line of work, fully cognizant of the fact that he was serviced to tip the scales of good and evil by flirting with those exact lines. The risks were high, but so were the rewards.

Now faced with a grand decision, thoughts bombarded him from every avenue of his consciousness—vivid images and narratives of fabricated children consuming him completely. Survival often rests in the hands of one's progenitor, and the fresh canvas that becomes the tapestry of their lives is shaped by an environment *not* of their choosing. Even if one *could* have precursory influence upon birth, they were still bound to fate. The ambiguity of the situation was stifling.

A sense of duty to aid the innocent youth was intensifying into an unexplainable and imperative obligation. He made the signal to his man, and they retreated like ghosts into the uninhabited region behind them.

***

Once the two men rendezvoused back with the other team members, the Chief gathered them for a discussion. They shared with them the details of the enemy encampment: machine gun bunkers, mortar pits, tripwires, an element of approximately fifty combatants, and possibly other unforeseen obstacles.

After sharing the militaristic details, the Chief shifted his tone and addressed his men calmly.

"Gentlemen, it wasn't definitive, but there were indicators of civilians living among the enemy." He paused momentarily to register the micro-reactions from his men before he continued.

"The position of this base is clearly a designed chokepoint. Satellite and drone footage should have picked this up, but this section is so narrow that the cliff face could have succeeded in concealing it."

The Chief lowered his gaze and shook his head in a gesture of frustration.

"We all got a visual of the river at this juncture, and even with dropping a lot of our *necessary* gear, we would still struggle to survive those rapids. We have a similar situation over there with the cliff. While we all have the ability to climb, we would have to, once again, sacrifice a portion of our kit to make the ascent, and we don't even have suitable gear for a climb like that. And, of course, due to the severity of the situation, we simply cannot turn back. A rock and a hard place, huh, gents?"

As the men sat quietly, waiting for their leader to continue, the surging waters of the river's rapids and the wind rhythmically beating off the cliff face demonstrated their eternal force. Nature's comical reminder to the men of the impending obstacles directly ahead. Also within earshot was the reverberation of each man's pounding heart, another indication of the potential innocent lives they could end with a simple radio transmission.

Dispassionately, their Communications Operator spoke first.

"I see no other option than to send rounds downrange onto their camp and sweep through and eliminate any survivors. We have a mission. Those people down there chose to be there."

He objectively calculated the variables and presented his position brazenly. Even his body language was noticeably tense and rigid in the dark mountains—vividly displaying impatience.

Though, the Chief was bewildered by his Comm. man's disregard for the potential obliteration of innocence.

"If there *are* children down there, they didn't have a choice."

"I understand that Chief, but there were no definitive details to indicate women and children. Yeah, we saw a soccer ball and maybe some clothes, but we toss the football around to each other back at base, and who's to know exactly what was hanging on the clothesline? What we *did* see was two machine-gun bunkers, a mortar pit, trip wires, and quarters to hold at least a platoon of enemy combatants. Would any of them hesitate to blow us the fuck up if given the opportunity?"

As the Chief pondered his next move, the other men in the team waited patiently. Since the Chief and the Communications Operator scouted the area, the rest of the team was at the behest of their knowledge. *Everything he said was correct,* the Chief thought. He had no proof of women and children living there, and every detail about the grounds proved to be fatal to the mission.

Secondary and tertiary options were horrid. They could not insert themselves into the rapids without suffering severe injury or loss of essential gear. Although the cliff face was a formidable obstacle, it could be accomplished with the *right* gear—gear that they had not packed for this particular mission. Encountering a tripwire in the particular scouting route only made the idea of sneaking by undetected pure suicide, as the area was arguably littered with similar obstacles.

The team faced a complex problem with no explicit or favorable options, only a range of severely negative ones. Achieving proximate surveillance on the bridge while advancing by undetected was vital to their success.

The limited space between the encampment, cliff, and river created a bottleneck that funneled anything approaching into a direct line of fire. Obstructions and patrolling sentries were arguably abundant on the perimeters. These obstacles dared any intruder to challenge Earth's brawn in either liquid or crag.

The Chief gazed at his men, searching their faces for an answer—an undeniable solution that was overlooked. Simple and elegant, that ensured zero casualties. He knew the reality, however. From this moment forward, everything would have to move swiftly and flawlessly.

"All right, gents, let's move further up the hill toward the cliff face to get a clearer visual of the camp. I want to borrow your rifle, so I can use the scope to verify no civilians are present before we give the clear to fire. Good to go?" The Chief asked, looking at each of his men.

"Roger that."

"Check."

"Let's get after it."

His men acknowledged as they quietly but quickly began to move again. They only needed to position themselves a couple of hundred meters from their current location to gain a better view of the enemy stronghold. From that vantage point, they would set up security and begin the call for fire that would rain manufactured thunder and lightning, obliterating most materials back to the basic components of matter.

Once again, the Chief and his team trudged up the steep incline, their footsteps crunching against the loose rocks and dense thicket. Despite the weight of their combat kit, they always moved with a purposeful intensity.

As they patrolled, the Chief could not escape the thought that there might be innocent civilians down there, unknowingly waiting to be slaughtered. He prophesied intense, terrifying scenarios of what he might encounter in the aftermath of the blast. He imagined sweeping through the midst of rubble and destruction, his senses overwhelmed by the stench of death. And then, through the carnage of splintered Earth and human remains, he comes across the small, lifeless body of a child, limbs twisted and broken.

I am in charge, he thought. *I would be responsible. I would bear this weight—forever.*

His thoughts again drifted toward her and the undeniable connection between them. How could he tell her and expect forgiveness? He could not imagine looking into her eyes and being truthful. *Oh, those eyes,* he thought. They reminded him of the color of the ocean in the early morning after a night of endless ferocity—perfectly complementing her personality.

He felt an overwhelming urge to dive into the seductive depths of her eyes but knew that he could never truly comprehend the power beyond the surface. Before, he was a driftless mass, but now her eyes lured him into a placid gravitational pull.

The solar system's chaotic beginnings eventually settled into calming, rhythmic beauty, leaving him to wonder if his life could also ease toward a harmonious routine? Something told him that only by keeping her in his life could he hope for any semblance of peace and letting her down frightened him more than any bullet that may pass by his head.

Tabula Rasa

***

After careful survey, they eventually positioned themselves in an optimal area to launch their assault. The Chief then exchanged rifles with his Sniper to scan the grounds for potential reasons to abort. His Comm. specialist grasped the laser rangefinder and examined the camp. The beams from the rangefinder reflected off the distant targets and precisely measured the distance based on the time of the round trip. Through careful calibration, they would supply a ten-digit grid and attain artillery measurements accurate up to a meter—deadly precision from afar. Clutching the receiver of the radio, the Communications Operator began his transmission.

"Spartan Main, this is Spartan One."

"Spartan One, send your traffic."

"Spartan One request call for fire, over."

"Spartan One, this is Thunder Six, standing by for fire report, over."

While listening intently to the progress over the radio transmissions, the Chief diligently scanned the area through the high-powered scope mounted atop the lethal Winchester Magnum. Thick beads of sweat ran down his face while his rib cage struggled to contain his thunderous organ. Vexing thoughts kept running through his head as the coordinates were announced.

If the worst happens, will I be able to live with myself?

"Grid: Six. Zero. Six. Four. One... Break."

What kind of person will this make me?

"Three. Nine. Zero. Four. Four... Break."

I never believed I would actually be confronted with something like this. He could feel the perspiration on his forehead forming a thick layer.

"Description: Enemy compound. Approximately fifty combatants. Machine gun bunkers. Mortar pits."

*What would **she** think of me?* The dreaded thought struck his mind again.

Scanning... Scanning... *What's down there?*

As the Chief surveyed the area, more disruptive thoughts materialized. He imagined himself hearing news of loved ones being decimated similarly. Since he believed grief was a universal constant, he wondered what would happen if he acted as the agent of these fatalities. Would the outcomes of completing their mission emerge as collective-good *grand* enough to justify the massacre? Without doubt, a futile measurement.

A momentary reflection for prayer passed through. The Chief paused to wipe the sweat from his forehead, clearing his vision.

When he returned his eye behind the scope, he homed in on a doorway as a silhouette figure appeared. A person. A woman! A woman holding a child—a mother!

"Fire for effect on my command."

"Abort! Abort!"

He had doubts that his dispatcher would obey his command, so he snatched the receiver from his grasp.

"Thunder Six, abort mission. Over and out."

"Raahhger that, Spartan One. Thunder Six, over and out."

The air around the operators was charged as the intensity of the moment sent an igniting current through them. Every muscle in their bodies was primed. Time stretched on endlessly, as it seemed that hours had passed since the first radio transmission. Inhaling deeply, the Chief handed the rifle to his Comm. Operator.

"Northernmost building."

Grabbing the rifle from his commander, he rested his cheek on the buttstock and situated his eye behind the scope. The man bit his lower lip as he scanned the area below, clearly unsatisfied with the recent transaction. He handed the rifle back to his Chief and simply uttered.

"Hmm. Guess you were right."

Immense relief poured over the Chief, but concurrently, he was vexed trying to comprehend the emotions of this man. Why did he seem to be so callous toward those lives down there?

The Chief locked eyes with his Communications Officer. A stare-off. A showdown. At that moment, the energy between the two operators was purely animalistic—primitive simian beings in the wild, championing for dominance. The Chief did not stare at him; he stared *into* him. There was blackness in his eyes. No story worth telling behind them, just a history of despair.

He eventually averted his gaze from his commander, knowing full well that he did not measure up to him. In any element that defines a man, his Chief had him bested, and his subordinate returned to submissiveness.

The Chief now addressed the team.

"Remove any needless gear from your kits, and we will bury it nearby. Prepare yourselves for some climbing, gents."

Chapter Three

His fingers were clenched so tightly they began to tremble, the tips turning a pale white as they often supported his entire weight. Blood dripped from numerous open wounds, quickly hardening in the cool night breeze that pierced his exposed skin. Despite the lacerations that marred his body, he remained resolute in ascending the imposing steep in the dead of night.

The four warriors climbed the formidable cliff face in complete silence, with only the menacing howl of the wind taunting them. Each gust was a violent assault, threatening to hurl their bodies into the dark void that beckoned from below. Clinging to the ledge, their cheeks pressed against the rough stone, praying the inches of earth they grasped to was enough.

Their crimson capes wavering in the wind mimicked individual flames taking on a life of their own during the ascent from hell. The stars and moonlight reflecting off their bronze shields and helmets resembled the crackling embers within these human infernos. In fact, their forthcoming objective would plunge them into a fiery abyss of unknown depths, leaving them all with doubts of a safe return.

As lifelong fighters with minimal convictions beyond a warrior's ethos, this objective symbolized the pinnacle of a lifetime. Presumably, as an assignment neither would return from, this represented the highest accolade a warrior in their society could achieve. To lay down one's life in honor of their culture and history on the glorious battlefield would solidify immortality. For those who devoted a lifetime preparing for death, the moment of its arrival becomes a source of pride and honor.

He paused briefly on the daunting slope to check on the three men below him. As the Igetis, he commanded this small syndicate of warriors. Fearless gladiators who had now ascended into an unnerving atmosphere, leaving behind the earthly realm and the first layer of clouds below. Looking down, he gazed upon a world obscured by a blanket of white as if it had vanished into a dream.

They found themselves in a barren, hostile realm where no creature should dare venture. The rock they clung to was cold and unforgiving. With minimal areas to rest, they knew death was certain below while unknown danger lay ahead.

Yet, there was not a shred of fear ruminating within these prodigious individuals. Fear was not a *feeling* but an expendable attribute that disbanded as they evolved past adolescence. The part of the brain that harbored fear was vacant and replaced with a deep understanding of one's capabilities. When experienced early and often, fear becomes a tool rather than a hindrance. By honing their ability to remain calm and focused in times of peril produced an air of normalcy when such situations arose.

As a result of abandoned dismay over mortality, the only concern is that it arrives ingloriously.

The Igetis received a nod of reassurance from his men and proceeded upward. Maintaining momentum up the precipice was crucial, but the Igetis knew that success necessitated more than physical stamina. He needed to cultivate a fierce determination within himself, a relentless drive that would carry him to the summit and *beyond*.

This mission, the darkness, the towering wall of ancient limestone were all just variables—exchangeable circumstances within the theater of life. Within him burned a desire for ascendancy, not just the climb but to conquer personal conflict and doubt. Every day presented a new chance to surpass yesterday's efforts while conquering new horizons.

Keep moving.

Although the Igetis had trained to the point where most actions had become automatic, these moments of danger still triggered an internal struggle. Occasionally, and often unexpectedly, an inevitable "gut" feeling would overrule logical thought, causing intuition to supersede while casting aside rationality and reason. Perhaps a signal from the depths of the subconscious—a suggestive whisper that possesses an unwavering compass.

As he ascended the merciless rock face, that sensation of a guiding voice in the back of his head grew more insistent. It served as a mental cue, warning him of potential dangers and guiding his movements with careful precision. With pure intuition as his key navigator, he climbed higher into the unknown.

The wind amplified its evening howl, its force intensifying with every inch the climbers gained. It buffeted them from all angles, determined to force a retreat. Despite donning helmets, sharp sand fragments sliced into the soft surface of their eyeballs, causing unbearable irritation as each grain burrowed its way into the delicate tissue. They blinked frantically, praying for tears to cleanse their vision, as it was impossible to shield their faces properly.

Even the slightest bit of relaxation of their muscles could prove fatal. The Igetis wondered if it could get any worse—keen to be put to the *test*.

***

Suddenly, the sky lit up with a blast of heavenly light. A proceeding crack of thunder exploded overhead, causing the mountain to tremble and send rocks toward gravity's assertive pull, demolishing anything in their path. The brief strike of illumination confirmed to the climbers that their exhausting and agonizing ascension was *far* from over. Then, as if on cue, the clouds released their moisture.

Situations of amplified adversity affect individuals differently. While most falter and retreat to the simplicities of comfort and routine, some push forward, struggling at every turn but power on. Several adapt and overcome with great vigor, and the challenges only intensify their will. And similar to the men ascending the cliff, the world also produces individuals who do not retreat; they push forward, conquer, and thrive in the face of struggle—all the while brandishing arrogant grins.

As each bolt of lightning pierced through the evening sky, the hardened faces of each warrior resembled similar smirks. Resilient faces that were now pelted with vigorous rainfall. The water weighed down their capes and made gripping the rock all the more difficult.

Each point of contact on the cliff required continuous reassurance as the next move guaranteed nothing. Any minor slip now would cause certain catastrophe. Such circumstances seemed unlikely to produce smiles on any human.

Perhaps their culture's stoic customs and lifelong rituals of enduring pain molded them into inconceivable warriors. Whatever the source, it yielded the perfect creatures necessary to achieve such an objective.

A sense of unease permeated the surroundings, causing the hairs on the climber's skin to stand on end. Simultaneously, they froze in their tracks as a fading crackling noise in the atmosphere captured their attention. The eerie phenomenon was brief—merely serving as a preemptive warning.

In an instant, their faculties were jolted as a fierce bolt of lightning hammered the cliff face precariously close, sending shockwaves through their bodies and leaving them reeling from the sheer power of the blast. The supersonic pressure wave from the strike caused the rock to come alive in horrifying fury. Boulders propelled outward with unimaginable force and speed. The vibrations were so intense that the colossal structure of Earth felt as if it might collapse with careless ease. All the climbers could do was struggle to maintain their minimal hold on the vertical terrain.

Looking down at his men, the Igetis realized he was a diminutive and an unwelcome guest on this towering inferno. The mountain continued to quake as the sky maintained its luminous eruptions.

Just then, in a spurt of lightning, the Igetis watched helplessly as his second in command, the Deyteri, lost his grip and began his advancement toward inevitable death below. From above, the

Igetis could only watch as things happened instantly, but to the Deyteri, time transformed.

Falling at the same speed as the heavenly water from above, he could almost distinguish each droplet's specific qualities. His senses were amplified, and every thought, action, and movement flowed effortlessly from one to the next. Panic was a distant sensation.

Just as swift as the flash of lightning, their Toxotai reached out and grabbed the Deyteri's cape. Somehow, he obtained a firm grip, and using all his strength and dexterity, he swung the unsecured man over like a pendulum.

When he saw the man's hands finally clutching a section of the cliff, he released his grip. The Deyteri was saved for another day. Regaining a steady posture upon the rock, the Deyteri knew he would have to thank his fellow warrior later, but for now—keep moving.

The Deyteri, the Igetis' second in command and closest ally, had been by his side since their early days of training, enduring countless hardships together. Despite the Igetis overseeing this mission, the two warriors were virtually interchangeable in military and leadership prowess, and the Igetis trusted him wholeheartedly. With many hours together, they forged a unique bond. So, when he nearly witnessed his demise, the Igetis felt something he had *not* experienced in decades—fear. As beings trained to endure pain and suffering without complaint, this unfamiliar surge of terror shot up his spine as he watched his oldest companion almost plummet to his death.

Although these warriors were practically vanquished of human emotion and reason, compassion for living creatures is difficult to eliminate, even for stoic mechanisms of war. These men *truly* did not fear death, but they bled sorrow on behalf of loved ones. Forbearance, neglect, and even personal loathing can be taught and self-imposed, but love for others is spiritual in nature. It would require cognitive miscarriage or the power of the gods to eradicate.

No creature on Earth held more influence over the Igetis' sensibilities than his one true love: his partner, his wife—his everything. Centuries of tradition within their culture were powerful drivers to summon the endurance and courage to perform his military duties, which were certainly held in the highest regard.

Yet, with each passing moment, he was driven by a single all-consuming desire—a lifelong duty to prove himself worthy of *her*. That was his true catalyst. Even with his outstanding accolades as a member of society, he could not fathom why she would bother to even glance in his direction, let alone love him back.

Fear of personal mortality was nonexistent, yes. However, his dismay stemmed from missing opportunities to share with her. Despite this, he had a reassuring sense that as time together in this realm shall conclude eventually, they would forever be one.

As the chaotic storm barreled down upon the Igetis, thoughts of his wife flooded his mind. Despite moments separated from each other, they always felt connected. To each of them, even the maximum time they were allowed to spend together on Earth was simply inadequate. Even if they were blessed with a long life together, they knew their hunger for more time would never fade.

And as though she were a divine observer with a grasp on fate, she turned the valve of torrential rain down to a gentle drizzle. The once ferocious gusts had now abated to a pale breeze, a faint echo of the turbulent winds that had previously threatened to hurl the climbers from the rock.

Despite their weariness, a common theme persisted—*is that the best you can do?* If there was any feeling of relief, it was that they could keep moving and finish the journey.

***

Climbing remained challenging and dangerous, but slow and steadily, the men progressed. The rain clouds still shielded most of the ambient light, but the Igetis could see something different as he peered upward. No longer could he only observe a structure of endless stone. The summit was near! He glanced down to signal his men, and as he gazed up again, he noticed something else unfamiliar. Something moving. *Perhaps, rainwater? A rock?*

Instantly, a wave of internal perception engulfed him. A sensation that was far more precise than the primary reaction to external stimuli—an intuitive warning. And as the ineffable motor inside him commanded him to move, the arrow barely missed his head. The adjustment saved his life, but the arrow penetrated his thigh and protruded out the other end, the tip inching inside the first layers of skin on his calf.

Another arrow fired at him forcefully. The Igetis swayed his body outward like a swinging door, maintaining a grip on one side. His momentum swung him around, facing outward now, back to the rock. Keeping a grasp on a small shelf he had managed to secure with his swinging hand, he now stood iron-crossed upon the cliff.

Without wasting a moment, he cried out to alert his men.

"Arrows!"

Instantly, the other men reacted, one of them frantically signaling to a small overhang nearby. The arrows began to hail down upon them in an onslaught of razor-sharp precipitation.

The men's junior warrior, the Stratioti, was the first to reach the ledge. With quick thinking, he jammed his shield into a slit in the rock, creating a more formidable cover from the attack. As the enemy projectiles swarmed down upon them, lacerating their clothing and skin, the Igetis remained in his outward posture.

His attention was drawn out into the darkened landscape that spread for miles beneath them—momentarily removed from reality to admire the enigmatic beauty before him. He knew he had minimal cover at his current position and needed to get to the established outcrop his men were developing, nearly twenty feet down and another ten feet to his right. *A savage distance.*

Barely hidden, the Igetis listened to the piercing sound of arrows impacting the scant cover of rock above him. The enemy was so close he could smell their foulness. His companions were able to commandeer their shields into the rock face to produce adequate cover from the barrage of arrows. The Deyteri gazed up at him, their eyes locking in a silent understanding of the only alternative—jump, a leap *into* faith.

Managing pain had become a habitual practice. The arrow through the Igetis' leg would cripple most men as their minds withered at the idea of jumping; however, a lifetime of discomfort made enduring the unbearable—effortless.

Of course, an arrow through one's thigh draws attention to the situation, but it was the constant graze of the arrowhead against his calf that tortured the Igetis. While the shaft was secured in his thigh, the arrowhead continuously found fresh skin to penetrate with each subtle movement.

The Igetis gathered the necessary details to execute his next move. He met the Deyteri's gaze once more, positioned firmly at the overhang's edge now, poised to assist him.

Arrows continued to fill the air, fractions of an inch away from their targets. Each hiss from a dart was a haunting reminder of the enemy's precision and the grim possibility of failure.

With the enemy closing in, they had no choice but to act decisively and take the fight to them.

With a nod of assurance, the Deyteri indicated to his commander that he was primed to catch him when he jumped. Surveying his surroundings one last time, the Igetis quickly calculated his options. Despite his damaged leg weighing him down, he prepared himself for a forceful leap.

His actions had to be swift and precise, with no room for error—remove his grip from the stone, project outward along the rock face, and lunge for his comrade. *It's now or never!* he thought.

He then made his move, and as he launched into the air, a sharp pain shot through his foot—an arrow had pierced center mass, disrupting his approach. He jumped, but his aim was gravely altered, and gravity immediately took over.

Undeterred, the Deyteri summoned his strength and skillfully leapt along the wall to a narrow shelf as arrows rained down around him. Just as he secured his footing, he extended his arm and grasped his friend's wrist with unwavering resolve.

Although the rain and sweat made for a horrible connection, and their grip immediately began to slip. Still, the Deyteri held on with *all* his might.

With one foot and one hand planted on the slick stone, the Deyteri watched as his friend swung deftly along the wall. The Igetis' body weight threatened to pull them both down, their grip weakening until only their fingertips maintained a connection.

With the last threads of strength in their hands unraveling, the Igetis scarcely planted the ball of his foot on a ledge directly below his friend. He was secured—for now.

A renewed sense of urgency overcame them again as the relentless storm of projectiles continued to rain down, forcing them to scramble for cover. Agony rippled through the Igetis as he rushed to safety. The arrows embedded in his limbs grazed against the rocky wall, stimulating the nerve endings to *maximum* intensity.

Refuge just a few more ascents away. With one last upward heave to shelter, the Igetis looked up and swiftly shifted his head as an arrow destined to pierce his eyeball ricocheted off his helmet, emitting a radiant spark in the dark night. He made one last minor maneuver and was finally under the cover of the rock and shields.

***

The makeshift shelter was as good as home in this situation. Ample slits and juts beneath the ledge, combined with the shields they had outfitted, provided a moment of respite, allowing them to catch their breath and reassess the situation.

While the Stratioti and Toxotai, the sole archer of the unit, cautiously peered around the edges to gather intelligence while evading deadly accurate arrows, the Deyteri offered to assist the Igetis.

"Which of these do you wish me to remove first?"

The Igetis was able to situate himself on the cliff in a formidable resting place with his back to the wall while putting most of his weight on his rear and uninjured foot.

The Deyteri moved lower on the rock and wedged himself into a crevice near his companion's wounded foot. The Igetis now grabbed the end of the arrow sticking out of his thigh and broke the back of the shaft and fletching off, tossing it into the night.

"Extract the one from my foot, and I shall attend the other."

Besides the elevated heart rate and heavy breathing, both men treated the situation with an air of stoicism—complete calm and composure overpowered natural human anxiety.

The Deyteri broke off the same section of the arrow embedded in his foot, and both men grabbed the remaining shaft and tip still lodged in his flesh. Eye contact—the Deyteri sounded off.

"One… Two..."

Both men yanked the foreign object out of the Igetis' body prematurely; the Deyteri knew the anticipation of such an event could be the most detrimental, while the Igetis was typically prescient of his friend's intentions. Profound human bonds seldom require verbal communication.

Either way, the two men's actions had the desired effect, as minimal pain was felt when removing the foreign objects. A steady flow of blood now gushed from the wounds, and the soothing warm temperature of the freshly discharged liquid accelerated his lightheadedness. They both removed sections of their capes and wrapped the cloth around the Igetis' injuries.

The wail of arrows battering into the shields above brought them back to the situation.

Keep moving.

***

The warriors needed to produce a strategy and execute it quickly. Desperate to gain a vantage point on the elusive foe overhead, the Igetis fought through anguish and a debilitating lack of strength on his left side as his adrenaline dwindled. A deep wave of trepidation overcame him suddenly; it was not anxiety over his injuries or the impossible obstacle above.

At that moment, he felt useless. Their clan of warriors was akin to their simian ancestors; once a member of the tribe no longer proved valuable, they were cast aside and neglected until inevitable death came upon them. Without a sense of purpose, one is adrift in life, lacking the motivation to take action and weather the storms of hardship and adversity.

High above stable ground, the severe weight of worthlessness hovered over him. He glanced down, still unable to see the floor from which they started their descent, and considered unburdening his men by hurling himself into the darkness below. And as if his men sensed his intentions, they shifted their gaze upon him.

The Igetis looked at each of them and then peered into the Deyteri's eyes.

"We still need you," was all he said to the ailing man.

Allowing himself to be vulnerable was measurably more arduous and required more strength than the Igetis ever had to exert in his previous exploits. He drew a deep breath from the early morning air and released his pride with a complete exhalation. *How can I still help?* he thought.

Keep moving.

The light of dawn was beginning to reveal the antagonists above. Sunlight was casting behind the enemy, creating discernible silhouettes.

While the Igetis was contemplating a plan, he peeked behind cover and had his first glimpse of the perpetrators. Presumably, they were a pair of sentries patrolling the surrounding area, and hopefully, it was just the two, and they had yet to call for reinforcements.

He then considered that impractical since most warriors would believe they were capable of extinguishing combatants in such an ideal situation.

When the onslaught of arrows ceased, the enemy began hurling rocks down in an attempt to dislodge the shelter of shields they created.

An idea emerged! They had one of the best archers in the unit—time to use him. He revealed to his men what needed to be done, and they immediately took measures to conduct the plan.

71

The Stratioti and the Igetis planted themselves on each side of the overhang while the Deyteri removed his cape, tied it to the Toxotai's cape, and then secured it around his waist. The other end was fastened to the waist of the Toxotai.

Acquiring a firm grip on the cliff, the Deyteri pressed his entire body into the precipice as his cheek kissed the cold stone. He needed to support the punishing weight of two men with minimal surface area to grip. The Toxotai directly below the Deyteri lowered himself slowly, attempting to cause as little stress on the powerful man supporting his weight.

Once he lowered himself to where there was no slack in the knotted capes and his body perpendicular to the wall, he fixed his bow and arrow. One arrow at the ready with another secured in his mouth.

Each man would have to work in unison to accomplish this plan. The Igetis *was* needed. They all shared glances and nodded in agreement—failure was not an option.

The Toxotai bent his knees into a squat position vertically on the rock face; an arrow pulled back with ferocious tension on the bow. Every vein bulged on the Deyteri as he clenched the vertical Earth, bearing the weight of two. Securing one's weight on the cliff face was an insurmountable challenge, and now he held the load of another man along with the weight of *his* life.

Instantaneously the two men on the flanks of the ledge peeked out to draw attention from the enemy. As anticipated, a barrage of arrows followed, one of which grazed the Igetis' shoulder, slicing through the first layers of flesh. Concurrently, the Toxotai propelled himself outward into the open air. The bounded capes and the strength of the Deyteri were the only elements keeping him from plummeting rapidly toward the ground.

Suspended in the night at full extension away from the cliff, he released the retracted arrow upward, slicing through the air with a whistle and a blur. With unerring accuracy, the sharp arrow impaled one of the enemy sentry's esophagus—silencing him for eternity.

As the improvised pendulum swung him back to the cliff, he removed the second arrow from his teeth. He was able to position it in the ready just before his feet touched the vertical rock again. Without delay, he shot himself outward once more. And yet again, the cinch around the Deyteri's waist tugged on his hips. He ground his teeth as his fingers held firm on the rock with extreme determination. The strain was immense, and as he struggled to keep his grip, he felt a sharp pain shoot up his finger as a nail splintered and broke free.

Out into the open air again, the Toxotai released the second arrow into the night. Even before the acknowledgment of his companion's demise and the hiss of the arrow were noticeable, the spear sliced through his jaw.

Everything was momentarily quiet until the second sentry's body came crashing onto the ledge shielding them. Briefly, the men got a glimpse of the man before he slid down; fletching and shaft of the arrow protruding out of his gaping mouth as the sharpened tip poked through the top of his head. His lifeless eyes seemed to stare at the men in bewilderment; *"how?"* was what they registered. His body eventually continued its descent into inevitability.

A collective laugh consumed the gentlemen on the cliff in the early morning light. The euphoria and elation were *not* from the carnage they delivered but the reality of their dominance over any situation thrown at them, and a wave of godlike strength coursed through their blood at that moment. Somehow, the plan had worked, and they were safe—for now. Resilience, creativity, and teamwork combined with immense grit created this indomitable force perched upon the precipitous rock.

However, the mission remained unfinished, and the men gathered themselves to continue their ascent. One limb virtually useless, the Igetis told himself, *to keep moving.*

***

Tabula Rasa

Each inch of ascension shot excruciating pain through the Igetis' leg. He possessed the ability to stifle the piercing bursts of agony, but he feared the weakness it delivered upon him.

They needed to reach the summit in order to properly triage his wounds, and fresh blood continuously seeped through his gashes, causing dizziness in a situation where absolute attentiveness was critical. His surroundings warped, his vision clouded, and every move was a desperate attempt to cling to life. On several occasions, his feet slipped, causing his head to slam into the solid surface he climbed—stymieing his focus even further.

Two of his men were directly below him, as one stayed by his side. In and out of consciousness, the Igetis somehow remained clutched to the wall. Images began to conjure before him. Visions of being home with his wife, lying in bed together into the long morning hours, a common ritual of theirs.

He could feel her warm skin on his now. Tasting her breath as their lips touch. Sitting up in bed, she straddles him, kissing his face and reveling in the closeness of their bodies. She then gently pushes him back, and he relinquishes his grip, falling. In slow motion, he descends onto the linens and cushions reminiscent of clouds, falling blissfully into the unknown, staring intently into her eyes before he closes his own. Falling.

***

A flickering light brought a confusing awareness back into his mind. The ambient light blinded him, but the cool ground on his backside offered comfort as his eyes struggled to open. He could hear rustling, but nothing made sense, memory muddled and bemused. The air was fragrant with a sweet, damp scent reminiscent of spring, providing a serene calmness.

Am I home? he asked himself. His initial attempt at movement ensued a searing pain in his leg, which immediately brought him back into focus and sent reminders of the evening's exploits. The Igetis groaned as he contorted his body slowly to position himself on his side.

All details flooded back into him as he regained composure, all but the final arrival at the peak. The sun had fully broken above the horizon and was soothing to the men after an evening fastened to a cold, wet rock. The Igetis blinked until his vision cleared.

His three companions sat close by, watching him vigilantly as they now held back grins upon his revival. He smiled back at them, relieved to be surrounded by such virtuous men, fully aware of what they had done for him in those last moments of the climb. Sentiments were unbefitting in this company, and the task remained, so little was needed to be expressed toward the men.

"Looks like *I* needed *you* instead. Let's keep moving."

Chapter Four

Rich rustic dunes enveloped the landscape in an uninterrupted panorama, and as the wind swept across, it left transient ripples in its wake. Soft ground lay underneath his feet as he seemed to glide over the terrain, his gait stretching far beyond familiarity. Even walking necessitated modifications. Due to the atmospheric conditions and the diminished gravity on this alien planet, a period of acclimatization to the new environment was obligatory.

The air tasted foreign to him, starkly contrasting with the familiar Earthly atmosphere. While it was *not* entirely "natural," it offered a sense of security. Each breath resembled a deep inhalation from a scuba regulator; an oddly satisfying sensation in the unfamiliar environment. Though unnatural, the first few successful inhalations prompted a calming acceptance.

While the composition was similar to Earth's, the atmosphere displayed a slight reddish hue within the blue sky as the sun broke the vast horizon—a dazzling portrait resembling the complexity of beginnings. *Better to witness beauty than to understand it.*

Hopefully, the precarious encounter with their adversary had not divulged their presence to other combatants. Bloodied and battered from the enemy's attack just moments ago, he was now healing rapidly due to the advanced medical kits they carried.

He could feel the zinc oxide nanoparticles in the hydrogel-based wound dressing working quickly and efficiently to close the deep lacerations on his leg. The composite bandage's warm fizzing sensation promoted wound diffusions' absorption, activating platelets and blood clotting almost instantly. These unusually rapid homeostatic processes allowed for quick and effective healing.

Ages ago, this type of injury would have required serious medical attention and quite possibly resulted in death. Now in mere minutes, he returned to full capacity.

Voyaging through this unfamiliar world caused him to reflect on the marvels of humanity's accomplishments. Previous generations seeded this desolate world with algae, which converted the water, nitrogen, and carbon dioxide into organic compounds. As the removal of carbon dioxide from the alien planet's atmosphere ensued, the greenhouse effect diminished, and surface temperatures settled to hospitable levels.

The atmosphere had not quite reached the normal nitrogen and oxygen concentrations to recreate Earth's atmospheric air, but he and his Strike Team could survive without breathing apparatuses. This terraformed world was now populated with a vast number of humans and various other species, an experimental subculture cultivated from the original cradle of civilization.

Now though, a civilization of mutinous inhabitants.

Tabula Rasa

As Earth has had countless generations of organisms collaborating in harmony and dissonance, this ecosystem was still in its infant stages. It was thrust into a condition of ecological balance previously forged over eons—evolution accelerated to a reckless pace.

In some regards, being unburdened by certain aspects of the past *could* work to one's advantage in shaping the future; learn but leave behind all the horrors of antiquity created by descendants. Slavery, war, racism, greed, envy, lying, and unnecessary violence could all be distant memories, as a change in environment could breed a societal character transformation. A fanatic new idea that this next iteration of humans had developed and practiced.

Intending to regain control over the central communications hub as well as the entry and exit ports, the Commander and his Strike Team had covertly implanted themselves onto the foreign planet.

The local insurgents had taken captive all the representative leaders from Earth who previously governed the peripheral world. This was in response to a widespread sentiment among the inhabitants of the infant ecosystem, as their patience waned and now refused to be subjected to the authority of a ruling power situated millions of miles away.

Earth had become reliant on the export of rare metals extracted from the soils of this virgin world and took advantage of their supremacy. For years, the obedient residents had reluctantly obliged orders from the commanders afar. Things were changing now. Revolution was in the midst.

***

Due to a combination of advances in science and technology and the global neglect toward the health of the planet of origin, the occupying nations joined together to create this alien land the Strike Team now stood on. For the first time in human history, the entirety of Earth's population agreed and worked together to bolster the continued existence of its species.

Throughout time, every generation has been challenged by resistors to change despite the abundance of examples that the world is eternally mercurial. Continuously evolving, *life* leaves disruptors in its wake, leaving them only to question their reticence to embrace change.

An organism will go to insurmountable measures to guarantee its survival. In the case of humans, they were required to enroll in unprecedented actions—unity. For the first time, it appeared terrestrial "intelligent" beings broke away from the "us and them" mentality, and a societal epiphany registered; *we* have to work as *one* to survive. Like the

Serengeti, after the rush of water saturates the soil, prosperity flourished for human civilization.

Working together toward progress and abundance eventually replaced survival necessities, which then further fueled advancements in science and technology that seemed unattainable only years prior. Colonizing a foreign planet was now the zenith of human accomplishments. But that achievement forged an age-old dilemma engrained in human biology. Separating the species so far apart rejuvenated the disparity among humans while constricting the evident and abundant similarities previous generations had also overlooked.

The primitive human brain had *not* advanced as quickly as its accomplishments and ambitions indicated.

Prosperity and abundance were cultivated for all, but once the reality that Earth and its inhabitant's survival relied on the output of the newly formed planet, division ensued. Working together for opulence evolved into working for *us*. Instead of teams representing occupants from both worlds, Earth sent subjects to regulate all activities, undertaking ancient tactics proven to be immensely flawed over generational attempts.

The architects of this global experiment envisioned a clean slate with the opportunity to learn from past experiences and cultivate growth and progress. But human behavior occurred—an incessant craving for its most precious commodity—more. Caught in an endless loop on the hedonic treadmill, it's easy to forget the philosophical principles of necessities.

The local inhabitants stood unwavering in their convictions and refused to succumb to the suppression imposed upon them by their matriarch planet. They revolted. They refused to sit idly by without representation of operations concerning existence within their realm.

As the banishment of Earth's commanding forces commenced and communication and exports to the origin planet ceased, Earth collapsed into a frenzied rage. Threats from afar landed on the flippant ears of the mutinously controlling forces of this planet. Earth had become dependent on them, and with their overpowering forces, they were perfectly capable of seizing power through violent methods, but not without severe damage to the vital facilities and habitat.

The celestial beings recognized Earth would not dare risk severing such a crucial limb of their social and economic systems and felt at ease with their positioning.

However, unbeknownst to the planet's occupants, the government of Earth had deployed a small unit of soldiers to infiltrate their domain. Instructed to subdue the wayward citizens and return them to the structure of subservience that the Earthlings desired.

Immediate action was crucial, and if Earth failed to secure command soon, all would be out of its grasp for the doddering planet. Therefore, his team was sent.

The Commander of this Strike Team narrowed his priorities, as those details had become superfluous to him. Parts of his mind seemed lost in a dense mist that relentlessly distorted his judgment, leaving him mechanical and devoid of emotion.

All his efforts were directed toward fulfilling the mission objective. But while the Commander covertly advanced his team to the target zone, his mind went to an infrequent location as a feeling of tenderness for the inhabitants welled up within him. Peeling back the layers of the particulars and narrowing his scope allowed a portrayal that transcended his perspective.

He then realized that was the first time he considered the introspection of the people he was sent to appropriate. This was a startling realization as his thoughts over the past few years had become increasingly clouded. A preoccupation with his own emotions neglected his gauge and dampened his ability to relate to others.

***

With a silent gesture, he beckoned his team to gather around him, their movements carefully calculated to avoid detection by any possible onlookers. The warriors were clad in sleek, state-of-the-art gear that epitomized technological warfare. Their suits, a seamless fusion of advanced alloys and adaptive fabric, molded to their forms like a second skin, offering both protection and flexibility. From their integrated visors, a stream of data flowed, displaying vital information and tactical overlays, granting them enhanced situational awareness and the ability to analyze their surroundings in real-time.

They had reached a hidden position that granted a clear view of the communications and launch site they planned to breach. But as the sun broke the horizon, its light crept across the sky with a steady, relentless momentum, and they no longer had the ally of darkness; the world around them was now exposed and vulnerable. There was even uncertainty about whether their presence on this planet remained undisclosed.

Their obstacle was a cosmodrome of gargantuan size—a true testament to the constantly assiduous collaboration between engineering and human ingenuity. During its peak activity, this spaceport shuttled and received no fewer than fifteen spacecraft per week, carrying passengers and cargo. Now, it lay dormant.

Just ahead stood the operations facility, encompassing the ports, logistics, and processing centers. Yet, it was the central command center—the Strike Team's primary objective—hidden within the walls. Extending to their right were the planet's communication and power grids, a boundless panorama of solar arrays, nuclear generators, and battery sources. An ocean of metal and glass bestowing new value to the term "man-made."

Located on the far side of the facility were the launch sites and fuel centers. Protected by a massive bastion, the fuel centers featured enormous electrolyzers that extracted moisture from the air, separating the oxygen and hydrogen—the primary fuel for the rockets.

A small fence roughly two meters high surrounded most of the compound, mainly used to protect the citizens and creatures inhabiting the area. Acts of violence or obstruction of the status quo were virtually nonexistent in this civilization, and little security was needed at any institution. Favorable conditions for him and his team.

Nonetheless, the wall was outfitted with a laser imaging, detection, and range scanning network. This system relays the surveyed data to an artificially intelligent 3D perception software program that classifies objects and determines if triggering an alarm is necessary. It also pinpoints the exact location of a threat, thus providing a complete and nuanced perspective of the compound's security perimeter. *Not* favorable for him and his team.

While located just outside the range of being detected, they prepped for their systematic insertion into the facility.

The Commander addressed his squad. "All right team, we are just under three kilometers from the wall. The laser recognition software is operating on a 905-nanometer wavelength that pulsates without interruption. We can't stop it entirely, but lucky for us, the techies have outfitted us with a device that can pulsate the same registered environment *just* scanned for about two minutes. Basically, we will be invisible to the sensor for a brief moment.

"In order for us to get into position and scale the wall before the sensors start working effectively again, we have to move quickly from this position and jump on the move, which I understand may create another issue. Traveling at that speed needed to beat the clock and avoid detection while jumping could make it difficult to control our landing—*if* we do land.

"I can position myself behind the team and secure each of us directly after we ascend above the wall. Like we planned, our sole objective is to activate the satellite controls in order to give Earth's command center complete control of their power grid. We all know the dimensions of that building inside and out, so if we get separated, make your way to the objective as quickly as possible. All it takes is one of us to activate the device, and I think we all know how outnumbered we will be.

"According to Earth's command, after today is over, they will lose the final satellite connection able to have a shred of contact and any control over this planet. We are the last hope. It won't be easy. It will probably be messy, but we have to get it done."

With that, he took a moment's pause to look at his team members, ensuring they all were clear in their objective.

"All right, activate your boots, and I will give the signal when to take off."

Since the atmosphere provided less gravity than Earth, running caused the time between each footstep to increase, keeping them elevated above the ground and reducing their maneuverability across the land.

To increase their mobility, the team would deploy two magnetized ball bearings composed of a flexible silicon material situated at the toe and heel of their boots. The bearings would manifest from nanoparticles embedded in the sole, lifting them slightly off the ground while sensors intricately connected every surface of their footbed to the ball bearings.

Resembling a hoverboard, the team's specialized footwear allowed them to make sudden movements through weight displacement, ensuring swift stability across any terrain. The rolling spheres attached to their boots also served as anchors, enabling them to maintain an established connection to the surface and effectively eliminating gravity's effect.

"Hey Commander, make sure you snag us and pull us back safe. We are all counting on those skills." One of his team members spoke up before departure, delivering a wink with the comment while prepping for takeoff.

Their Commander coldly grinned back but in good enough humor before belting his command. "Remember, we have two minutes—ready for launch in three...two...one. GO!"

They activated the temporary laser-imaging disabler and then bolted forward on their MagBoots, kicking up a plume of red dust in their wake. With each push, the Strike Team screamed across the surface of the strange planet, navigating around the lethal obstacles scattered throughout the ecosystem. Zipping over the landscape, they would be a perplexing blur to any onlookers.

The Commander glanced swiftly at his watch—they had one minute to reach the wall. Just as he returned his gaze forward, the automatic mechanism in his brain initiated a state of alert with a massive rock approaching! Absolutely no thinking, pure instinct.

With only milliseconds to react before impact, he quickly shifted his weight leftwards, allowing only his right boot to slam into the stone, torquing his body into a rotational frenzy. Everything turned into a mosaic blur. Fluids suspended throughout his vestibular system were beyond disrupted, which severed his balance and spatial orientation, forcing him to calibrate with what minimal sight he still had.

The only certainty was that he was still upright, spinning on the bearings. Amidst the trepidation, his body's automatic response prevented him from being hurled across the desert like a rag doll. It was as if a dormant part of his brain came to life, enabling him to maintain composure and stability in the absence of analytical reasoning. He reacted and shifted his weight down into his heels, slowing his spin and momentum. A cloud of red dust exploded into the air as if a comet had struck the surface.

The Commander achieved stability, but his composure was spinning on-axis. Focusing seemed impossible as he struggled to return his balance to equilibrium. Another signal from his brain then alerted him to the sensitivity of time. He batted his eyes and spotted his team members on the blurry canvas that was his sickened vision. Head down again, he leaned forward and took off after them—*thirty seconds until exposure.*

Approaching the wall at high speeds, the three comrades ahead readied themselves to jump while the Commander lagged far behind. To soar over the wall, the resilin in their boots would have to "react" as they sprang forward—a synthesized protein found in many insects and now embedded within their boots allowed them to propel distances up to five times their height.

Since time was an issue, they had no choice but to leap at full speed. Moving that fast and the considerably low gravity, there was no predicting how far they could project themselves if not intercepted—*ten seconds until exposure.*

The Commander purged forward, knowing time was defeating him—*five seconds until exposure.* Charging ahead, his other senses were coming back online. Rusted dirt spewed as he carved his track in the terrain. *Four.* The Commander watched his team vault into potential oblivion. His analysis indicated he would arrive too late. *Three.* If he idles, they are lost forever. He prematurely ascends, doubtful he will make it. *Two seconds until exposure.* He reaches for them—a hopeless distance. *One.*

The laser activates.

The laser's sensors were miraculously out of reach. With the Commander barely clearing the wall, he and his team remained suspended, levitating into uncertainty. The team flailed about as they gravitated further away from safety.

It was now or never to secure their fate. A current of panic and despair charged the air as the squad advanced further away. Suddenly, they each felt a sharp tug at their waist, halting their movement. Remarkably, they were snagged by their belts, with a single finger from their Commander's hand, despite being several meters away.

Like a serpent's tongue, his fourth finger swiftly extended and latched onto a nearby pole, securing their anchor to the surface.

Slowly, he and his team descended back toward the ground in the faint gravitational atmosphere.

As they reassembled, the Commander's arm returned to natural form. His entire left arm resembled a metallic muscle in both image and tactile quality. Once entirely flesh and blood, this appendage was now transformed into a fearsome weapon that set him apart from his fellow hominids.

***

As a predominantly pacifistic society, this generation was unacquainted with war. Only a small outfit to police homeostatic disruptors and a space fleet were necessary. The space fleet were stewards of planetary travel—coast guards of the cosmos, trained to breach any rogue shuttle and occupy either planet interchangeably. Perpetual travelers. And in case of alien invasion, they were the first line of defense. Fashioning himself within this lifestyle, the Commander faced a hostile scenario only one other time, which nearly cost him his life.

With his fleet at the time, the Commander was tasked with intercepting interplanetary thieves who had seized a cargo ship of metals being shuttled toward Earth with the intent to hold ransom. With superior technology, the space fleet's spacecraft could disable the vessel's controls and attach themselves to any ship for inspection once positioned at a certain distance.

Travis Lane

Eventually, he and his team caught up to the space bandits and docked themselves alongside the stolen vessel. Detaching from his pilot's harness and swimming through the zero gravity chambers, the Commander proceeded to board their craft. He moved his way up to the docking mechanism, which separated him from the criminals, and with a signal, a series of metallic clanks and whirs ensued as the first door opened.

As he approached the intermediary of the two crafts, a jarring alarm sounded, causing him to halt in his tracks. He quickly placed a hand on the ceiling to alter his momentum and prevent himself from floating further. As he pivoted back toward his team, the criminal's ship detached! The emergency doors activated, sealing the vessel instantly and *anything* in its path.

It is common not to immediately feel an amputation when administered so suddenly. Only when he spotted the floating blobs of blood did he realize his left arm was missing. He examined the stump where his arm used to be and almost admired the surgical detachment, and then a brief pulse of thought struck him—fragile.

With the shred of sensibilities still available, the Commander assumed he would faint in such a situation, so he acted as such, but the attempt to escape the pain and shock was hopeless. Unable to break out, he returned to the center of chaos and began to wail.

92

The other crew members floated toward him, but their approach was violently disrupted as the shuttle convulsed from the explosion of the thieves' ship. The foolish attempt to discharge ruptured a hole in their emergency seal, causing a drop in pressure inside the shuttle cabin. This led to a malfunction that ignited the liquid hydrogen.

An eerie silence followed the bright flash and explosion. The space fleet's ship remained intact as the thieves were obliterated into millions of fractions, now representing cosmic trash destined to scour the endless void of space for eternity.

The other members of the space fleet finally reached the Commander, wrestling him into submission from his erratic flailing. As blood spewed from his severed arm, globules of crimson danced about, steadily filling the cramped confines of the spacecraft while constructing a kinetic collage of horror.

Acting quickly, the crew sprayed the nub with hydro-gel nanoparticles designed to clot and heal. In an instant, the wound was cloaked in a firm layer of dressing, though not without leaving its mark in a maelstrom of mayhem. For the Commander, losing consciousness arrived *too* late but welcomed, nevertheless.

The Commander awoke in a hospital on an interplanetary space station. He could feel the gravity pulling down on him due to the station's rotational movements—a satisfying awareness. His surroundings were adorned with gleaming metal surfaces and streamlined medical equipment. Soft futuristic lighting bathed the room, while the faint hum of advanced technology moaned in the background.

Once the initial confusion subsided, the reality of *why* he was there swallowed his spirit. The covers that hid his disfigurement taunted him, and he lacked the strength to inspect. He was aware that the Cyberphysician would 3D print a replica of his arm using his DNA, but the idea of possessing a partially "artificial" limb was still profoundly unsettling. He lay there, quiet and still, breath shallow, with his gaze fixed on the ceiling, yearning for the familiar sanctuary he had so foolishly surrendered.

A phantom feeling in the fingers of his severed arm reminded him of the brain's unforgiving nature. The vast network of interconnecting neural structures in his brain refused to acknowledge his arm's defectiveness, taunting the emotional reasoning parts of his mind, which were absurdly creating the illusion that his fingers were wiggling underneath the blanket. *How strange.*

The Commander found it even more bizarre to notice the blanket moving in sync with his fingers' "phantom" sensations. He then flung the blankets across the room to reveal his arm for the first time. No, not *his* arm. The components of a human arm were there: fingers, hand, elbow. But this was not flesh and blood;

instead, a gray, fibrous material was pulsing and shifting in every direction with the slightest instruction. Reeling from the unexpected sight, panic took over, and he shot out of bed.

Completely unrestrained, his artificial arm stretched and twisted, thrashing about, and destroying the room and all that came in its way. Hospital equipment and furniture slammed and shattered into the walls, floor, and ceiling. His screams were a violent blend of terror and fury—a conscious seizure—feeling every bit of his epileptic destruction.

As his arm continued to contort and convulse, its movements seemed to be fueled by a malevolent force writhing in agony and desperation. The chaos brought in a flurry of technicians, unexpected by his premature revival and mayhem, and had it not been for the prompt action, he may have easily killed himself or others.

Upon awakening the second time, he realized he was restrained and monitored by a team of strangers. They proceeded to inform him of the "consensual" surgery conducted after his accident. Using artificial fibers derived from spider silk, scientists designed an advanced compound capable of immense strength, elasticity, and energy-absorbing capabilities. By combining that material with synthetic neurons intertwined with his own, the doctors had equipped him with a vicious bionic weapon. The Commander was no longer fully human.

With the healing process nearly immediate, he began training in the subsequent weeks to control every aspect of his arm. The biomimetic material allowed him to transform his new appendage into nearly any configuration, and due to the immense elasticity, any manifestation his arm embodied scarcely diminished the strength of the substance.

With refined dexterity and speed, he could discharge each finger up to three times his height in opposing directions, facilitating a lethal organism in close quarters. While this new "tool" proved helpful and, at times, exciting, he would often stare discouragingly at it. The eerie cinereal alloy. Supernatural convulsions incessantly denying any respite. That sickening nexus of human tissue and spider silk matter. Every detail was an unsettling departure from his humanity while pulling him closer toward a state of aberration engulfed in delirium. Thus, he removed himself, and alone he remained.

***

Collecting their bearings, the team gathered near the wall and prepared to make their subsequent movements toward the command center. The urgency of the situation left no time for reflection on past events.

"Move!" The Commander ordered.

Mobilizing their MagBoots again and launching ahead, they arrived promptly at the nearest section of the building. Their eyes darted around, searching for the entrance necessary to breach, and once spotting the robust hatch, they wasted no time infiltrating.

Employing his insect-derived arm again, the Commander compressed his hand to a durable gelatinous form and effortlessly seeped through the narrow cracks in the door. The malleable nature of his appendage found its way through the labyrinth of crevices like a river forming fresh tributaries on the dry landscape.

Once penetrated within the fissures, he manipulated the locking system, and with a satisfying hum, the lock disengaged.

Guns drawn, and at the ready, the men began their approach on foot. Roaming the hallways of the lower level, they poured in and out of rooms, scouring for anything worthwhile.

Turning a corner, they were confronted by two unidentified figures. Both groups froze in a moment of tense silence. Without further delay, the Commander and one of his team members quickly fired their guns, dropping the unarmed targets where they stood. The bodies quivered and convulsed before eventually settling lifelessly on the cold, hard floor.

Each man was armed with an electron gun powered by a miniature nuclear reactor. A magnet was fixed to the barrel, generating an electromagnetic field that propelled a precise cluster of electrons toward their intended target with pristine accuracy and ample distance. The electrons, traveling through the magnetic field as a medium, would remain in their tightly packed formation until they reached the desired destination, inflicting a temporary paralysis upon impact.

Society, at one point, had deemed it more "convenient" to immobilize people with an electric shock rather than deal with the ghastly aftermath of bullet-ridden bodies.

The Strike Team sprang into action, bounding the two temporarily paralyzed individuals before pressing on. Moving with a blend of caution and speed, they glided down the hallways, clearing each room without hesitation. Contact was made, so it was time to move fast.

Four more adversaries emerged before them, wielding electron guns of their own. The next second, a barrage of clustered electricity blasted toward them, and the team retreated around the corner, seeking cover. Flashes of light were colliding and ricocheting off the walls around the team as they waited for their turn on the offensive.

The Commander, standing second in line, exchanged a glance with his comrade in front of him before barking out orders.

"Run the rabbit!"

With a nod, the team member leapt from behind cover, drawing attention to himself as the Commander acted in unison. As his ally darted across the hallway, the Commander spun around in a kneeling position to face the mayhem and discharged his arm in a flash. Like a frog's tongue, he snatched one of the combatants from several meters away, the constriction squeezing him to the brink of death before hurtling him into another opponent with a destructive force that rendered both useless.

Meanwhile, the team's nimble "rabbit" fired precise shots from his electron gun, stunning the other two and clearing the way ahead—for now. Recent events had brought unwelcome awareness of their presence, leaving no time to waste on cuffing the unconscious foes.

As they advanced to the end of the corridor, they reached the entrance to a vast atrium, with stairs on each side leading to the second level. Atop the pair of winding stairs awaited transport to the command center with access to the elevators.

Barely crossing the threshold into the atrium incited a sudden hailstorm of electrons showering upon them. Electric currents crackled and hissed, searing their skin, and leaving trails of tingling heat in their wake from the photoelectric effect. The team staggered back, gasping for breath, and reeling from the sheer force of the power unleashed upon them.

Two of the team members activated their MagBoots and fired out into the opening, back-to-back, commencing with a rotational ballet as they discharged their weapons at full capacity, eliciting a tornado of spewing electrons. Moving with fierce agility, they darted around the room, taunting their opponents with bold moves while striking them down with pinpoint electron shots.

Suddenly, the Commander noticed someone moving down the stairs quickly. In one swift motion, he discharged his hand to grab the assailant's weapon and rip it from his grasp, but he remained clutched to the pistol grip, causing his body to launch through the air like a discarded rag. The Commander swiftly pulverized the firearm before retracting his arm back; he then turned to his remaining team member next to him.

"Grab on!"

His ally swung their arm over the Commander's neck, and in a fluid motion, he extended his synthetic arm upwards and clasped the balcony railing above them. Effortlessly, the two warriors ascended above the mezzanine and swung over the railing as they skillfully evaded the continuous bombardment of electrons.

Without losing momentum, they deftly returned fire, neutralizing the remaining impediments in their vicinity.

Upon reaching the elevators, the Commander turned to check on his two comrades below, who had stopped maneuvering around the atrium and were now pinned down by a legion of armed guards and situated behind a desk waiting for the inevitable. Just as he turned to assist them, an array of electrons zipped by him, nearly striking his face. Another pack of guards approaching from the hallway were on the assault and forced him to retreat.

Overwhelmed with a sense of helplessness for his team, the Commander reluctantly followed his last remaining member into the elevator. They knew that it only required one of them to activate the power controls, but neither held out hope for a successful return from the mission.

Heavy breathing and the hum of the fast-moving elevator were the only noises for a brief moment of solitude before the doors opened and guns were positioned at the ready again.

Emptiness and silence in front of them. The placidity was palpable, but it only added to the growing tension. They stepped out of the elevator, lurking cautiously down the hallway and preparing for another wave of activity. Passing by closed doors, they slowly followed the signs in the corridor to the gateway ahead.

As the two stalkers kept their focus ahead, a woman soundlessly appeared behind them from a door they neglected to clear. A melancholic exhale was all they heard before the mysterious woman sent a charge of electricity through them strong enough to cause paralysis, while also sending them both into a state of comatose.

***

In his idle state, the Commander *knew* he was in a dream. He was caught in a liminal space longing for continuous reverie—procrastinating consciousness because *she* was there.

'Wake up, my Love.'

He heard her gentle voice say to him slowly, drawing out each syllable as she commanded his revival.

'Wake up, my Love.'

He clung to the sound of her voice, letting it wrap around him in a warm embrace, and for a moment, he could almost feel her beside him in bed—a haven where the world seemed to fade away, and they were left residing within a celestial kingdom crafted by the might of their passion. It was the one solace he had left.

Whenever he dreamt, the image of her face had become elusive, obscured by a veil of vulnerability. Terrified of her witnessing his weaknesses, his subconscious reflexively pushed her away. Her voice was all that remained now.

'Wake up, my Love.'

The sound echoed once more, but he fought wakefulness.

'Wake up.' Harsher this time… Her voice was never harsh.

"WAKE UP!"

Catapulted from his blissful memories of his wife to a partial state of wakefulness, he struggled to regain his composure. The intensity of his yearning for her magnified exponentially, his chest physically aching with a profound desire to lay his eyes upon her beauty. His mind would not permit it. His faculties had yet to fully recover, but as his blurred vision crystalized, a silhouetted figure materialized. *Am I still dreaming?* he wondered.

With the prospect of an ill-fated destiny drawing near, nothing occupied his thoughts more than seeing her one last time. As his perception sharpened, the figure in front of him came into astonishing focus. A woman carrying herself with undeniable confidence, her movement exuding a quiet strength that commanded attention.

She *was* in front of him!

He was suddenly jolted with disbelief—electroshocked back to reality. His reaction caused him to lose balance on the chair to which he was tightly fastened and helplessly fell backward. Flailing about on the ground, he frantically attempted to free himself and deploy his synthetic arm. Through his grunts and struggles, a laugh that he knew all too well caught his attention.

His arm was sutured together by magnetized cuffs, rendering it useless except for the ability to extend his fingers arbitrarily. Two individuals behind him eventually lifted him back upright, now facing his former lover.

"I didn't know I could still knock you off your feet like that." She said to him, still giggling.

"W-Wh-What the hell is going on?"

"It's good to see you too, my Love."

He looked down at his confined limb. *How could it be?* he considered as his mind raced with total perplexity. Words were attempted, but he remained speechless as she spoke again. His mind struggled nearly to the point of fainting as he absorbed the situation.

"I understand that this is very surprising for you right now. And while I would prefer to consult over details concerning us, we simply do not have time for that, and we rea—"

"I'm sorry!"

His thoughts were scattered, and he struggled to make sense of any of it. But deep down, he knew he had to accept the truth—*everything* was his fault. Overcome with emotion, he impulsively apologized. Built up sentiments through countless nights of personal deliberation, he simply could not hold back. He apologized for taking a job that kept him away for so long and making her assume he did not desire to be with her. He apologized for refusing to see her after his accident, disappearing without a trace, and for never contacting her. Most of all, he was apologizing for who he was.

She crossed her arms and scowled at him in a practiced and refined stare. Eyes watering but holding her bearing as her piercing gaze, reminiscent of a stormy horizon, held a depth that hinted at both wisdom and determination.

"Did you really think I wasn't going to accept you after this?" Gesturing to his arm.

Of course, she understood how he felt and thought. She knew everything about him. The poor woman probably ached more for him than she ever did for herself—she was indeed a genuine soul.

"I couldn't accept myself." He said, guilt lacing his voice.

"How could you be so naïve to think I wouldn't still want you? Still want to have you, talk to you, laugh, cry, every damn thing with you! All I fantasize about is seeing your eyes when you return. I lo—"

"I'M A MONSTER!"

He shook his head of matted black hair and attempted to elevate his gaze, but through his shame, he failed to make eye contact. She could sense his contrition for yelling, and remained quiet, allowing him to carry on.

"I can't even look into my own eyes. I fear to gaze at yours and witness the looks I would receive."

"How could you let your vanity get in the way of something so special?"

"It wasn't that. I didn't feel human. I felt detached. I feared you pitying me."

He finally summoned the courage and relaxed his wayward eyes on those pair of fearless orbs staring right back at him.

"I was scared you would stop loving me."

She wiped a tear from her flawless, rosy cheek and glanced away. Inundated with a flood of feelings, frustration was the initial emotion capable of summoning words.

"To think that I would stop loving you is the greatest insult of my life. I will never stop loving you... We must move on, though."

She stepped back and turned around, attempting to secretly wash away another tear. As she about-faced, she filled the Commander in on the puzzling details.

"I have been working at the command center here for several years. I moved here about a year after you stopped talk…" choked up, she finally continued, "…after communication *ceased* between us. Once you arrived, I was notified immediately. We pretended not to have our systems up upon your entry to hopefully bolster your arrival at this building as promptly as possible. We expected this sort of operation to be conducted by the authoritarians of Earth.

"Oh, your other team members are alive and well. We have them downstairs in a similar garment you are donning. We absolutely don't *intend* to cause harm to any of you. Having said that, there will need to be some agreements between you and I."

Deep down, he felt like he had so much to say to her, but he felt utterly shameful. All the pain and pity he felt over the years from his deformity would have been healed by her. Although, she appeared to have no more to say on the subject, and now they were stuck in a most unusual circumstance of deliberation.

"We know about the override system. We know that they would send a team to activate it. Those problems have already been solidified to our benefit. If we all don't come to an agreement before the final interconnecting satellite is disabled, *they* will be completely detached. All the interplanetary stations are under our control, and Earth lacks the resources to send even minimal munitions toward us. There is nothing more Earth can do but negotiate now. And *you* are going to help *us*."

"What could *I* possibly help with?"

The Commander inquired, knowing now that he was just a pawn in this game and playing that part was his only choice.

"Interestingly enough, Earth *does* have one last trick up its sleeve. They installed a failsafe mechanism here at our command center that acts as a kill switch to all our communications satellites. If this permanently deactivates, it will signal the satellites to leave orbit, sending all our communication out of existence. We will no longer be able to contact Earth but also the communes on the interplanetary stations. With no contact, they will be stranded out there alone—forever. Without resources delivered, they cannot survive. Hundreds of thousands of innocent people will be left to patiently expire in the void of space. Earth was willing to give up so much, just for control."

"I still don't understand… what can I do here?"

"The failsafe is guarded by a plasma shield, operated by high-powered magnets, creating a frequency of electromagnetic radiation. It is impossible to override here, and the barrier is too

108

thick for us to insert any useful material in there with appropriate dexterity to disable the mechanism."

The Commander gently nodded his head as he realized his purpose now. He felt almost reborn. A definitive purpose pervaded his being and the shackles of vulnerability detached, allowing him to rise to the surface of enlightenment.

His arm that caused so much emotional torture would be the mechanism that gives this planet salvation. He required no more musing—that was how it was with her. So easily could he stray from rectitude and then be reeled back in by the sheer force of her compassion.

He had allowed himself to be controlled by outside influences for far too long, slipping comfortably into the role of merely existing as a cog in the machine, no matter what its purpose. He looked at her and confessed.

"I'm the enemy. I selfishly left you to pursue my desires. I chose my own feelings over yours when I decided to disappear. I came here to thwart your rebellious actions. I am not even human! I. Am. The. Enemy."

"You are *not* the enemy! I know you better than you know yourself. You've created this *being*. This alter-ego of who you really are. This..." She said, gesturing to his arm, "does not affect this..." then placed her hand across her heart.

She then signaled to someone behind him, and the next second, he felt the magnetized cuffs deactivate and fall to the ground. He stared between his legs as she approached him candidly. Kneeling in front of him to catch his stare, she grabbed his human hand as her other hand rested upon his engineered protuberance.

No nerve endings, but somehow, he could still feel her warmth. He stared into her. He knew those eyes, but they still contained so many surprises—a boundless galaxy of love and warmth. No matter how far he strayed, she would pull him back, showing him the path.

The Commander breathed in clarity for the first time in ages. He was aware that his synthetic arm had roboticized his mind—obeying orders without pause. Still attempting to hold on to that shred of integrity, he could feel his judgments becoming clouded. *He* was the wayward one. Doing the right thing takes more effort than a simple cognitive suggestion, especially in the act of leadership. It requires reflection. It requires patience. It requires empathy. Unfortunately, it is sometimes all too easy to justify and confuse doing the right thing as doing the right thing for "me."

Her pureness saved his discarded soul. Looking into her eyes was all that was required to unequivocally know what to do. A tear crept down his cheek as he nodded at her.

Tabula Rasa

The Commander knew Earth should not have complete control over a society so far away. He knew it was wrong of them to take advantage of their resources. He knew allowing the satellites to be disabled would arguably cause the deaths of thousands of innocent lives. He knew this because she knew this. Her eyes lit up a fragmented void of darkness that he was too scared to illume himself. It was time to light that fire once again.

Part II

"There is nothing noble in being superior to your fellow man;
true nobility is being superior to your former self."

- Ernest Hemingway

Chapter One

The leather strap around his neck felt heavier than usual. The rugged and frayed material rubbing against a defined area of skin was saturated with sweat from multiple intervals of intense use. He paced. Fastened at two ends, the strap held the tool that dangled near his waist as he marched back and forth with fanatic anticipation. Sweating.

More akin to a detachable body part than a piece of hardware, the device became indistinguishable from man or machine when operating at optimal capacity. However, incessant trembling tormented his hands, and it was impossible to operate when his fingers failed to perform each microsecond command efficiently. Falling behind or creating dissonance with his other group members may cause irreversible damage. He knew this, and therefore, he was pacing and sweating—and now vomiting.

"Whoa ho, ho, buddy. I suppose better here than on the front row, huh?"

"Fuck, I can't do this." He said in between heavy breaths.

"Relax, my man; you're the best."

Hunched over, the strap was wrenching harder on his neck now as he expelled the remaining fragments of his stomach contents.

While his shirt hung unbuttoned, he inspected his tight-fitting jeans and leather boots for any discrepancies. Gradually, he uncurled himself through a reluctant groan, allowing the tool to position in front of his designer belt buckle. With his head still bowed low and his peripherals obscured by his wild and untamed hair, he ran his eyes over every contour. *It* was all he knew.

The 1961 Fender Stratocaster emanated a sultry Tahitian Coral shade; its weathered and worn body was a testament to the tumultuous journey of a wild and willful spirit. Passed through many previous owners, it had never found a master until he laid his hands upon the alder and Brazilian rosewood that comprised her magnificent body. He was the Guitarist.

As seasoned musicians, he and his band had played gigs in just about every dive bar and rundown club in the city, but tonight had the potential to reshape their destiny. Cultivating a niche but burgeoning following, the four rockers had finally persuaded a record producer to attend their next show—a rare opportunity that is unlikely to recur in a musician's career. A door that once unlocked, can only be opened through originality, talent, and grit.

His perceived lack of talent was the primary factor behind the regurgitation. Playing alongside the three other members was a daily source of gratitude, yet the weight of self-doubt constantly loomed over him as incessant thoughts plagued his psyche. *You're a phony—an imposter. You-do-**not**-belong!*

Despite the encouraging inclusion, he was crippled by the conviction that he was unremarkable and a mediocre musician at best. His band was aware of his insecurities and grew irritated by their persistent manifestations during live performances. Resembling a melodic corpse, he stood motionless on stage—an act incongruous with the rock and roll music and image the band strove to convey.

The other band members consented because he *was* good, and they all believed his playing meshed well with their style and that self-assurance was imminent. However, numerous gigs together had diminished their confidence as he remained lifeless on stage.

They could no longer tolerate a statue onstage with them, aimlessly strumming away on the guitar. They needed animation—a magnetic performer who commands the stage with an alluring presence while emanating a sexual aura that ignites the audience through the hypnotic melodies of their six-string.

Those circumstances coalesced, and at that moment, the other members' nervousness stemmed more from *him* than the usual anxiousness of a live performance. He knew this, which propagated his uneasiness. The cycle continued—he paced, and he vomited.

Anxiety and fear amassed control as he felt marooned in solitude—entirely unfit to solo this burden. Bent over, lips moist in bile, he timidly gazed at his band members.

Clad in either skintight jeans or leather pants, all three were shirtless or donning sleeveless tops that showcased their rocker physiques. Finely groomed hair brushed over their bony shoulders, emaciated from a lack of nutrition—unmistakably punks.

With the band currently on stage commencing their final song, the countdown to their own performance had officially begun. In mere moments, they would face a packed house of hundreds of critical music aficionados along with the *one* individual controlling the fate of their music careers.

Their Singer abrasively rolled his eyes, conveying his displeasure at the sight of the Guitarist's condition. The Drummer took a deep drag from his cigarette, exhaling a cloud of smoke that obscured his face before he turned and walked away. The Bassist knew better.

Being his oldest and staunchest ally within the band, the bass player had a keen understanding of the Guitarist's strengths and limitations as a musician. While the Bassist persistently acted as an advocate on the Guitarist's behalf, he recognized the trepidation over live performances. Still, despite the palpable nerves, he remained a bastion of strength and confidence when the Guitarist failed to summon it internally.

Tabula Rasa

The Bassist advanced toward him, lighting two Benson and Hedges in his mouth before passing one on to his friend. Continuing the graceful ease of a rock star, he pulled a fifth of whiskey from his back pocket and took a lengthy swig before handing it off—expelling the cloud of tobacco only once the whiskey had firmly settled in his stomach.

The speakers pulsated vibrations of rock and roll, causing the fans to *feel* the music. Caught up in the throbbing rhythm amplified their hysteria and enthusiasm toward radical measures. The thought of stepping out into that energy with the duty to maintain and hopefully elevate could break even the strongest of wills.

"I know what you're thinking." The Bassist remarked while exhaling another puff of smoke.

The Guitarist remained silent, sensing that his friend had further thoughts to share and opting to drown the last of the whiskey while nervously smoking a cigarette as he listened.

"You think you are going to ruin this for the rest of us, don't you? You know, you can be like a chainsaw sometimes. Agonizing to get started, but once going—*you* do all the work. Since day one, your thoughts haven't changed, and we still want you around, right?"

The Guitarist pulled hard on his cigarette as he continued to gather his thoughts, exhaling through his nose and reluctantly nodding while standing upright to face his friend. Having his full attention now, the Bassist's soft-toned eyes glanced upward, retrieving distant thoughts in order to convey his message.

"Do you remember when we were kids, and we used to jam together in your parents' garage? We were absolutely terrible and obnoxious, of course, but we jammed so long until the strings on our guitars felt like razors that chewed our fingertips raw, sometimes even spitting blood all over our damn instruments."

The Guitarist grinned feebly and nodded at his friend.

"Yeah, man, I remember those days."

"Good, cause I never told you how important those jam sessions were to me. I admired you so damn much. You seemed to know everything about the guitar: every scale, chord, and just about every damn song. You drove me to be a better guitarist. I wanted to play on *your* level, know what you knew. You still do that for me."

"We were just kids playing around in the garage. This, out there, determines all of our futures. Jamming in a garage with you is different than being on stage in front of the world." The Guitarist argued.

He polished the rest of the whiskey and lit another cigarette. The spotlight would soon be on him, and the alcohol failed to assist with slowing his rapid heartbeat.

Groupies and sound technicians passed by them in an undulating current as the concert demanded constant movement.

The Bassist continued his rousing speech.

"I am trying to get you to understand two things here, man. One, you still work your ass off and know more than anyone about music and especially the guitar. During our practice sessions, we have to play down to you. You're *that* good! More importantly, that makes us all want to be better. You are the fucking mechanism for the rest of us working our asses off. That's invaluable. Please, understand that."

Another half-grin shaped across the Guitarist's face, as no human is immune to persistent flattery.

"Secondly, I absolutely *love* playing with you. The reason I have the confidence to go up there and rock out in front of a bunch of strangers is because I know my brother is right there next to me. I use those memories of us uninhibitedly rocking the fuck out in the garage to bolster my confidence on stage. The beautiful screaming ladies in the crowd helps too, obviously."

He delivered a wink with *just* the right amount of arrogance to remain charming before continuing his monologue.

"What I want you to do tonight is imagine it is just the two of us playing as loud and fast as we possibly can until either our fingers bleed too much or the neighbors call the cops. That is the only damn place your mind needs to be. Be there with me, and let's capture that *flow* where everything in the universe is shut out, and only *us* and the music remains—just jam with your brother, man."

The Guitarist took another drag from his cigarette and realized he had exhausted it in only three puffs. His eyes were red and damp from tension, but he felt sustained, strong even. He surrendered to his eyelids, where he then transported himself back to the safety of his garage.

A thick haze of exhaust filled the air—hostilely blending with the spicy aroma of sweat, hormones, and possibility. The ugly and stained rug cushioning their bare feet provided a soft landing as they jammed. Scraping together every penny from odd jobs afforded the cheap amplifiers that now shook the walls to their foundations. The rustic tool shelf behind them provided an inferior backdrop as they faced the closed garage door, outfitted with posters of their favorite bands. With adrenaline in the driver's seat, they would slam and kick anything upright and proper into "artistic" disorder amid their emulations of *true* rock and rollers.

He noticed his heart rate dropping as his confidant's words created a sanctuary that provided a much-needed remedy.

Self-doubt can often fade away through the confidence of others. Just as a tree's branches grow and sway from the stresses of their environment, spirits can be broken or strengthened through trials and tribulations, yet always anchored by the resolute trunk of *purpose*—the entirety, though, reinforced by the roots of one's supporting cast of associates. True greatness is *never* achieved through sheer solitude.

The Guitarist straightened his posture, brushed his hair away from his face, and locked eyes with his friend, emitting a renowned state of confidence. His stare was penetrating and almost frightening—a fierce intensity of a warrior bracing for battle. The Bassist drew back in exhilarative surprise—his friend had finally emerged!

"That's my boy! You're alive! Have one more smoke with me, and let's find some more whiskey to chug while Drummer boy goes up there and does his thing before we join."

***

They each ignited two more cigarettes and passed around a bottle of whiskey as the Emcee wrapped up the applause of the previous band and began to introduce them.

"All right, ladies and gentlemen, let's keep this marvelous evening going with our next band. Locally born and bred, these young rockers are on the precipice of greatness. Rockers pure of this generation—style, class, charisma, talent. They have it *all*. And gentlemen, if you don't hold them close, they will have your girlfriends too. Let's give it up for *Blank Slate!*"

The crowd gave an incurious cheer as their band had *not* nearly reached household status. A sense of lethargy was settling over the room, sapping the energy and leaving the audience listless; the once-vibrant atmosphere now hung in the balance as the lack of vitality reached a tipping point.

Suddenly, the lights faded to black, and as the room plunged into darkness, a collective gasp rippled through the audience, their emotions a symphony of surprise, fear, and thrill. Conscious of the fact that showmanship was as crucial to their performance as the music itself, the band had sweetened the set manager's deal with some extra cash and recreational pharmaceuticals to ensure that their stage instructions were precisely executed.

In the blackout that enveloped the entire venue, the Drummer covertly walked on stage and positioned himself behind his percussive instruments. With a quick swig, he downed half a beer before upending the bottle and watching the remaining liquid splash onto the polyethylene that made up the skins of each Toms and snare drum. After discarding the bottle into the unknown, he positioned his drumsticks delicately but steadily in his hands. He then gradually began spinning them with a flick of his nimble thumbs, listening to the *whoosh* of the anthropogenic rotors as they prepared for takeoff.

With a deep inhale, he launched into his performance, hammering out two thunderous beats on the bass pedal before crashing down on the cymbal, triggering a brilliant flash of light illuminating the Drummer for only a brief moment before fading to black again. Only a momentary lull in the darkness before he struck again!

Every subsequent drum lick became progressively more intricate and nuanced as the lights strobed to life with each crack of the high and medium Toms. The barrage of explosive strikes from the drumsticks propelled geysers of beer skyward in the flashes of light, allowing only a momentary glimpse of his enigmatic form to the crowd before disappearing once again into the shadows.

He then unleashed a flurry of lightning-fast licks that sent shockwaves through the air, building to a thunderous crescendo that echoed with raw passion before falling silent in a moment of tense anticipation—the calm before the storm.

Travis Lane

In the pitch-black again, the darkness was broken only by the gentle, pulsing thump of the bass drum, gradually building in intensity. Each tap growing more pronounced. Boom. Boom. Boom. Boom. Louder and louder as *something* was rapidly approaching in the darkness! It was a calculated design to build an ambiguous tension in the room.

All of a sudden, the stage was flooded with light as the Drummer began tearing into a collage of melodic pandemonium. Beer, sweat, spit, and hair flew uncontrollably around him as the bludgeoning sound penetrated the crowd to their bones. Under siege and unable to escape, a wave of divine energy showered upon the gathering from the satisfying anomaly of rhythmic chaos.

An eruption of cheers nearly engulfed the intense cadence of his drum solo, and as he continued his melodic onslaught, he unleashed a torrent of sound that left the audience dazed and deafened.

Backstage, the three other members prepared for their entrance as each one's foot or head rhythmically bobbed while the packed house continued to roar in excitement. The power of the music swept over the Guitarist, and the sounds of the outside world became a mere shadow in the background of his consciousness. With his friend's help, he was able to transport himself to a place of refuge where the sole focus was the *music*—something he undoubtedly understood.

Tabula Rasa

As the lights dimmed on stage, the percussive exhibition grew more subdued, creating a veiled, muted ambiance where the rest of the band would make their entrance. The Singer and Bassist climbed the steps first as the Guitarist took one last drag of his smoke and flicked the smoldering butt into oblivion before joining his ensemble.

The music commenced immediately as the group established themselves on stage, leaving no room for idle chatter or nonsense—only rock and roll. The Guitarist exchanged a glance with the Bassist, who nodded back in a tacit form of communication that incited a feeling of ease and sanctity. They were *present* in their house of worship.

With his friend's words echoing in his mind, the Guitarist felt a soothing calm surge through his veins as they began to rock. Shutting out the world around him, he elevated to a transcendent realm where there were zero inhibitions—completely free to be *himself*—a microcosmic haven for expression, where outside of it, authenticity is often met with resistance and disapproval. The oppressive force of judgments and insecurities had formed a suffocating shell of anxiety and fear, smothering his natural essence while possibly stifling his creative spirit. But benevolence and trust had removed his shell, allowing him to emerge as his true self once again.

While some musicians thrive on engaging with the audience, the Guitarist found a genuine connection with his instrument and the messages it conveyed through harmonizing within the melodic currents. The way he fused with his guitar was nearly hypnotic to witness, and the audience could only watch in awe at how he poured his emotions into the instrument. During extended solos, he would throw his head back, eyes sinched tight, and mouth agape in rapture, evoking a sense of micro-orgasmic bliss with every note he played. The lights behind him produced a heavenly aura as he towered above the audience—elevated to divinity, while pure envy permeated the room.

The other band members were equally entranced by this *fresh* musical expression from their Guitarist. Precisely the breed of guitar player needed to bring the audience alive, an adhesive that bonded the rest of the elements of their ensemble to create an artistic force irresistible to all. Throughout the performance, the Guitarist and Bassist would meet in the middle of the stage, facing each other in an intimate engagement of musical dialogue. Their rhythmic unification evoked the nostalgia of their garage sessions, and a vibrant expression of enthusiasm evinced with every note they played.

Watching the performers radiate joy was infectious, and the audience could not resist being swept up in the moment. The energy level had reached maximum capacity, threatening to burst the seams of the building. Every occupant was in constant motion, lost in a trance-like state and dancing with reckless abandon.

After a successful setlist, the band took to the stage for one last encore song. A ballad that begins with a slow, smooth rhythm, preparing the listener for a luminous incline of rock! The last two minutes featured an intricate guitar solo in A-minor pentatonic scale—the final sendoff—a lasting aftertaste the audience would be left with; essential to be flawless in order to properly satiate the masses.

At that point in the song, the Guitarist positioned his fingers and began to command his instrument. In an instant, the guitar's electrical signal was jolted to life by the magnetic pickup that surged into the preamp's transistor. It was then transformed from a minuscule whisper into a roaring, full-bodied wave of sound. His hands confidently explored every inch of the guitar's body as his fingers caressed the strings with a precise amount of intimacy and intensity.

From the stage, the Guitarist peered out on a sea of obedience as every soul clung to the seductive notes his fingers rapidly struck, and with each resonant tone, the audience was transported to a realm of sanctity, and *he* was their guide.

As his anxieties gradually faded away, his confidence reached new heights. He was reborn, and the eyes of everyone watching were awarded the masterful inauguration. Roars of approval. The crowd's energy was a unifying force, and he harnessed it to solidify their bond. Guiding them now toward climax, his screams echoed in sync with his guitar as it belted out each tone flawlessly before finally settling on a soft, punctuating strum of the A-chord to consummate the evening.

***

Backstage, the band erupted in cheers and triumphant embraces to celebrate their remarkable performance. The Guitarist basked in the praise he was receiving, not only for his flawless playing but also for the magnetic new persona he had unveiled that evening. As they reveled in the exhilaration of their success, they passed around a bottle of vodka, savoring the heady rush of adrenaline still coursing through their veins.

Their celebration was abruptly interrupted when a bevy of beautiful young girls entered, their presence emanating a youthful elegance. Among them, the record producer himself, resplendent in his slim-fitting, single-breasted continental suit, approached with a shuffling gait. With a cheesy grin stretching from ear to ear, the Producer sauntered over to the young musicians, shaking hands with each of them.

"Well, gentlemen, that was… something."

The band remained quiet as the *suit* sized them up.

"How long have you four been playing together?"

"About a year." The Singer replied.

"Do you have *any* representation right now?"

"We book all our gigs personally."

"Okay."

As the Producer continued scrutinizing them, the four men struggled to focus amidst the flock of voracious mavens gathering around, giggling, and eyeballing the performers. This was an orchestrated sequence that the Producer had performed on numerous occasions with the male musical youth.

Closely observing the effects of the commotion, the Producer struck at the opportune moment.

"Do you gentlemen have plans this evening?"

"No, Sir."

"Okay. Well, I have a routine get-together at my place up in the hills nearly every Friday—a small gathering, of course. With a more comfortable setting, we can further discuss your future in the music industry. My assistant will give you the details." With that, the Producer cast a glance over at the dazzling young women and continued. "It seems that you have made some lovely new fans this evening. I don't think it would be polite to disappoint them by not showing up tonight... Or disappoint me... See you soon, boys."

After the Producer left with his group of sirens, the men stood there silently for a while in disbelief until the Drummer finally spoke.

"Whoa! Did you guys see the blonde in the skirt?"

"Shut up! We need to take this seriously... but yeah, of course, I saw her... Shit, though... I'm fucking nervous about *all* of this. We have no idea what to expect and haven't a clue what is and isn't a good deal. All we know is music, and neither of us really even seriously considered this moment—did we?" The Singer exclaimed, looking exasperated with only the thought of what potential the future may hold.

"The only thing we have to do tonight is charm him, act like rock stars, and *don't* sign a damn thing. We can call around tomorrow and inquire about what we should do before we make a commitment. Honestly, guys, let's just enjoy tonight and not make complete asses of ourselves."

"But we're rock stars. We need to be...a little rowdy." The Drummer chimed in.

They exchanged smirks and nodded exuberantly, reveling in the prospect of a wild evening of rock star antics ahead. Their boisterous agreement was unexpectedly disrupted by the arrival of a stern man donning a charcoal grey flannel suit. With a determined gait, he approached them, handing them a business card with an address scrawled on the back, his stare unwavering as he delivered it, before swiftly retreating from the room.

"All right, fellas, let's pack our shit up and head on over there."

***

As they drove their ragged van onto the cobblestone driveway, their eyes widened in awe at the three-story Jerusalem stone mansion before them. Centered in the driveway stood a fountain suitable for a select location in Versailles. Circling around it led to two towering Italian Cypresses that granted admittance into the mahogany double-door entryway. While the exterior exuded elegance, the interior was rife with debauchery.

The concern about their attendance and overall appearance that gripped them earlier quickly dissipated as soon as they laid eyes on the revelry unfolding before them. The abundance of riches had not prevented the presence of vice, and the exhibit of depravity was in plain view. A mountain of cocaine lay atop a Steinway & Sons Fibonacci grand piano—perhaps an unsettling sight for Heinrich's eyes. Bikini-clad women darted around the sprawling compound, disappearing and reappearing from the seventy-foot infinity pool and multiple jacuzzies scattered throughout.

Unlimited booze and drugs were on offer, providing a fitting setting for true rockers. No strangers to excess, the band had previously indulged in any medicinal ingredients available. But amidst the opulence, they were introduced to a whole new level of extravagance. Once mere bottom-feeders, they now found themselves swimming in the top-shelf of substance abuse.

Navigating through the orgy of perversion, they were overwhelmed by the sheer magnitude of the experience. No turning back now as the night's proceedings readily began. Rubbing shoulders with Hollywood's elite. Playful banter with lingerie models. Downing shots with world-class athletes and attempting to make as much cocaine vanish as the politicians could. The band had made *it*!

As they circulated among familiar faces, the four rockers were suddenly drowned out by a slurred but assertive English voice that seemed to cut through the room, commanding everyone's attention.

"Oi 'erd ya fuk-kuz put on a s-some kind of show tonigh, eh? Where's ya guitarist, then?"

Everyone, including and especially the band members, was acutely aware of the person addressing them. Arguably the best living guitarist in the most famous band was demanding their attention in his inebriated stupor. For the past few decades, the music world has been hopelessly trapped in the enduring shadow cast by the legendary rocker standing before them now. His prodigious talent earned him accolades and a coveted place in the Hall of Fame well before manhood, elevating him to a godlike status that surpassed the worshipped figures of antiquity.

Idolized for his partying as much as his talent and artistry, the Rock Star stood before them just as they all had imagined he would look—androgynously sexy with somehow a powerful suggestion of masculinity. With chiseled cheekbones and piercing eyes that seemed to hold a hint of mischief, his appeal was coupled with an undeniable magnetic aura, commanding attention in any room he entered.

"Where's ya f-f-fuk-kin axeman?"

"Right, ah, right here!"

The moment the Guitarist spoke to his lifelong idol, he immediately felt a sudden wave of sobriety wash over him. They locked eyes. A visible agony etched itself into the man's features, causing the Guitarist to question if he was gazing upon a slice of heaven or hell. Regardless, as the Rock Star's magnetic, smoldering eyes bore into the Guitarist, he felt a rush of adrenaline along with a sense of unease, as if he were poised to embark into uncharted territories. His piercing stare told the Guitarist he could take him to a place he had never been.

Travis Lane

With a menacing swagger, the Rock Star closed in on the Guitarist, his hypnotic eyes fixed on his target. The Guitarist tensed, half-expecting a fistfight, but to his surprise, the Rock Star threw his arm around his neck in a playful but rough gesture while flashing a disarming smile.

"Y'fuckin' cheeky bastard! A lil birdy told me ya know what ya're doin' up there."

"Ah, maybe. Maybe a little."

"Ah, fuck off, mate. I was chuffed to 'ear about your bloody prowess on stage. An' ya know what? Maybe I'm knackered, too damn tired of being the bloody *best* anyways. Maybe I'm ready to pass my torc- my th-throne or whatever. Who gives a toss, eh?"

Tugging on his collar, he pulled the Guitarist away from the curious onlookers, eager to speak more intimately with him. As they embraced, their foreheads touched, and the Rock Star's rough stubble grazed the Guitarist's cheek; his noxious body odor assaulted his senses, reminding him of the stench of decay that fills a hospital room of the terminally ill—rotten. His eyes were hollow and sunken like two black holes had swallowed up his entire face, obscuring his peripherals. Exhaustion etched every line of his face, making him appear years older than his actual age, a testament to a life with limited moments of peace.

Vanquishing his slurred speech now as if it were all an act, he spoke with a renewed sense of authenticity and conviction.

"Listen, mate, I know this all seems glamorous, but it's a fake. It's all bloody fake. Everything 'ere is ah…temporary. Like waves crashin' on the shore, onleh to retreat to the ocean." The Rock Star drew a deep drag from a cigarette that seemed to appear from nowhere and expelled the smoke in an exasperated groan before continuing. "Oi, it's a magnetic force that relentlessly reminds ya of yer own insignificance, wearin' ya down until ya're nothin' but shattered remnants of yer former self. Ya get me? Truth is, no one gives a toss about ya, and chances are they *never* will. Look, I'm tellin' ya this 'cause I wish someone would have told me before. But. But ya'r music, mate, *can* be real. Ya know, even with all that beauty that comes with music, sometimes, though, I ah, I just want it all to go away. For it to be… quiet—forever... For all of you to shut the bloody hell up!"

His voice echoed through the room as he turned to face the crowd, drawing uncomfortable looks from the other guests. Giving everyone a contemptuous glance, he then turned back to their private conversation.

"Only numbin' yourself remedies the bloody bullshit you endure day in and day out. What more can I say? Truer words have never been said—I don't know, maybe. Anyways, I want ya to come with me, mate. I want to show ya something."

Travis Lane

The Guitarist was no longer awestruck by this larger-than-life figure confessing to him. Instead, he felt a twinge of pity for the aging rocker. Over the years, the Guitarist had learned so much from this man's music that he could not resist a private gathering with his *once* idol. However, the Rock Star seemed to act as if the Guitarist had no choice and whisked him away to a vacant bedroom.

***

Inside the room was a catalog of intellectual carnage. Books, pamphlets, drawings, and sheets of music were scattered about in a design that suggested madness—or genius. Dark burgundy and midnight blue curtains obstructed the outside world, creating a harsh, isolated alcove. The California king bed sat untouched while an assortment of pillows and blankets covered the floor.

The most conspicuous feature, however, was the staggering collection of empty liquor bottles and drug paraphernalia. It was difficult to fathom how a human heart would still be beating after such abuse. At the center of the rakish collage, on an immaculate emerald velvet chaise lounge, gently rested a 1939 Gibson J-35 Sunburst. With its spruce top and mahogany back, sides, and neck, and finished with the famous dark sunburst hue, the guitar was a work of art. Light as a feather, the wood would vibrate with a marvelous resonance, producing a timber melody that surpassed imagination—a guitar of the gods, bequeathed to the hand of man.

"I knew ya'r eyes would go straight to the Gibson."

"That might be one of the most beautiful things I have ever laid my eyes on." The Guitarist responded, unable to take his eyes off the splendor.

A mournful sigh billowed from the Rock Star. He then sauntered toward the lounge chair and gazed at the guitar with a crestfallen expression as though bidding farewell to a dying friend.

"It's difficult to put into words, mate, but I have always felt that this instrument has been the one constant in my life to truly love me. She's been a friend that's challenged me, pushed me, supported me. Without *'er*, I'd be lost and alone."

"You are one of the most cherished and loved musicians of all time."

"What did I tell ya downstairs, mate? It's all bullocks, innit? It's all temporary. Even love, yeah? People fall out of love all the time, don't they? There's nothin' eternal about it. What a bleedin' typical word." Collapsing into an armchair, the Rock Star exhibited his weariness. "Anyway, I'm not lookin' for a pity party. I brought ya up 'ere for a reason. Obviously, this ain't my gaff, but I stay 'ere quite a bit. The *suit* lets me keep this room, and I'm 'ere more than my own place. I hate 'im, but I trust 'im, kinda. And what 'e told me tonight shocked and pleased me…"

"What did he say?"

"He said 'e saw *me* on stage tonight. Not literally, obviously, but a version of me—in ya. He wouldn't bullshit me with somethin' like that if it weren't genuine. Other folks are sayin' similar things. Made me happy when I 'eard all of it; cause I think I am ready to be done. It's my time to go. As the Greeks pass on the torch, I pass on to ya—the Gibson." The Rock Star announced, gesturing for him to pick up the instrument.

"Absolutely not! I cannot accept that. One, I am not even remotely on your level in any capacity. I'm simply a nobody, a loser. Two, you can't be don—"

"I've bloody well made up my mind, mate. It just feels right, and this is *my* decision. Ya can accept it *or* bugger off outta my room and continue hangin' out with all those lifeless wankers downstairs."

The Guitarist stood in stunned silence, completely taken aback by the unexpected incident. It was a moment he had fantasized about since childhood—a personal and intimate encounter with his idol. He had imagined countless conversations with the man, down to the most minor details of their clothing, as they conversed and reached mutual understandings on musical interpretations. But now, as he stood face-to-face with his hero, the moment felt broken. The glamourous façade hid the emptiness inside, and the absence of any true enchantment made it clear that the rocker's spirit had been vanquished long ago.

The Guitarist attempted to shake himself out of his daze. *Wake up*, he thought. Within one evening, he had encountered a lifetime of experiences, and the magnitude and velocity of the life-changing events left him feeling shocked and immobile. One night, and his entire reality had shifted. *What can I learn from this? How should I act?*

"I will ensure that this beautiful instrument gets the proper care and attention. I absolutely promise." The Guitarist's eyes were resolute as he finally accepted the gesture.

"Ha, I know ya will, mate. I told ya, first time in my life in a long time that I felt I was makin' the right decision, and I am happy with it."

They stared into each other's eyes in the compassionate silence they had forged. The Guitarist realized that the Rock Star had shown him heaven, but an inferno eternally present existed deep within. As in the universe, opposing forces were necessary for balance. Little did the Guitarist know that his idol was about to take him on a journey to the darkest depths of *his* hell.

"Alreet, mate, that bed over there looks proper comfy to me. I reckon I'm going to relax the only way I know how. I'm sure ya've done the gear before, so feel free to join me in getting a little numb."

"I actually never have. Is it as good as *they* say?"

"Ha, well… It's the *fucking* conduit to God. Lightning bolts don't harbor that much energy." He paused to gather distant thoughts. "In reality, though, maybe it's always just foreplay."

The Guitarist was acutely aware of the horrors behind the drug and had always been consistent with refraining from prior temptations. However, at that moment, he found himself considering his options. He had indulged in other drugs in the past without issues, and how could he turn down an offer from his idol, who had just gifted him arguably the most precious guitar on the planet? It was *just* heroin, after all—*how bad could it be*?

Only all those thoughts were lies—lies he told himself. Self-justification is more powerful and dangerous than any explicit lie. He had convinced himself that what he was about to do was the best thing he could do, maybe even the right thing. In fact, it did not take long until he told himself that it was the *only* thing for him to do.

It was a human flaw that enabled the mind to minimize the consequences of mistakes and bad decisions upon prolonged deliberation. He was stepping onto a slippery slope that would be nearly impossible to stop once in motion, forming a continuous loop of cognitive dissonance; mental hypocrisy—torturing himself by dividing himself.

He examined his idol, gripped with apprehension, but eventually submitted with a smile and a nod, fully aware that there was no turning back now. The Rock Star instructed him to lie down on the chaise lounge, pledging to guide him as he makes contact with God and fully commits to his therapy. The Rock Star went to the desk, pulled out a small leather bag, unzipped it, and removed the necessary contents in order to *escape* this world: a needle, a spoon, a small bag of substance, a lighter, and a tourniquet. With so little effort, why hesitate to tread that path laid out to reach heaven?

After preparing the needle, the Rock Star positioned the tourniquet around the Guitarist's bicep and carefully located a suitable vein. He held the syringe with one hand while he grasped the Guitarist's forearm with the other. The Rock Star's hand was ice cold, as though human blood ceased to flow through his veins.

Before proceeding, he looked at the vulnerable man lying on the couch and seemed to silently apologize for what he was about to do, but knowing it was "necessary." It was like a doctor administering chemotherapy to a terminally ill patient—this will

141

be your *only* remedy henceforth. The Guitarist navigated his mind for something, someone to help. To stop him, save him, and show him the righteous path, but there was no answer—not yet.

The Rock Star dropped his head near the Guitarist's arm while puckering his lips; he blew a soft whisper across his skin as he injected the needle into his bulging vein with ease—barely a pinprick. The Guitarist watched as the substance disappeared into his bloodstream, instantly feeling a sense of warmth emanate throughout his body. As the Rock Star removed the tourniquet, tidal waves of unimaginable rapture engulfed his body, pulsating with euphoria.

Oh my god, he thought.

He immediately became lost in the unexpected rush of pleasure, utterly unaware that he was capable of feeling so much by feeling nothing at all. He eventually welcomed the blackness behind his eyelids and gently evaporated into blissful oblivion.

***

His revival was enigmatic. He returned from his condition of complete disregard, but his return was *not* to Earth. He was dead, and he knew it. No, absolutely certain of this fact, as the figure before him was an *angel*. A comforting aura of light encircled her head, accentuating the faint, chestnut undertones of hair so lusciously inviting, beckoning him to bury his face and drift off into a peaceful slumber for eternity. Her serene presence held him spellbound, and he found himself unable to look away from her eyes, which appeared to capture the essence of all four seasons in a single gaze. The joy of spring. The warmth of summer. The comfort of fall. The intrigue of winter. Yes, he was dead, and he made it to heaven. A gentle sound escaped the angel's rose-tinted lips.

"You can call me Love."

"I couldn't imagine a more proper name. Am I dead?" The Guitarist asked, almost in a whisper.

"Dying is easy. Being brave enough to live, now that takes courage."

The realities of his surroundings started to crystalize as memories of his intravenous therapy with the Rock Star resurfaced, yet he found no trace of him. He was *not* dead, but he still felt the embrace of heaven. The angel sat on the couch by his feet, gently placing a hand on his leg as he regained his composure. Her beauty grew more radiant with each passing moment as his mind regained clarity. The curves of her face reflected the light and revealed shadows in the way men like da Vinci strained their minds over to perfect. Far more than a beauty of a generation, as the universe was incapable of sculpting a more perfect combination of molecules even with an infinite number of attempts. She was a unique masterpiece of creation.

143

"I *really* thought I was dead."

"It is far too early for you to leave."

"In all my years, I think I actually agree with you on that. Well, *my* Love, my name is—"

"I know who you are. I was at your show. I must admit, I was quite drawn to you and your performance…"

He sat up, the soft cushions of the lounge giving way beneath him, and he leaned toward her, closing the gap between them. A noticeable blush surfaced on her perfect face as his heart rate nearly doubled in a single interval. New waves of euphoria flooded over him as he breathed in her intoxicating perfume and, for the first time, encountered the soothing warmth of her body next to his—far more potent than the bewitching tar injected into his bloodstream. A full-body high that cocooned him in an ineffable sense of solace. Confused about these sensations, he considered the drugs. Why was he feeling this way? Was it not obvious?

The brain's emotional region sends signals via pathways by activating neurons to create pleasurable sensations. Drugs mimic this process, becoming the only welcomed guests down that path, dismissing all other sources of enjoyment, even the most notable of influences. He longed for this woman sitting next to him, but the opiates had already rewired his brain, and despite the inexplicable sensation that consumed him, the needle held an irresistible allure. The path may seem straightforward, but without a guiding light, one will surely stray into darkness.

"You have a perplexed look on your face."

"It has definitely been an *interesting* evening—lots of, ah, surprises."

"One moment can alter the course of a lifetime."

"Important to cherish every second of it then."

She looked at him with a shy grin, immediately causing him to smile back in response, his own expressions mirroring hers. With a final lingering look, he had to avert his gaze, the weight of emotions almost too much to bear.

As his eyes scanned the room, they eventually landed on the Gibson sitting next to him, and he realized the instrument remained untouched since it was gifted to him. So, with gentle hands, he wrapped his fingers around its neck and instantly sensed the depth of the guitar's soul. Rubbing his hands across the textured wooden seductress charged him like a battery. With each caress of his fingertips, a jolt of electricity seemed to shoot up his arm, priming him with the energy required to play. Finally, he cradled the guitar in his arms, positioned at the ready. He took a deep breath and settled his palm on the bridge as his fingers hovered above the strings. For a moment, he hesitated, waiting for the guitar's approval. Returning his gaze toward the angel next to him, he flashed a grateful smile and began to play.

I yearn for that moment, my final escape

A feather cast off, fallen from grace

Seconds will pass while memories are made

But it won't be long 'til you forget my name

A fractured soul may walk among

Veiled in the shadows of what once was

Each light is so bright I run for the cave

These thoughts will subside, once I escape

Entirely unfit to banish these thoughts

And I'll tell you I'm fine, but I'm probably not

Echoes of grim memories must be numbed

I don't need that push cause I've already jumped

And just when I thought I was on my last breath

Tabula Rasa

Your eyes may have pulled me from the grips of death

Now take my hand and show me your bliss

It's time to escape this barren abyss

As the final notes echoed through the room, he glanced at his arm and saw the dried blood from the earlier injection. Self-pity rose within him, but he pushed it back, ignoring *all* his wounds.

"Wow. I-I kind of can't believe my ears right now. That was beautiful... but so very somber. When did you write that?"

"That just happened *right* now. I can't even explain it. I couldn't even help myself. The words and music just poured out of me; it felt almost like I had to get out of the way."

She graced him with a warm smile, and they simply sat there and absorbed the moment together, sharing the surrounding air of wonder. With all the thousands of hours he had spent holding a guitar, not once had he ever produced a melody so effortlessly. Within the cosmic dance of destiny, every diminutive event holds weight somewhere in the movements of life, but at that particular interval, her mere presence kindled his fire—a *muse* of galactic proportions.

Setting the guitar down, he took her hand in his, the warmth of her skin calming him as he lay back on the lounge. They shared

147

the moment, no words necessary, just the comfort of each other's company in that period of time and space. As he held her, the Guitarist wished the world would freeze and allow them to stay in their embrace for eternity. He battled the temptation to remain conscious, but his weary eyes eventually surrendered to the darkness. And, regrettably, his soul still craved another *dose.*

Our whispers, our touches, now fading to black

Growing weak and frail, I begin to crack

Judgments clouded, it's still my mistake

*I chose not to flee; I chose **not** to escape*

Chapter Two

Knock. Knock. Knock. The thumping sounds struggled to integrate with the hazy, dream-like state.

"Excuse me, Sir."

Knock. Knock. Knock. Each noise muddled and confused his faculties.

"Mister, we need you on set. They are asking for you. I am sorry, but can you please answer your door?"

Knock. Knock. His heavy eyelids refused to budge as a monumental hangover greeted him upon awakening. As he lay face down on the floor, his initial observation was the dry oatmeal-like substance that covered his pillow. A pungent and sour odor filled his nostrils as he took his first conscious breath of the day, immediately recognizing the familiar smell and contents on his face—a recurring theme in his current lifestyle. *Well, I guess better facedown to avoid choking,* he reasoned.

He allowed his tongue to venture out to absorb the dried substance from his lips, and somehow, a satisfying hint of whiskey was registered, sparking his batteries. As he strained to lift his one-thousand-pound throbbing head off the ground, his senses were a mist of disorder and uncertainty.

He sought a bottle that had not been depleted of its emancipating substance. Now conscious, it was time to replenish.

Knock. Knock. Knock. The unexpected noise jolted him, and a necessary clench was required to prevent the involuntary discharge. Disoriented and startled, he fought to regain his composure.

"Sir, are you awake? They really need you out he—"

"Give me five minutes, asshole!"

"Yes... but... okay, Sir."

In the throes of disorientation, he berated someone or something without any awareness—still fully captive to the weariness after a night of revelry. Fighting to gain control over his eyes, his vision remained at the center of a nauseating vortex, but as the blurriness dissipated, he realized he was still in his trailer on the set.

Rolling onto his back, he stared at the ceiling with a despondent gloss blanketing his eyes. And like clockwork, the same thoughts went through his head in moments like these: *What happened last night? Why do I keep doing this to myself? You worthless fuck, are you ever going to stop being such a worthless fuck? Just end it already! Only then will you be...* His futile self-pitied thoughts trailed off as "no one" cared or would listen.

Eventually managing to hoist himself to an upright position, he was able to absorb the chaotic atmosphere surrounding him. A liquor store's worth of empty bottles littered the floor, while zip-lock bags containing a motley selection of drugs were mixed among the clutter—an obstacle course of emphatic inebriation.

As he morosely sniffed and extracted the last drops from any bottle within arm's reach, his attention was suddenly diverted by an unexpected sight. Jutting out from beneath a tousled heap of blankets on the other side of the cramped trailer, a pair of pale, naked butt cheeks caught his eye. Startled, he paused and squinted, trying to make sense of the development. *Shit, I hope she's alive,* he quipped.

On all fours now and in the final stretch before dragging himself upright, it dawned on him that he was almost completely exposed, with only his briefs left hanging at his feet. Sifting through the scattered clothing, he became puzzled as it seemed the only garment unaccounted for was the enigmatic girl's underwear.

After a repressed cough, his hand traced a path up his face, fingers kneading at his temples to ease the throbbing pain. His hand ascended higher, and with a restless motion, he tugged at his hair, his fingers tangling in the strands until he finally solved the mystery of the girl's missing unmentionables. As he made contact

151

with the lacy scrap of fabric tangled in his messy locks, he gave a disconcerting tug and removed them from his head.

Another proud moment, he mused with a revolted sneer.

Maneuvering through the chaos on the floor, he managed to find the bathroom and *finally* commenced with a painful but gratifying release. He splashed water on his face, and after rinsing away the filth that had accumulated from his indulgence, his eyes met with the image of the creature that plagued his thoughts, the seducer of regrettable exploits. *I have to live with this asshole*, a question he posed to himself for effect. Face to face with the unflinching image, he felt a powerful impulse to lash out, to punch the eyes out of the individual looking back at him, break the nose, cave in the skull until the twitching and breathing flippantly ceased. *Only then would I...*

It was a cruel irony; his livelihood depended on his face, yet he could not bear to see his own reflection. He stared pitifully at himself, at the over-defined cheekbones and the slight upcurve of his nose; without blinking, he inspected every millimeter with excruciating harshness. Every imperfection, every flaw, even the unnerving symmetry seemed to taunt him, daring him to look away, to yearn for someone else to appear in that reflection.

After inspecting his entire face, he reluctantly approached the nucleus of his own sight, his timid gaze beckoning with endless depths that mirrored back an eternity of *transcendence*. There was zero recollection anymore—a mimic, just a vile shade of his former self. Of all the negative ways he described himself, a *liar* struck him the most. He lied to get what he wanted from others. He lied about his substance abuse. But his self-deception far exceeded any deceit he perpetrated on others.

A burst through his trailer door interrupted his contrition exercises.

"Big-time-movie-star! Where you at, my man?"

The annoyingly sprightly voice of his Manager shattered the fragile peace of his hangover, sending his headache to peak levels. The throbbing delivered strobe light flashes of memories from the previous evening, which started piecing together in the Actor's mind.

Due to the success and newfound acclaim, the Actor was nominated for a prestigious award, and he and a group of "friends" had celebrated the evening quite rapaciously. Currently filming a new picture out of state, he contemplated whether violating his trailer on the movie set was a better idea than ravaging his hotel room.

With a despondent demeanor and a pounding headache, the Actor vacated the lavatory, finding his manager, a man with carefully parted thinning blond hair and a starched shirt that

153

seemed rigidly formal, still reeling from the abundance of debauchery displayed in the small trailer.

"I see you continued the party well into the *following* evening."

"Evidence would suggest you are correct."

The Manager pointed at the face-down body on the mattress with a furrowed brow. "Ahh, that's not the girl I saw you with last night?"

"Yea, I don't know who that is either…" The Actor rolled his shoulders dismissively, fully expecting this predictable behavior. Suddenly, a brief memory resurfaced, crystal clear in his mind for only a second; he *did* have a chance encounter. The warmth of a fleeting memory surged through him, only to be swiftly subdued by the numbing effects of his "medicine." One thing he was certain of was that the emotions stirring within him did not originate from the lifeless form lying before him.

Unfortunately, the evening lost all remnants of sober awareness. The details and sensations smeared into a mélange undulation, entirely in rhythm with the constant fluctuating barometer that comprised his most turbulent emotions—day after day.

"Is she alive?" the Manager questioned, concern lacing his voice as the figure had not moved since his arrival.

"Honestly, I don't know. Haven't checked yet."

Tabula Rasa

With slow and cautious steps, the two men approached the young woman's motionless frame, examining her for any sign of life. But as they drew nearer, a sudden and startling blast of gas escaped from her flawless posterior, jolting the men with surprise and prompting them to a hasty withdraw.

"Well, that's good enough for me. Let's get the hell out of here."

***

The Actor hastily threw on a pair of faded jeans and a plain white t-shirt, eager to escape the confines of his trailer. As the two men stepped outside, the sun's final rays of the day settled on the Actor's face, and momentarily, the warm embrace exiled the burdens of existence. With fleeting seconds left, the Actor bid farewell as it dipped below the horizon, only then to carry on with his day apathetically.

The two men walked toward their first destination, the wardrobe trailer, where his manager launched into a detailed and nauseating itinerary for the evening ahead. Once the climactic shoot wraps up tonight, they would be boarding a private jet with a gaggle of gravy trainers who perennially clung to his manager—a group the Actor long learned to detest. Still, he held onto them like a persistent rash, scratching the scabs and preventing any healing. Upon setting down at the airport, they would head back to the Actor's house and have a celebratory welcome home event.

The Actor had little regard for the Manager's words. He was anticipating a good, uninterrupted sleep in his own bed. He had a plan. He would isolate himself by locking his door and letting the raucous partying continue outside. However, he had previously attempted this strategy, only to ravenously fill his nasal cavities with stimulants, denying him the rest he so badly craved.

Upon arriving at the wardrobe trailer, the Actor took his first step up the stairs but immediately recoiled, nearly collapsing off the platform. Gasping for air, he clutched the handrail and began violently expelling a cocktail of self-prescribed poisons onto the ground. His body seized up in an intense spasm, leaving him paralyzed with eyes bulging and tears streaming down his cheeks. He continued to expel every substance from his stomach until the dry heaves indicated the tank was empty. The Manager's indifferent attitude was evident in how he rolled his eyes and tilted his head, his gaze fixed on the Actor as if examining a mere asset. When he asked if the Actor was okay, he gave him a sarcastic thumbs-up, spat, wiped his lips, and attempted another ascent up the stairs.

Without so much as a greeting to the staff, the Actor slumped down in a chair inside the wardrobe trailer, hoping to catch a few moments of sleep while getting his makeup applied. As he stared wearily into the mirror, the chief of wardrobe, an older woman with stern features, stared at him with a distinct grimace.

"Yea, I know—I look like death." The Actor rolled his eyes at her.

"No, this reaction on my face is from how you *smell*."

"Right. That checks out. My apologies."

A hushed discussion occurred among the staff before a few of them handed the Actor deodorant and a bundle of baby wipes. The Actor could see the pity and disgust impressed on their faces as they handed over the hygiene materials. He reluctantly accepted and began to clean himself while they prepared his accoutrements for the film.

***

Brimming with electric vitality, the Actor burst through the trailer door, transformed into a new man. He was adorned in a perfectly tailored pinstripe suit, and looking fresh and invigorated with help from a stimulant in the form of a white powder, he now exuded a surge of confidence and vigor. Marching with swagger, he strolled over to the filming area, eager and ready to work. As the fine powder tunneled its way through the rolled-up banknote and into his bloodstream, it ignited a fire that engaged thrusters,

157

sending him skyrocketing. With superhuman powers and intense focus, he was officially revived.

After a conversation with the director and a few other crew members, he made his way to the backseat of the modified midnight-black GAZ Volga parked in the dilapidated industrial site. Sitting there in silence, the Actor began some ritual warmups. Rolling his neck in circles, he exhaled slowly, humming until depleting all the air from his lungs, and then repeated. He was going through the scene in his head, imagining himself performing the lines with visual-spatial accuracy. A true master of his craft, he held the art and the dedicated workers in the industry in high esteem and thus always committed himself fully to every role.

Sitting in the middle of the seat with a camera on him, he slipped into his character's identity—a determined "liberator" disguised as a Russian gangster. Two bodyguards positioned themselves in the front seats of the vehicle. The director readied the set, cued the fog machine, creating an eerie, isolated presence in the evening's darkness, and...

"Action!"

The Volga silently glided down the dark, deserted roads within the industrial park. Moving slowly, the car suddenly swerved to a stop as one of the bodyguards succumbed to a severe sickness. The

Gangster peered cautiously out the windows into the indiscernible evening, his senses on high alert.

Once parked, the two bodyguards exited simultaneously to resolve the issue. But before they had time to question the sudden and violent illness, they were each dispatched by two precision bullets. The suppressor fitted to the assassin's rifle transformed the energy created by the blasts, converting the noise into heat and rendering the shots fatally silent.

The Hitman had covertly poisoned one of the guards earlier, attempting to eliminate any suspicion of a planned attack. Meanwhile, the Gangster sat obediently in the backseat, only hearing the faint thud of two large bodies hitting the ground. Even though the gunshots were not heard, the Gangster's instincts told him he was being hunted.

Anticipating the imminent danger, the Gangster unholstered his Makarov PMM pistol and pulled the charging handle back to confirm that a round was chambered.

He sat there with gun in hand, ruminating in bewilderment about the "reality" he found himself in. As a rogue "emancipator," he had traveled back in "time" to the Soviet Union during the height of the Cold War. Embedding himself deep within the highest echelon of Russian intelligence, he intended to use his secret access to detonate all programmed nuclear warheads with the ultimate goal of eliminating all life on Earth.

Suddenly, a voice resonated from outside the vehicle.

"Za char ud ur rasa, aderphee."

Though not the Russian he was currently accustomed to, the language was one he was quite familiar with. "I know it's you, brother."

A sinister grin spread across the Gangster's face before he delivered his retort.

"Erla Za."

"As do I." The man he was conversing with in the strange tongue was not just his brother but an identical twin. When they were infants, they experienced the phenomenon of cryptophasia, leading them to develop a language only they understood. Their identical twinship also functioned as the enabling factor for their ability to traverse "time." During a brief period in the womb, the boy's thalami were connected via a thalamic bridge, which facilitated the exchange of blood and brain activity between them, enabling them to synchronize and share each other's sensory information. Typically observed exclusively in conjoined twins, this remarkable occurrence allowed the boys to live separately but

remain "connected." An aberration that confounded them their entire lives until they learned that it was all just a glitch.

Recently, a stunning revelation emerged—life on Earth was not what it seemed. Instead, everything was part of an advanced computer simulation, controlled and manipulated by an advanced species beyond human comprehension. This groundbreaking discovery was kept hidden from the public, as the researchers believed global anonymity was necessary until further information was gathered. Using a powerful supercomputer with the capacity to link to human brains had exposed this truth. Through countless experiments, it was discovered that conjoined twins were able to pierce through the veil of reality and linearly access the simulated timeline. This was possible by a connection between their thalamic bridge. Conjoined twins were a subtle glitch in the simulation and provided a link outside human reality. The Gangster and his Hitman were the only two non-conjoined humans with this ability.

Traveling forward on the timeline, the Gangster had witnessed a stark vision of the future—a cataclysmic environment far more ominous than any apocalypse humans had prophesied. Faced with this terrible fate, the Gangster believed he had a duty to act as humanity's "savior." The only way to accomplish this was to remove all of life before the inevitable arrived. And so, the Gangster transported himself to the height of the nuclear arms race in the Soviet Union, providing a perfect opportunity to carry out his grim mission. With a push of a button, he would extinguish all of life in their illusory world.

"I think it's time you joined me outside of the car, brother."

The moment of reckoning had finally arrived, concluding with an inevitable showdown as old as "time." The eternal struggle between good and evil hinged on a conflict of passion and reason, with the emotional and logical paths of introspection vying for dominance.

With a practiced touch, the Gangster holstered his pistol underneath his suit jacket and exited the car.

"Cut!"

With a bustle of movement and haste, the crew took up their positions, readying themselves for the upcoming shoot outside the vehicle. Amidst the flurry of activity, the Actor was able to steal a quick moment to inhale some revitalizing white powder. After ensuring everything and everyone was settled into place, they readied the set.

"Action!"

Right on cue, the Gangster emerged from the vehicle and stood cautiously at the rear of the Volga. Through the fog, a darkly clad version of himself appeared before him.

His stunt double filled the role of the twin being as they filmed the same scene earlier in the week where the Actor portrayed the twin.

"How did you find me?" The Gangster asked in utter disbelief.

"When in our lives has one of us done something without the other knowing?"

"Well, you've always been the better one—somehow. I was hoping my red herrings would have disrupted you a little longer. I knew you would be looking for me."

"You left me with few options."

"Well, you didn't see it."

"You told me everythi—"

"It doesn't matter what I told you! What I told you was only a fraction of the horror I saw… that I understood. You weren't there to witness…to be consumed by the unspeakable terror, where every nerve in your body is electrified with fear."

The Actor's words were infused with raw emotion, as his haunting stare brought to life the nightmares engraved in *his* mind's eye. The bleak depths of the human psyche are known only to those who have peered into the abyss, and the Actor bore witness to the unspeakable sorrow that lurks within—he considered his darker than others. Always in decline but never hitting bottom.

As the Actor delivered his lines, an effortless tear accumulated around his eye, summoning personal emotion to portray the essence of his character.

"If you saw what I saw, you wouldn't be trying to stop me. You'd be helping me!"

"I can't deny that I don't understand the images you've seen. But can anyone truly understand the intricacies of someone else's analyzes and interpretations of the world around them? Simulation or not, we are all unique, and we all view our world differently."

"Anyone who could understand what I know would not think differently than me."

"I am aware that what you experienced was alarming, but I share the exact same DNA as you, and I view it as an opportunity to solve a problem. So, you can't say that anyone would feel the same way. We discovered a glitch, so that gives reason to believe that there are other glitches and either what you saw was not real or there are solutions around it."

*"Even if there is a **one** percent chance of that reality occurring, we must avert it!"*

"I agree, but we should look to solutions before the easy fix of decimating our entire existence. This simulation, or whatever our reality is, is, in fact, our reality. We are still conscious beings to the limit of our understanding, and I believe that is more than enough to prolong our existence. We still have the ability to adapt to uncertainties to create a better way of life. We need to use the strength of others to bolster positive change instead of amplifying the individual weaknesses and vulnerabilities each of us carries."

Dialog from the script specifically designed to captivate the audience while punctuating a theatrical message. Staring intently at the supporting thespian, the Actor was primed to deliver his climactic speech, intended to render tears from all viewers. His lips moved, but the words were suddenly too heavy to project. His surroundings vanished as his vision blurred and his peripherals tunneled. Then, complete silence. No air. He dropped to his knee first before fully submitting to gravity's pull.

"Cut! Medical, on set, now!"

Initially, a hush fell over the set as confusion seized control. A rush of personnel eventually came to the aid of the Actor as he attempted to regain his composure before nearly stumbling once more. Two helpers arrived on each side to prop him upright. The energy in the atmosphere was more pity than worry, and he felt it—a pit of despair.

After enduring an onslaught of annoying questions, he finally managed to dismiss the mob and retreat to his trailer, shuffling away with a demeanor of degradation.

The strange woman had thankfully vanished, and all that remained was the dilapidated by-product of the previous evening's sins. Overwhelmed with distress and humiliation, the Actor sank into the couch inside his trailer. He buried his face in his hands, tears flowing immediately and promptly escalating to hysteria. He was stuck in a form of paralysis where he felt his chest tightening, unable to catch his breath, and gasping for air between sobs. Each inhalation of air felt thin and suffocating, as though he was breathing through a straw. As the tears streamed down his face, he crumbled in on himself, wracked by cries of self-pity—feeling vile about the diminutive nature of his circumstances.

The crushing weight of his selfishness piled onto the already solidified mountain of anguish, and he swore he would be buried alive by it all. Living with *himself* became an ever-increasing problem as thoughts of divergence constantly swam throughout his head. *Living with*? He thought back to earlier when he stared at himself in the mirror—*who was this unwanted resident endlessly causing conflict?* He mused inwardly, pondering whether harmony and balance between his internal divides were even possible.

Once again, his Manager plowed through the door at another low point of introspection. The Actor quickly employed his thrilling acting skills and transformed away from the sorrowful soul he was so accustomed to. His sleeves were wet from wiping tears away, a detail his Manager would surely ignore.

"All right, man, due to some technical issues and your, um, incident, they are shutting down filming until the middle of next week. We will head on back here shortly for some much-needed vacation." He explained the situation outside, then continued, "Here, I thought you might need more of this," and handed the Actor a small vile of cocaine before detailing the rest of the agenda for the day.

"A private plane is waiting for us at the airport with a group of lovelies to join us. There will also be a couple of people accompanying us to talk to you about doing some advertising and keeping that revenue stream going. Shortly, we will be back at your crib and really get the party going."

When he started letting other people manage his life, he felt like he had abandoned his old self to a distant memory; submitting to subservience had amputated his spirit. A manipulated shade of his former self was all that remained. Far too many blank spaces in his memory over the last few years to even qualify as a functioning human. He even struggled with remembering what happiness felt like.

"Whatever. Let's just get out of here."

***

A self-induced haze overshadowed his travels back home. Reality was often collateral damage when the Actor attempted to suppress his thoughts and feelings. Images flashed of filling his nostrils and stomach with stimulants and depressants, a cocktail necessary to walk that fine line of manic-depressive.

Conscious enough to make a minimal assessment of his situation, the Actor gazed at the unfamiliar faces that filled his house and the neglect they displayed for his personal space. The inebriated wave that darkened his thoughts was subsiding, but agony neglected to sleep in. Instantly despondent as misery owned a sizable piece of real estate between his ears.

He shifted his weight, hoping to gain enough momentum to stand up and grab the bottle of whiskey in front of him and summon a much-welcomed comatose state.

"Hey, where are ya headed, buddy?"

He ignored the probe. He had a plan. Snatching the bottle and darting through the crowd, disregarding any human engagement, he withdrew to the bedroom.

Stumbling down the halls, the Actor bumped and knocked over decorations he never made a choice on. Even his own house felt like a movie set—everything *was* fake. Securing the handrail, he closed his eyes and attempted to transport himself over the obstacles. Opening his eyes revealed the staircase still ahead. He groaned and began his ascent. His body seemed to recognize the intentions of his mind and attempted to fatigue itself out of willpower.

His plan involved starting a bath in his freestanding acrylic oval whirlpool and pouring himself a full glass of bourbon neat. Once he set things in motion, he sat the glass of bourbon next to the tub on the reading stand and checked the temperature of the water. Moving back into the bedroom, he began to undress, still shielding his imperfections from nobody but himself.

In languid movements, he proceeded to his dresser and slowly opened the top drawer, waiting for the detonation. Shifting the perfectly folded underwear aside, he eventually felt the cold steel on his skin. He secured his hand around the grip of the Sig Sauer and presented it in front of his face, inspecting every detail. He had a plan.

Once returning to the bathroom, he put the pistol on the stand and stripped off the remainder of his clothes. He stared at his imperfect naked body through the floor-to-ceiling mirror beside the tub. Malnourished and weak, skin so pale and nearly to the point of translucence. A hurricane-induced hairstyle, arranged and displayed in such fragmented ways. The Actor's eyes shied away from the mirror's glare, unable to confront the harsh reality of his reflection.

Fueled by rage, he then seized the gun and swung it at the glass, smashing the mirror with the pistol grip and sending shards of bladelike crystals scattered throughout the floor. Looking down at the razor-sharp mess on the ground, he leaned over, picked up a piece the size of a toothbrush, and set it down on the stand along with the pistol. Still panting from his outburst, he slowly eased himself into the warm water. His plan was in motion.

Sliding down into the chasm of the tub only to have his nostrils above the water, he started to ponder what it might feel like to drown and if one could do so voluntarily.

With a determined commitment to his plan, the Actor felt an unusual calm wash over him, as if the weight of the world had been lifted from his shoulders, the walls of his doubts and fears came tumbling down, and he could finally take a deep breath and exhale, knowing that his anguish would soon be over. At that moment, he was entirely at ease, his body limber and fluid, like the water surrounding him. His mind had fully returned to the *now*, while the past was forgotten and the future was irrelevant.

Lifting himself, he reached slowly toward the pistol but landed on the glass of bourbon. Sipping the nectar gradually, he savored every sensation on his tongue, along with the slight and pleasurable burn. He basked in the feeling of happiness that engulfed him, musing on whether it was the serene atmosphere he had carefully crafted or the relief of knowing that his pain and fears would soon be vanquished. This wave of strange elation washed over him, sending shivers down his spine in the warm bath.

Returning to the situation and remembering *why* he was there, he put the glass down and impulsively grabbed the pistol. His mind spun like the rapid acceleration of a turbine engine. Memories came on a reel, but somehow all at once, and then suddenly, everything went blank.

"Fuck it!"

With his final words hanging in the air, he forced the barrel of the gun into his mouth, feeling the icy steel against his tongue— his final earthly sensation. He squeezed his eyes shut tightly before pulling the trigger with fierce determination.

No explosion, no pain, nothing. The pistol's grip safety impeded his finger.

"Motherfucker!"

Frustration boiled over, and the Actor let out a dreadful roar of fury as he slammed the pistol back on the stand. His entire body clenched as if every drop of moisture within him congealed into a solid mass. He strained to release his voice again, but all that escaped was a hoarse, inaudible howl that seemed to vibrate in his chest—a reflexive behavior before the actual pain set in. He wept uncontrollably as he regained control of his temporary paralysis. Bawling into his eyes, he felt defeated—once again.

"Please, just let me die," he begged.

He wept uncontrollably for several minutes, gasping for air while battling to control his emotions.

Once the shock of his failed attempt subsided, the Actor reconvened and envisioned himself bleeding out slowly in the warm bath, imagining it to be comparable to falling into a deep sleep. Painless, soothing, and less messy. Glancing over at the piece of glass he placed on the stand rejuvenated his ambitions, and he took one last swig of bourbon before he grabbed the razor-sharp piece of glass.

Holding the sliver of glass in one hand and hovering it over his other wrist, he noticed something peculiar. He saw strange eyes staring back at him, their reflection shimmering in the tiny piece of glass barely big enough to reflect *only* his eyes, obscuring the rest of his face. For so long, he had looked at his reflection in the

172

mirror, focusing on the perfections and imperfections without ever daring to look deeper within himself.

A sudden and unusual rush of sensations flooded the despondent man, leaving the Actor feeling unlike himself. The eyes that met his were not only unfamiliar, but they also seemed to speak to him. *You are not alone,* they whispered, revealing a dichotomy of consciousness. So much said with so little. It was as though a part of himself emerged and reminded him of the internal alliance, a union in pursuit of a shared vision.

At that moment, through a profound and unexpected act of introspection, he compelled a part of his essence to detach from the consuming darkness that had plagued him for so long. The rush of adrenaline and energy that followed the failed suicide attempt could have led to any number of outcomes. Perhaps, the brush with mortality and the fragility of existence was enough to breathe new life into him. Regardless, in an instant, he was overcome by a sudden shock of resurgence that left him reeling with its astonishing power. Rather than being overwhelmed by tumultuous emotions over living with himself, he now felt buoyed by the support that was available to help him carry his burdens, creating a novel surge of hope.

The Actor felt a void being filled, a sense of completeness, as further self-reflection blossomed in his mind. He contemplated his problems and ultimately came to the realization that he would never be able to conquer them unless he brought them to light and faced them head-on. Memories of loved ones and their impact on his life inundated his mind, which also highlighted the deep sense of responsibility for the roles he plays in their lives as well.

By relinquishing control of the steering wheel and failing to navigate his course, he had veered dangerously off course and found himself stranded far from his intended path. Regaining his position in the driver's seat would empower him to chart his own course. *How did I slip so far from control?* Frustrated with his lack of awareness, he scolded himself for his ignorance. Toxic relationships and poor choices had left him mired in negative emotions. He now recognized the need to sever ties with indifferent or harmful people and reclaim control of his external environment. With sudden clarity, a vision for self-improvement took shape. First step: get rid of his manager.

Emerging from the bathtub, the Actor snatched up the gun and made his way downstairs.

***

With nothing but bare skin and a gun, the Actor strode into the room where the interlopers had congregated. Yet, it was his dangling member that caught the attention of everyone present, leaving the Sig Sauer pistol all but forgotten.

The Manager seemed to assess the situation in its entirety and immediately attempted to ease the tension.

"Hey, big guy, everything okay? A lot of *tools* you have out right now."

"Shut your damn mouth!" The Actor never raised the pistol to the firing position, but with a flick of a wrist, he hinted at the possibility of non-compliance. Adrenaline coursed through his veins, fueling his unwavering determination.

The Manager made another feeble attempt. "What's the problem?"

"Not another single word out of you!" The Actor emanated a fresh aura of confidence, liberating himself from the addiction that once sapped his strength. A potent force of electrifying hemoglobin rushed through his arteries, propelled *not* by some narcotic but by an inner fire ignited by a novel determination.

The Actor's eyes narrowed as he fixated on the Manager.

"You are undoubtedly one of the worst individuals I have ever allowed into my life. Since I became associated with you, you've manipulated me and encouraged this behavior solely for your benefit."

"I really don't think th—"

"I told you to shut your goddamn mouth! I am in control now. No one thinks or acts for me anymore. I know I am responsible for my actions, but you are *not* my advocate. I need to get rid of your toxic ass. So, get the hell out of my house. Oh, and if it wasn't already clear—You. Are. Fired!"

As the words reverberated throughout the room, the Actor maintained his piercing stare at his former manager, his eyes conveying a message louder than words could. Slowly and discreetly, several unwanted guests ambled out of the room and out of his life. Those who remained stood around, unsure of what was expected of them. A few continued sipping their drinks while glancing around at the others, waiting for guidance.

Recognizing that his development still necessitated the aid of others, the Actor knew he needed to get to a rehabilitation facility. He then turned to a random young woman, and with the gun pointed at her like a wagging finger, he spouted demands.

"You! You need to take me to rehab *right* this instant. That place that's uh, that's not far down the hill from here."

"Yes, whatever you want, just please, please, for the love of God, don't hurt me." The young woman nearly began convulsing as she wept with wide eyes. Bewildered by the woman's frantic response, the Actor failed to recognize that his finger-wagging with the Sig Sauer in his hand appeared to be a terrifying demand from a deranged nudist. Without delay, he lowered the weapon, placing his hands behind his back and leaning forward to convey an air of obedience and compassion.

"Oh! No, no, no. This is *not* a demand, and I understand this looks... threatening. Let me try again." The Actor delivered a laugh, but it only made him appear more unhinged. "Ma'am, *can* you please drive me to the closest rehabilitation center? I believe there is one down the road just a ways. After I put pants on, of course, and put the gun away."

He gave the skittish young lady a charming wink and grin, hoping to ease her worry. Thankfully, her lips curled in response, mirroring his expression. The silent affirmation filled the Actor with a burst of delight.

"Thank you so much, dear. You have no idea how much that means to me." He smiled at her, then turned toward the crowd, "The rest of you freeloaders, get the hell out of my house before I *do* start shooting."

The nuisances in his life scattered like cockroaches, fleeing in the wake of his newfound clarity.

As he sprinted up the stairs to get dressed, he was unable to refrain from grinning at the shattered glass fragments on the bathroom floor. Sometimes, a mere change in perspective can have voluminous consequences.

***

The initial stages of rehab mirrored his drug-filled binges: paying little attention to the mundane details of life, slipping in and out of consciousness, and being overwhelmed by fear and uncertainty. Days dragged on, but weeks passed in a flash. Nights were sleepless, soaked in sweat and consumed by the persistent agony in areas of his body he was unaware *could* even feel pain, embracing it eventually as it remained the one constant in his present existence. Despite it all, the Actor persisted, determined to emerge from the darkness and reclaim his life.

Once the physical symptoms of withdrawal began to subside, the Actor found that the road to recovery became much less daunting. The relief the Actor experienced upon discovering the root causes of his addiction was like being reborn—the tentacles of dependence released their grip, and he returned to the surface.

The mutual support among the other patients fostered an environment of heartfelt concern, creating camaraderie through shared experiences. Troubled souls helping troubled souls.

During his rehabilitation, the Actor rediscovered his compassion and empathy for others. A wave of support and outreach from fans motivated him to recover quickly and return to the world stronger than before. Supporters often described their trials with addiction, and some even fed off the Actor's "courage" to seek recovery of their own. But he could not help but feel despondent as his fame and success marginalized his flaws. In contrast, others who fall victim to the same winding road of fate are relegated to the gutters of society and acknowledged only as inconveniences to be avoided.

***

During the early days of sleepless nights and severe tremors, the Actor had a conversation with a fellow rehabilitator that often came to mind.

On a haunting wakeful night, the Actor slipped out of his room and ventured to the rehab center's back patio. Despite the sweatshirt and fleece blanket draped over his shoulders, the cool evening breeze sent chills down his clammy skin.

The only other wakeful wanderer on the terrace was an elderly gentleman donning sweatpants and a faded cardigan. He sat still, seeming lost in thought as he stared up at the vast expanse of the early morning sky.

Needing comfort or distraction, the Actor walked over to the man.

"May I join you?"

The older man simply looked up at him, smiled, lowered his gaze, and nodded. His face was etched with deep lines and wrinkles, not from the passage of time but weathered from misery. The Actor sat and followed his gaze, curious about what had captured his attention. He was not sure what to look for. Still, sitting quietly and enjoying the comfort of someone else's presence was peaceful.

Basking in the soothing stillness of companionship, the Actor marveled at how he could admire the vastness of the universe while simultaneously being aware of the microcosmic surprises constantly unfolding around him. *Where does consciousness land on the spectrum of astronomical and atomic?* He found himself exploring provocative queries. *How can we have the capacity to contemplate far beyond the expanses of one's reality all the way to the diminutive origins but then struggle to appreciate the present?* These thoughts, which were familiar echoes in his current environment, caused his mind to pulse with awareness.

The comforting voice of the gentleman beside him abruptly halted his reverie on the mysteries of life.

"You know, most people don't realize this, but stars are in constant conflict with themselves." With a momentary pause, the older man shifted his gaze to the Actor, and a simple glance drew his eyes to follow his own upward to the starry sky. The old man continued speaking, his words carrying an air of wisdom and experience. "The collective gravity of a star's mass causes it to *pull* inward. If there were nothing to prevent it, the star would continue collapsing until it became its smallest possible size. But there is *pressure* pushing back against the gravitational collapse of the star. And that pressure is, of course, *light*, my friend. Due to the nuclear fusion at the core of a star, it produces an enormous amount of energy. The photons push outward as they make their voyage from inside the star to the surface, a journey that can take thousands of years. When stars become more luminous, they expand outward and become red giants. And when they run out of light pressure, they collapse. They collapse down into white dwarfs... Even on the grandest dimensions of our universe, we find internal conflicts."

The two men smiled at each other, introduced themselves, and continued a brief session of small talk. The air was crisp and comfortable, and besides a few pleasant sounds from nature, the two men were in complete isolation.

After reaching a level of comfort, the Actor questioned the man's reason for being at the treatment facility.

"Well, my friend, I've actually never used a drug in my life, and I hardly touch the booze." The older man swallowed something difficult before he continued. "My wife died suddenly... about five years ago, and shortly after, my only daughter started using heroin. It didn't take long before it took her over. The usual routine: denial, rock bottom, apologies, exploit loved ones—repeat. I finally exhausted all my money into paying for a stay here, the best rehab hospital one could ask for, one last-ditch effort to save my little girl."

Pausing once more, the older man peered upward again, looking into the infinite void but zeroing in on specific coordinates as if he knew exactly where to address his thoughts.

The Actor felt entirely pitiful at the level of pain he felt relative to this man. Comparisons were never warranted during his treatment, but he believed empathizing with the tormented gave him the necessary perspectives. When indulging in his own desires, he had isolated himself while amplifying idiosyncratic and mundane details. Now, with an unceasing commitment to compassion, the Actor identified with his elder—two heartbeats, struggling to keep the motor running.

A noticeable glaze coated the older man's eyes as his eyelids quivered to contain their release—muscles strengthened with time. Somehow, he managed to speak, each word a labored effort that demanded more air than he had to give.

"My daughter passed away two weeks before her spot opened here... What was I supposed to do? All the typical people would come to me and say how sorry they were and be supportive and do this and that, but what you're receiving from them is... ahh... unusable, I suppose. It's impossible to exhibit that much empathy to feel how low someone is at that moment, especially when you haven't had those experiences. And I didn't want to be around anyone that wasn't as defeated as I am. So, I decided to use her place here and surround myself with other people currently at their bottom."

"I-I simply can't imagine. I am so sorry to hear about your family," the Actor offered, baffled by the revelation.

With a polite shake of his head and a wave of his hand, the older man acknowledged the statement, recognizing there was nothing else to be done or said.

"My wife was the love of my life—truly perfect for each other. You know, the only way I can explain it is that she and our daughter were the absolute lifeblood of me. Every decision I made was for them, giving me a higher purpose than I could ever fathom. That's what you need, my friend. I know you have your talents, but you need to find that one person or one thing that consumes all your love and attention."

As he listened to the words of the hardened gentlemen beside him, the Actor began to ruminate on the elements of his passions. Reflecting or sensing a premonition, he felt a strong desire for a connection, a union that would ignite a passion and steer him toward a higher purpose.

The older gentleman continued.

"It will take time, and I will never be the same, but life goes on; not the same life, a harder, more complicated life, but the gift of life is still there. That *can't* be ignored. And out of respect for *them*, I won't swallow up and die. I will continue to try and make positive impacts in this life because I know how significant their influence was, and I must make up for those losses now. That is precisely what they would have wanted. My wife used to have this saying that she would declare, 'You should always remember in bad times,' and then she would say, 'Especially in good times...that this too shall pass.' I always loved that idea. I will never get over this agony, and I don't want to because that means I will have forgotten about them. But if I don't continue on, then I will be ending their lives all over again. They deserve so much more."

As he shared his story, the Actor knew there were many ways to interpret it, and he found strength in the man's resilience in the face of loss and his unwavering dedication to those he loves; from the Actor's perspective, that took far more strength than kicking a bad habit and improving one's vanity. Unlike the older man, though, he had the privilege of being a source of goodness to his loved ones who were still alive. They would serve as the catalyst for his influence on the world.

"You're on a journey, my friend. And you have to realize that at the end of the day, it's not what you do or create that makes the most significant difference. It's how you make the people around you feel. That's it."

"Some journey. Landed me in rehab with sweaty, sleepless nights, and I don't know if anyone needs or even wants me anymore."

Turning toward each other, the two men held each other's gaze for an extended period, exchanging a sense of comfort and warmth through their eyes; the older man's eyes, swollen and red from incessant sobbing, retreated deep into their sockets.

Although his time in rehab was changing him, this particular evening, in the quiet darkness just before dawn, became the brightest beacon cast down the Actor's path. Even when everything that mattered was lost, the strength to keep going was a testament to the human spirit's resilience. It not only filled the Actor with courage and empowerment, but it also ignited a glowing devotion within him, reminding him of the strength of his convictions.

The older man smiled, stood up, and said one last thing before retiring to his room.

Travis Lane

"Life is tough right now and filled with many uncertainties, which can and will be absolutely frightening—I get it. But remember, my friend; this *too* shall pass."

Chapter Three

The sun's rays radiated with unusual vibrancy on this particular stretch of Earth, casting a luminous hue upon the verdant landscape. His wide-brimmed, deep burgundy, velvet hat with gentle curves tilted at the precise angle on his head to defend against the scorching radiance. An abundance of noises and smells from the countryside emanated throughout the crisp afternoon air.

As the rouncey pulled his carriage, he plucked the silk strings on his lyre, creating a harmonious melody that blended seamlessly with the rhythms of nature. His mind was attuned to the details of his surroundings, and he transformed them into captivating musical expressions, like a form of coordinated and effortless synesthesia. To him, music was akin to painting, allowing him to capture the essence of the invisible and bring it to life. A true genius and polymath, he possessed a masterful way of interpreting the world around him.

The Master was returning to the city, embarking on the second act after a tumultuous beginning. Having distanced himself from the public world of art and science, he now felt ready to resume his work. Following some recent artistic achievements, the Master had isolated himself from the world. Inspiration had been elusive, and he felt himself trenching a divide between reality and illusion.

Regrettably, his private struggles had come to public attention, exposing his vulnerabilities for the world to see.

While his actions had unquestionably damaged his reputation, the Master held onto a beam of optimism that he could restore his standing. The course of a decision, whether good or bad, is molded by the specific circumstances surrounding it, but posterity ultimately renders the final judgment. Devoid of options and aid, he departed the city, retreating to a reclusive existence until he could secure gainful employment again.

Taking in the panoramic countryside, the Master felt renewed with optimism and ambition for his return. As he rode through the farmlands, he finally reached the outskirts of civilization. Irrigation canals and fields of basil, chamomile, coriander, and sage filled the air, which then blissfully navigated to his nostrils. Plucking the strings of his lyre with acute precision, he skillfully mimicked the distinct aromas that permeated the air, allowing any listener to envision the scene in exquisite detail.

Emerging from his self-imposed exile, the Master was now brimming with renewed confidence and vigor, ready to take on the world once again. Mindful of his rare talents and opportunities, he resolved to use them to leave a lasting impact.

Despite his exile, the Master remained a dedicated worker, eagerly anticipating the opportunity to showcase his latest creations to his peers. One of his recent projects was the design of a clock featuring a fusee, which utilized a cone-shaped pulley with circular grooves, much like a bicycle gear. The cord, attached to a mainspring barrel, was wound around the fusee from bottom to top when the mainspring was wound all the way up, allowing both apparatuses to spin in unison as the cord unwinds from top to bottom onto the barrel during operation.

However, the clock was more than just a mechanical marvel. On top of both the fusee and barrel, the Master had attached a cylindric canvas painting around the winding arbors. The fusee displayed a portrait of a young man, while the barrel showed an older man. As the clock unwound, layers of drawings behind the cylinder canvas shifted the image of each man. While the clock ticked, the young man would slowly appear older as the old man on the barrel shifted toward a younger-looking man—depicting the regularity of repeating events, such as the ebb and flow of a wave.

The Master was consumed by another personal project that had taken over his life. Amid his "banishment" and self-pity, he encountered an individual who disrupted everything. This encounter shattered his logical vision of the world and replaced it with a mysterious façade. Overwhelming sensations vanquished reality, leaving only desire in its wake. The Master's typical empirical methods and deductive reasoning failed to account for these emotions, and his profound cognitive computing ability seemed superfluous in understanding the situation he found himself in.

The novel desire he felt frightened him, actually, and he attempted to retreat to familiarity and reason. But what truly lingered in his mind, more than any repetitive rote memory, was the visceral sensation that arose whenever he imagined the *eyes* of the enigmatic individual. He had sketched and painted hundreds of versions, each iteration pleasing him in its own way, yet he yearned for the genuine pair that remained elusive. No matter how wonderfully brilliant each brushstroke was, he could only produce a mediocre rendition. And as his obsession grew, he questioned whether it was the longing to create a perfect rendering or to gaze upon the real ones yet again.

The city hummed with the bustle of production and trade as a heady blend of aromas filled the air. Silk merchants and guild members exchanged information on dye ingredients and trade with neighboring cities, while music and theater acts vied for attention with street performers and demonstrations. Houses and buildings constructed of wood and woven strips were then coated with clay and horse dung. The urban commotion created a cacophony of almost deafening noise—town criers, church bells, and traders calling out their offerings. The result was a dizzying array of activities designed to activate all the senses.

A constant surge of excitement blossomed within the Master as he returned to the welcoming familiarity of his surroundings. After multiple back-and-forth letters to several studios, one of the guilds had cautiously accepted him to join. Despite concerns over his past altercations and potential difficulties, his skills and ambitions were deemed worth the risk.

Though the other masters would be hesitant, they recognized his ability to influence and inspire the younger acolytes. With a long-standing rapport with numerous religious and royal patrons, the studio devoted its efforts to producing paintings, altarpieces, murals, portraits, and other projects for many years, ultimately establishing a thriving and revered workplace.

As the Master's carriage pulled up to the studio, a mix of emotions washed over him. Pulling directly up to the anterior of the studio illuminated a mix of emotions for the Master. He was immediately greeted by a swarm of eager apprentices, their hands calloused from endless hours at the easel, each vying to assist him with his belongings. However, he also noticed the glares of other masters, who looked on with disdain from a distance; their attire was modest and marked by the stains of their craft.

Despite the mixed reception, the Master knew he had to comply with the guild's stipulations. As a newcomer, he was required to live with the apprentices until he established a steady stream of clients. Although this was a typical requirement, it was not without its challenges.

According to the Agent, his presence among the younger artists would arguably bolster ambition and excitement. As the studio supervisor, the Agent's primary responsibility was to represent, promote, and sell the artists' work, allowing him to have the final say on any business regarding the creative professionals.

As the Master and the protégés began to unpack his gear, a young, curious-eyed pupil approached the commotion, making the proper acquaintances with a mixture of awe and admiration.

"Val'rous aft'rnoon, t seemeth yond thee shalt beest w'rking with us."

"Aye, so it seemeth."

The Student, his youthful enthusiasm subtly etched in the curve of his eager smile, reveled at the prospect of engaging in the crafts with such a masterful artisan. The Master's rapid and triumphant success in his professions was unmatched, and his premium and highly popular work inspired many young artists. His pioneering constructs were widely regarded as the epitome of excellence and tenaciously sought after by aspiring artists eager to emulate his success.

A faint grin spread across the Master's face as he remembered his humble beginnings but quickly pushed the thought aside. He knew that hard work and dedication were the only paths to success, and he was determined to recapture his former glory.

Upon one of his trips to unload his belongings into the studio, the Master caught a glimpse of the only man in his profession he truly admired. This dynamic antagonist was an unparalleled source of knowledge and expertise, leaving the Master in awe of his rival's skill. Despite their fierce competition for the same services, the two men rarely exchanged more than passive-aggressive subtleties during their chance encounters. As their eyes finally met from across the way, the two rivals exchanged a non-verbal message of mutual respect and admiration, silently acknowledging the potential impact of their shared experiences—whether a force for good or ill, its influence remained uncertain. With a subtle nod from the Scholar and an equitable gesture from the Master, it was time to get to work.

***

Experiencing the inner workings of a workshop was akin to witnessing an art form in and of itself. Communal spaces were designed to bring together a wide range of disciplines, from painters and sculptors to mathematicians and scientists, all united in their pursuit of new ideas and techniques while enabling the convergence of art and science.

Under the watchful eye of their masters, young artists honed their skills, explored uncharted methods, and pushed the limits of what was possible. In this environment of healthy competition and cooperation, ideas flowed freely, and creativity knew no bounds.

And though the rules for the young artisans were strict, they felt free to explore and share their thoughts, knowing that they were among a community that valued and respected their contributions.

The guilds' diverse pool of talented individuals brought together a wealth of knowledge and skills, fueling a never-ending stream of revolutionary innovations. A painter and sculptor's eyes, trained in the human form, working with a physician, brought forth depictions of unparalleled accuracy and beauty. Altarpieces would be designed with great beauty and architectural perfection as various experts assembled around a single project. Work was an ongoing enterprise as most craftsmen lived within proximity and rarely detracted from conversations about the creations inside the studio.

Amidst the chaotic exchange of arts and sciences, the Master found himself alone, tucked away in the corner of the main studio room. Struggling to concentrate on his work, he studied the commotion before him, envious of the exchange of brilliance he was *not* included in. In the company of other visionaries, he experienced moments of pure bliss as they collaborated to create something extraordinary. By bouncing ideas off each other, they discovered solutions to previously unknown problems. The sport of conversation and debate enhanced everyone's understanding of the world, and when provided with a proper platform, beautiful art came to be. Reignited with passion, the Master yearned to escape back into that communal *flow*.

Beside his easel, he placed his aging pendulum timepiece, hoping to capture attention and generate conversation. Alas, no one noticed its delicate craftsmanship, and he spent the next hours quietly and methodically adjusting his workstation before the Agent approached him with a steady purpose.

"Art thee getting comf'rtable with thy accommodations?"

Faced with the degrading demotion to protégé status, the Master felt his confidence falter, undermined, and disrespected. Yet, he refused to succumb to despair. Instead, he gathered his bearings and resolved to working hard to alleviate any dissonance within the guild. His approach would be one of humble subservience, biding his time until he could rise again.

"I couldst not beest happi'r with this opp'rtunity and mineth owneth current accommodations."

"Val'rous! What art thee w'rking on at thy moment?" The Agent sauntered around the workstation; arms held lightly behind his back as his eyes meticulously assessed the surroundings.

"While on mineth owneth, um, sabbatical, I devis'd a h'rologe with an aesthetically pleasing depiction of the aging of sir and the relation to repeateth occurrences."

"Int'resting. I am sure the oth'rs wouldst liketh to seeth thy w'rk."

The Agent departed as quickly as he arrived, abandoning the Master before he was prepared for the conclusion of their meeting. Previous feelings of exuberance had now begun to dissipate, and he yearned for the solitude he once thought he loathed.

The Master's attention drifted to the clock, which the Agent had hastily disregarded. A sudden urge to smash it on the ground and give in to a thunderous rage seized him, tempting him to destroy everything in sight until he was satiated with his torment or too exhausted to continue.

As an alternative, he chose to triumph over his agony. The Master inhaled deeply through his nose, and after a long, tranquil pause, he exhausted the putridness of his pain—embracing his restrained composure.

Struck with the realization that his swiftest return to a paid artisan was by creating portraits or busts for wealthy patrons, he began his quest, gathering an array of human forms to study and perfect. Undeterred by the means through which he obtained his subjects, the Master delved deeply into the intricacies of every body part. The Master studied how light was reflected and absorbed in each area, using this knowledge to create the most realistic descriptions with each brushstroke. Scientific studies were equally important to him as his artistic activities; while having a keen eye for aesthetics was necessary, recognizing the dynamics of structural anatomy and physiology was equally vital.

The Master often considered the importance of understanding the growth of an individual and the expression of emotions, crucial knowledge that allowed him to capture the true essence of his client's portraits at any given moment. This attention to detail often left patrons joyfully tearful at first sight of themselves.

***

Shortly after accommodating himself within the studio, the Master wasted no time in enlisting the aid of the Student to assist him in pitching his paintings to a wealthy merchant in the countryside. Together, they gathered an assortment of the Master's lifelike depictions of the human form, ranging from sketches to fully-realized canvases, and set out to procure employment.

As they made their way to the merchant's lavish estate within the carriage, the apprehensive Student struggled to overcome his nervousness and engage in conversation with his revered teacher. After mustering his nerve, the Student found his voice.

"What w're thee doing while hence, Mast'r?"

Scornfully analyzing the juvenile, the Master relished in a moment of dominance before retreating from the fervent persona. Yearning for the warmth of human companionship, he flashed a smile at the eager Student and delved into a captivating recollection of the projects he had crafted during his absence while showing the most personal praise for his clock design.

"And as it unwinds, it grants did lie'rs upon the images, shifting the sir's visage to and fro, all at the behest of timeth."

"I am marvel'd by such a notion and eag'rly anticipateth the opp'rtunity to beholdeth it. Might I inquire as to wheth'r thee has't any oth'r endeav'rs yond thou art currently pursuing?"

"Nay, nothing imp'rtant."

The Master never spoke of his fixation on the eyes, for it was too intimate to reveal. It was well-known that the artisan world was a haven for vulnerability and emotion, a place where the heart ruled the mind; however, this particular project held a special place in *his* heart—keeping those ideas archived. Time and experience had taught the Master the art of embracing his true self as the embodiment of his essence to the world, a challenging task that demanded great introspection and resilience. Yet, despite his tenacity, he shrouded that very being into obscurity. But with the ebbs and flows of life's current, this was now the period of his revival.

Upon arriving at the sprawling 90-acre estate, a hush of awe enveloped the Master and Student. The stunning variety of well-crafted botanicals, laid out in a meticulous design, left guests spellbound. Rising regally above the verdant flora was a pristine white stone mansion, its Lauze stone roofs and symmetrical proportions showcasing an artistic and structural masterpiece. The grandeur of the estate was set against a backdrop of a vineyard landscape beyond human replication—nature's confident shrug of effortless splendor.

Visitors were greeted by a colossal front door, exquisitely designed to entice them inward; beautifully handcrafted African mahogany served as the partition between royalty and commoners. Above, towering stained-glass windows that rivaled a cathedral offered a breathtaking visual. While below, marble ponds bestowed a bountiful display of exotic fish, adding a touch of enchantment to the already mesmerizing surroundings. Every detail was carefully tended to, as neither a single leaf nor blade of grass was askew, all thanks to the tireless efforts of an army of laborers who meticulously manicured the grounds.

Servants, dressed in drab clothing, quickly assembled around the rouncey and began assisting with unloading the Master's work. Once inside, the extravagance only intensified. Paintings and sculptures adorned the opulent interior, and household fixtures were created from the rarest metals.

The two artisans were ushered into the dining area, where a sumptuous feast was spread out for everyone to savor. Meats, cheeses, fruit, and pastries were all displayed decoratively, far beyond the needs of the guests present. At the head of the table, a robust man clad in the latest haute couture fashion gorged relentlessly as a servant introduced the two guests, ushering them into the lavish dining hall.

After a perfunctory introduction, the Noble dismissed the window of opportunity to greet the men properly, opting to smugly gesture for them to enter instead. He was a revolting specimen, oozing constant vile, with a body that seldom hindered his constant perspiration. His stench permeated through the aroma of the elaborate spread, and as the Master watched the Noble devour a pork rib with unbridled gusto, cannibalistic thoughts invaded his mind. Finally, with a morsel still in his mouth, the Noble spoke with a lack of decorum.

"Ahh, the talent. Welcometh."

"Val'rous aft'rnoon, Sir."

The two artisans spoke in unison as they respectfully bowed to address the man of elevated economic stature.

"I seeth those gents hath sent a neophyte and the dissident."

The Noble forced a brutish laugh, taking a ludicrously large bite of a succulent turkey leg, heedless of the scattered bits of spittle and flesh that flew from his gaping mouth. With no sense of decency, the Noble brazenly continued speaking as if his insatiable appetite was more pressing than the courtesy of his guests.

"I supposeth those gents has't not much respect f'r mineth own wanteth and desires down at thy studio."

Standing up straighter, the Master spoke confidently.

"With all due respect, Sir, I believeth those gents hath sent thee two of the finest artists not only the studio but the city can off'r."

"Is yond so?"

"This young pupil hast shown extreme progresseth in various fields, arguably a top perf'rm'r. And myself? Well, despite one's feelings ov'r mineth actions, the value in mineth owneth w'rk is premium."

Without uttering a word, the Noble continued devouring his rations, his eyes locked in a challenging stare with the Master. The Noble's contempt for miscreants, which the Master was now labeled, was evident, and his anger seethed at the Master's presence.

The Master was certain the man had already made up his mind about any potential business between them. Still, he remained steadfast in his conviction to captivate him with his charm and sublime craftsmanship. He refused to falter in his pursuit of success—he pressed forward.

"I am w'rking again f'r a reasoneth. I was *not* imposed to an int'rval of exile. Twas initally believeth to beest p'rmanent. The requesteth f'r mineth owneth w'rk was too ov'rwhelming to keepeth me hence. I am backeth because I am the most wondrous… sir."

The Noble's fiery glare softened, and surprisingly, his thin lips twisted into a wry grin. At the sight of this, the Master felt delighted, recognizing that a mere reminder of his expertise was enough to ease any doubters.

The Noble rose to his feet, abandoning his half-eaten turkey leg and snatching up his chalice of palm wine. With an arrogant strut, he ambled over to the two men, his extravagantly purple robe trailing comically along the floor as he swayed back and forth. Halting just a step away from the Master, the Noble gazed up at the unyielding figure before him and declared.

"Thou art one arrogant hound! How dareth thee cometh into mineth owneth house and speaketh so proudly of theeself."

The unexpected retort made the Master flinch backward, and he quickly interjected to defend himself.

"Sir, I assureth thee yond p'rsonal and business particulars shall not affect the quality of mineth owneth w'rk. Mineth owneth whole purpo—"

"Thee hark to me! I shalt not payeth any amount of currency 'r mineth owneth timeth to someone who is't acts so bellig'rent. The way thee walketh in h're so confidently and arrogantly disgusts me, and I shalt did spread the w'rd of thy pitiful aroma until nay one hires thee and thou art once again expell'd from existence."

Stunned by the shift in momentum, the Master recoiled further from the rabid brute. A fiery urge to retaliate nearly consumed him, but he knew that even uttering a single word could result in his ultimate defeat and put a swift end to his awaited comeback.

With his mouth open and tongue pressing on the inside of his bottom teeth, the Master was primed to strike, and when he folded over the petite figure, his brow furrowed, his senses homed in on his prey with animalistic precision. But despite his initial impulse to fight, he realized that sometimes, walking away was the only way to win.

Retreat was inevitable, as the Master knew not every battle was worth the fight. With a slovenly bow to the homeowner, he turned and walked away, leaving behind the fruitless confrontation. As the two artists mounted the rouncey and rode off into the horizon, defeat was accepted, but the Master vowed to hone his skills for the battles to come.

***

The ride back was silent except for the rhythmic sound of hoofbeats and the gentle rustling of leaves; the pair of artists rode side by side. They were lost in thought, each pondering the recent events, and the Master wondered if the Student shared his dismay at the Noble's aggressive behavior.

Unable to contain his frustration any longer, the Master turned to the Student and spoke in a pragmatic and urgent voice.

"Yond horrid Sir hast nay business speaking those w'rds to me. To us."

He waited for the Student to respond—yielding his opportunity, the Master continued his rant.

"An irrational sir liketh yond hast nay business receiving mineth owneth w'rk anyways. Yond gent shalt beest s'rry at which hour ev'ryone is yearning f'r me."

Silence continued to hang in the air, broken only by the monotonous sound of horses' hooves on the cobblestone. The Master exhaled another defeat and resumed his introspection on the situation while the young pupil remained aloof and indifferent.

The silence in the carriage was oppressive, magnifying the tension between them with each passing moment. As they rode on, the claustrophobic space seemed to shrink even further until it felt like no more air was left to breathe.

With a full breath gathered, the Student finally spoke up.

"May I speaketh openly, Sir?"

The break in silence startled the Master.

"Prithee."

"Thee believeth yond the Noble was irrational, but I disagreeth…"

The Student paused for consent from his pedagogue.

"Besides a briefeth mention of me, thee hath spent the entire timeth talking only of yourself and what *thee* can off'r. The guild hath opened their arms to thee, and thee still only bethink of yourself. Not once didst thee mention how w'rking togeth'r with all the artisans, scientists, craftsmen, and oth'rs can produceth the most sup'rb w'rk. Haply if 't be true 't beest true thee allud'd to the teamw'rk and collection of thoughts and ideas w'rking togeth'r, *we*, not thee, wouldst produceth the most wondrous w'rk, then that gent might has't been m're receptive."

Another astonishing occurrence rocked the mind of the Master, forcing him to question his perceived omniscience. *Might mineth owneth grasp of these events beest misguided?* His earlier victories and recent resurgence from the abyss had filled him with unwarranted confidence, leading him to believe that he was entitled to success.

As they journeyed, the discomfort inside their transport grew more intense. The Master struggled to find solace and instead resorted to staring blankly out the window, his cheek resting on his fist, overwhelmed with embarrassment and defeat. As he reflected, the Master endeavored to adopt the perspective of others, seeking to understand a different view of the world. He tried to imagine what the Noble and Student were thinking during their previous interaction. He imagined what the studio's agent thought about accepting him even though it was an unpopular move. Maybe his acceptance was *not* due to his "superior performance" or "knowledge" but something else entirely.

The Master acknowledged that past triumphs do not secure future success; they only serve to elevate one's confidence. He berated himself for his inability to discern these self-evident truths and questioned whether a genuinely exceptional mind would have overlooked such basic principles—humbling reminders of one's limitations. Nevertheless, he found solace in the newfound awareness that every individual perceives the world through their own unique lens.

Even more illuminating, the Master considered, was the realization that a mere youth had bestowed upon him this particular gift of enlightenment. The illusion of mastery is often shattered by the timeless truth that sometimes, the most profound education comes from the unadulterated, unfiltered vision of the youth. With unwavering conviction, he set his sights higher, knowing he could be better, and he would prove it—to the world and himself.

As the carriage jostled through the crowded streets, the interior remained silent, and the Master continued staring out the window at the eclectic individuals careening about their day.

Suddenly, something caught his eye, and he bolted to life. Without warning, a sublime intuition signaled the arrival of a vision immediately before he *actually* saw *them*. He shouted to the coachman to halt the rouncey, his hands trembling with excitement as he fumbled with the door handle.

The Master's descent from the wagon was both awkward and undignified after he finally managed to pry the door open and tumble to the ground. Momentarily stunned and disoriented, he lifted himself to search for the source of the electrifying impulse that had spurred him into action.

Elbowing his way through the throngs of people, the Master spun around in every direction, straining to catch a glimpse of the elusive treasure. His heart pounding with excitement and frustration, he berated himself for letting *them* slip away again. A burst of exhilaration shot through the Master's body as he caught sight of the irresistible eyes. Despite the surrounding chaos of the busy streets, the eyes leaped out at him like a bolt of lightning illuminating a dark forest. The details of *her* face had now been fully revealed to him, and he found himself entranced by how her features seamlessly blended, forming a portrait of pure, organic beauty. Never abashed, her cheekbones were prominent and exotic, resembling the contours of cherished landscapes. The sharp and definitive ridgeline of her nose eventually guided one's gaze to the swollen, forbidden fruit of the forest—lips thick and sensual and so tempting to taste.

But nothing demonstrated greater power than the intensity of her *eyes*. The waves, currents, tides, and storms, all the forces of the ocean were prominent in her penetrating stare. He felt numbed and charged simultaneously, entirely at the mercy of the elements.

Oblivious to the world around him, lost in the hypnotic pull of her eyes, the Master was awed by her power and was unable to resist a smile to break free from his lips. Filled with a new sense of purpose, the Master felt determined, destined to uncover the identity of the elusive beauty who had upset the delicate balance of his existence.

***

Back at the studio, the Master stood tall at his workstation, meticulously assessing every aspect of the face that complemented the enigmatic eyes he had been obsessing over—time to work. With every brushstroke, he breathed life into his creation, imbuing it with an unparalleled luminosity and texture.

Although typically customary for specialized paint preparers to handle the dyeing process, the Master was far too fastidious about leaving anything to chance. As he ground the pigments in the marble muller, he calculated the proper amount of linseed oil to create his ideal texture and luminosity. The oils allowed for a far superior delicacy in the colors because the translucent colors could be layered, creating a wide range of tones. Scrutinizing over this task with every iteration of the eyes that he painted, he felt he had finally created the correct shade.

The Master's brush quivered with anticipation as it approached the canvas. His inaugural stroke was an act of sheer determination, a declaration of his unyielding commitment to bringing his vision to life. With eyes closed, he transported himself back to the moment on the street that had ignited his desires. Every detail, every nuance of the scene, was burned into his memory, and he worked tirelessly to recreate every microscopic element upon the canvas.

Time stood still as the world continued to turn around him. Lost in concentration, he was oblivious to the events unfolding around him. People came and went, their conversations barely registering as he tuned out the world around him. Hunger, thirst, and exhaustion were mere trifles in the face of his unrelenting passion. Only the sound of a specific phrase uttered in passing was capable of catapulting him back to reality and out of his creative trance.

"I recognizeth those eyes."

"P-pardon me?"

Uncertain about whom he was talking to, the Master stepped back from his painting, which felt as if he was emerging from the canvas, elevating from the depths of his designs. Naturally, his focus was drawn to his subject's eyes; despite the intricate detail, the contours of the face remained unfinished, leaving an indiscernible portrait. Although, his work made it entirely unavoidable to become lost in the ocean of possibilities those eyes offered.

The Master pivoted and saw the Scholar standing over his shoulder with a mesmerized inspection of his canvas. His posture, though slightly stooped with age, maintained an air of regal bearing, mirroring the dignified poise of a great maestro of the arts.

"I hath said I recognizeth those eyes."

"Thee wilt beest mistaken."

"Nay, Sir. And, I might not but sayeth, but those art undoubtedly the most p'rfect rendition of human eyes I has't ev'r seen."

The Master, still returning from the ethereal realm of his creative space, struggled to comprehend the words and their origin. Though the weight of the man's compliment was substantial, he could not ignore the need to address the statement regarding the owner of such captivating eyes.

"How doth thee knoweth whom these eyes belongeth to?"

"I liketh how thee didst addeth so much detaileth to the lines and veins 'round the eye to maketh it m're expressive." With soft strokes, he traced his fingers along his lengthy beard, the subtle gesture revealing a contemplative nature as he pondered.

"Aye, I appreciateth yond. I'm s'rry, didst thee heareth mineth owneth inquiry?"

"I believeth the m're imp'rtant questioneth is wherefore art thee so imm'rs'd with painting those eyes, hmm?"

Slightly annoyed by the dismissal of his question, the Master reminded himself to be calm and collected. He was pleased to have started a dialog with the Scholar, and if he held information about the owner of these wondrous eyes, he could oblige his interrogation.

"I has't seen those eyes twice, anon. Those eyes englut ev'ry didst biteth of mineth owneth waking bethought. A f'rv'rnt obsession regurgitat'd through mineth owneth brusheth."

The Scholar was noticeably charmed by the man's honesty. Unbeknownst to the Master, the Scholar had kept a keen eye on him since his arrival. Although he could only claim to understand a fraction of what the Master had been grappling with, he felt a profound empathy for the struggles and triumphs that defined the man's artistic journey. As he witnessed the Master incessantly working while the other guild members came and went from the studio, his rich curiosity exhausted him to the point where he had to inquire about the obsessive endeavor.

"I wilt sayeth. Thy obsession with this painting inspires me."

"I appreciateth thy acknowledgment, but I wilt eke commence with bringing w'rk to the guild."

"I disagreeth. I has't faith yond if 't be true thee showeth this amount of passion towards any projecteth, the w'rk shalt cometh to thee."

"Possibly."

With a hint of skepticism in his voice, the Master offered a dubious retort.

Suddenly, he remembered the first words the Scholar had uttered with his unexpected interruption.

"How can thee recognizeth these eyes?"

"One doest not f'rget such a set of eyes so easily."

Angry at the Scholar's equivocation, the Master feverishly lapsed into an incessant interrogation.

"Pardon me, might thee elab'rate furth'r? How doth thee knoweth who is't these eyes belongeth to? Art thee ribbing me? thee wilt bid me who is't this is if 't be true thou art telling the truth."

With the hyperactive questioning the Scholar was receiving, he could not help but grin, which agitated the Master even further, reddening his face and bulging his eyes in response. The dilation of the man's eyes prompted an idea. He widened his smile and spoke softly to the Master.

"Cometh with me. I wanteth to showeth thee something."

Bewilderment consumed the Master. His eyes flicked around in disarray as to find the answers to his questions and the direction of where the conversation was heading. But as the Scholar turned to depart, the Master eventually withdrew his internal probing and followed in his wake.

The two literati strolled amidst the throng of craftsmen, scientists, and experts in various fields. The Master followed obediently behind the Scholar, still simmering with resentment over their conversation's abrupt conclusion.

Though he never explicitly admitted it, the Master held the Scholar in high esteem and aspired to emulate many facets of his work—a feature that functioned as a catalyst for his conscientiousness.

At the Scholar's workstation, he rifled through a set of drawers, emerging with a drawing portfolio. With a quick gesture, he invited the Master for a closer look. The folder contained a breathtaking array of facial drawings and paintings, each a masterpiece in its own right. But it was the eyes that held the Master's attention, enticing him in like a moth to a flame. As he gazed upon the illustrations, the Master felt a sense of jealous awe wash over him.

"These art wond'rful."

"Thanketh thee. Thanketh thee."

From the faintest sketch to the most intricate paintings, the Scholar's work indicated distinct brilliance and tenacity. The Master was struck by the level of detail the Scholar had painstakingly rendered onto each surface, a testament to his profound skill and unwavering commitment to his crafts.

Flipping through the booklet, the Scholar explained how he had dissected countless different eyeballs from multiple species, intending to sketch from the *inside out*. He informed the Master that through his studies, he concluded that the iris played a crucial role in regulating the diameter and size of the pupil, thereby controlling the amount of light reaching the back of the eye.

The Master listened in rapt attention as the Scholar delved deeper into his obsession with the human eye; mostly consumed with understanding what was "behind" the eyes—a chasm that remained beyond the reach of any scalpel. Not only were there drawings of multiple eye colors but many with extreme dilation and contraction.

In the end, the Scholar had mastered the replication of the human eye.

"I didst wanteth to giveth thee the paintings to possibly assisteth thee with thy um, endeav'r. Thy passion is motivating, and i desire it continues."

"These art all unbelievably brilliant."

As the leather-bound folder changed hands, the Master felt a pang of envy shoot through him. This man was his rival, competitor, and enemy of sorts, and now he was willingly handing over years of assiduous personal work, an act of courage and confidence that the Master could only admire.

The two men stood there, silent except for the shuffling of papers and the sound of their own thoughts—drawing conclusions about the situation and each other. Though gratitude filled his heart, the Master believed that expressing it would only underscore his vulnerability and the extent of his jealousy. So, instead of thanking him, the Master attempted to bring levity to the situation and sought to glean as much information as possible.

"Tis fine, so art thee going to bid me who is't's eyes those belongeth to?"

The Scholar offered a fleeting laugh.

"In due timeth. I am sure thou art acknown of the artisan competition approaching soon, c'rrect?"

"Of course."

"I has't didst concludeth yond if 't be true thee award'd most proficient artist, then I shalt bewray to thee the myst'rious individual who is't bears those eyes."

The Master's mouth curved upward in amusement, with his lips parting enough to signal the acceptance of the challenge.

Both men stood there grinning at each other. Each conveying a different sentiment but aligned in their commitments. They were both driven by a deep-seated need to explore the mysteries of the human form, to capture its essence and beauty. They were both artists but also scientists by virtue of their qualities.

The Master finally gave a confirmation nod and shook the Scholar's hand. He then motioned for the Scholar to join him at his workstation, eager to discuss other projects that occupied his mind and heart.

They were two very diverse personalities, voyaging down different paths, trying to answer the same questions. The Master was determined to reach his goal of being a superior artist. Through the valleys of his struggles and hardships, he clung to the unwavering belief that his resilience and achievements would conjure from within him an unbreakable spirit fueled by a relentless drive that would only yield once victorious outcomes emerged.

Though the requisite elements of success were firmly grasped, it was only after coming to a profound realization of the empowering effects of positive external influences that the true value of these catalyzing forces was embraced as an indispensable component of the journey toward triumph. While advocates can offer invaluable guidance, it was the Master's most implacable adversary that ultimately fueled his ambition.

In his relentless pursuit of personal excellence, the Scholar served as a formidable rival who pushed him to continually surpass his limits. Even as the Master tried to temper his emotions, the very idea of meeting those wondrous eyes that had so enraptured him sparked a blaze within his soul, igniting a fierce longing to achieve the impossible.

Chapter Four

Sitting in stillness, he felt the subtle vibrations on his bare feet. The walls of the diminutive chamber appeared to be trembling at the same rhythm. Looking around, he wondered if the room caving in on him was a better alternative to what lay ahead. *No, get those thoughts out of your mind,* he asserted to himself. His nerves disrupted rationale.

This was the pinnacle, the capstone, the culmination of his journey—only seconds away. Innumerable moments of defeat and despair littered his journey, yet he knew there was no better place to conclude it. His ascension toward greatness, the bitter tastes of failure and despondence, the resurgence; all of it only worthwhile—to close out on top.

As his gaze wandered to the wall clock, he felt the final surge of anticipation wash over him as final preparations were required. He inspected his personalized electromagnetic suit, ensuring it was tightly secured to his body. Within the suit, electrons connected to his entire muscular system, which were designed to monitor his physical capabilities, tracking every exertion and discomfort he endured, indicating his power gauge levels. The more effort he exerted or pain he suffered would deplete the power gauge, eventually rendering his suit and other equipment useless. Though the attire enhanced his physical capabilities, it weakened the same as his flesh and blood.

Seated, he slipped on his boots, inspecting each one before sliding his foot into the device. He ensured the two magnetized ball bearings located at the toe and heel would be deployed effectively, allowing him to travel the terrain efficiently and move at expeditious speeds.

Next, he positioned his helmet securely over his head, tightening the straps with a satisfying click. As he turned the power on, the face shield came to life with a flicker of light. A kaleidoscope of information appeared before his eyes, each indicator a glowing point of data, the most important being his and his contender's power supplies.

As the walls of the small staging room continued to tremble with palpable energy, each tick of the clock built a crescendo of excitement and anticipation. In just a few moments, he would step into the pod that elevated him to the surface. Within seconds of stepping into the shell, he would be transported from complete solitude in the small room to the middle of a colossal arena with nearly two-hundred-thousand screaming fanatics and seven other determined contenders. The walls shook even harder from the masses above, pounding away with the thrill of the impending competition. The Athlete was ready.

The surface of the arena was the stage for an electrifying display of human aggression and athleticism. As soon as the games commenced, the eight participants would spring into action, racing around the massive arena at audacious speeds, scavenging for weapons to use against their adversaries in a no-holds-barred melee. A formidable force field separated the gladiators from the spectators, as objects and humans became lethal projectiles. The dynamic venue was a chameleon, constantly shifting its shape and form, with obstacles and levels that added layers of complexity to the frenzied battle.

This skirmish was only the first of three rounds to determine the ultimate winner of the coveted title. After the tumultuous clash, the eight contenders would be ranked by points, positioning them for the second round—an adrenaline-fueled, death-defying race. Placing high in both the arena and the race was pivotal to securing a solid position for the final, daring round. It was a game like no other, a true test of skill and grit—a game they called Sparticon!

For the Athlete, one thing was crystal clear; winning the championship was crucial. However, his rival agreed to a wager that rested on the outcome of the first event. If the Athlete placed higher, his opponent would introduce him to an individual that occupied every crevice of his mind. The Athlete was wholly preoccupied with this individual, so much so that he found himself scrutinizing every aspect of their hypothetical interaction. He analyzed every potential conversation topic, rehearsed every word in his head, and ran through every possible scenario until he was confident he would not make a fool of himself. The prospect of meeting this person had become as vital as winning the championship.

The clock on the wall signaled that the time had come to enter the pod. At a slow and stately pace, the Athlete approached the transportive cocoon. Stepping in, he surrendered himself to a realm of countless uncertainties. As the capsule sealed him in, he felt a sense of finality. The world outside fell away, and all that remained was the sound of his breathing and the steady beat of his heart.

With a sudden jolt, he could feel himself elevating toward the surface, and the anticipation was now palpable. Moving gradually, the mechanics hummed beneath him, their steady thrum punctuated by the escalating roar of the fans. The fog on his face shield suggested the rapid pace of his breathing; his hands trembled with unease.

The Athlete drew a deep breath and closed his eyes, imagining the arena stretched out before him—envisioning his initial moves. At the outset of the game, a single error could shatter both victory and possibly life. In this fast-paced arena, humans hurtled forward at speeds upwards of one hundred miles per hour, wielding weapons and braving hazards at every turn. To prevail in this contest, a contender had to be swift, nimble, cunning, and creative. With its unparalleled grandeur, *Sparticon* reigned supreme above all other sports, standing unrivaled as the undisputed main event.

As he emerged from the mechanical esophagus and into the stadium's bright lights, his pupils dilated in wonder at the stunning display of human ingenuity. A vast, bustling sea of people surrounded him, awash with the vibrancy and energy of life itself. The deafening cacophony of screams, pounding footsteps, fireworks, and music shattered his focus and disrupted his game plan as he had mere seconds before the match began. Angry at his desultory, he quickly absorbed everything he could before it was too late.

"Commence!"

The announcer belted through the sound system.

More explosions of fireworks lit up the sky. As the eight contenders scattered and planned their attacks, the arena came to life and began to shift and move—its very foundations pulsing with the energy of their struggle.

Roughly fifty meters away, a weapon rose from the ground, elevated by powerful magnets. The Athlete's eyes locked onto it, and he launched himself forward. Another contender had the same idea. Both competitors leaned into their stride, allowing the ball bearings on their boots to propel themselves with blinding velocity.

They arrived at the weapon simultaneously, each grasping for the electrically charged baton designed to deliver debilitating shocks to the recipient. Clung together, the two athletes spun and weaved in a chaotic dance of combat, each trying to wrench the weapon from the other's grip. Punches and knee strikes landed with bone-breaking force, but neither competitor could gain the upper hand.

The two fighters scaled a curved wall, defying gravity as they pushed their bodies to the limit. Advancing higher up the wall eventually caused them to lose their balance, and as if hitting an invisible ceiling, their bodies tumbled back to the flat surface below. Just as the fighters were regaining their bearings, a shockwave grenade landed with a deafening boom between them. With no time to react, they were hurled through the air, the electric baton flying haphazardly out of reach. The crowd of thousands bellowed a thunderous gasp as the Athlete struggled to bring his mental faculties in order. The other contender and the baton were nowhere to be seen, lost in the chaos of the explosion.

With a sickening jolt, the Athlete realized that the early incident had already depleted much of his power, and he felt it. But he could not afford to dwell on that now. With fierce determination, he looked ahead, ready for whatever the arena threw at him next.

As the mêlée raged on, the Athlete knew he needed a new strategy—and fast. The arena was a frenzy of activity as opponents clashed and fought with all their might, their every move scrutinized by a rapt audience.

The Athlete, grateful to have evaded further harm, sprang to his feet and took off down a narrow path, his mind racing as he searched for a new weapon with cautious eyes. With each passing moment, his chances of evading detection dwindled, his power gauge registering the lowest of the eight.

As he tore down the narrow track, the crowd's deafening roar amplified in his ears, signaling the tumultuous events unfolding within the stadium.

Suddenly, a large portion of the arena began to shift and contort. The track just ahead of him enclosed as the adjacent ground shifted and became the ceiling, trapping the Athlete in a perilous situation—forced to go through the tunnel or ascend above.

As he approached the makeshift underpass, another contender appeared at the other end and immediately darted toward him while wielding a deadly shock hammer. Weaponless, depleted of strength, and with limited options, the Athlete pushed himself to go even faster, knowing that his survival hung in the balance. Unable to reverse his course quickly enough to escape, the Athlete's only chance was to reach the enclosed area before his enemy and jump onto the upper level.

A single, solid strike from a shock hammer would surely result in a certain defeat for the Athlete and a swift exit from the competition.

The Athlete analyzed the distance and his approaching adversary, his heart racing. It was going to be close. He hunched over, muscles tensed, and sprung forward as fast as he could. The space between them was closing rapidly, and he knew he had to make a move soon; however, jumping early might also prove lethal.

Closing the distance rapidly, the contender positioned the hammer to strike. Just as they were about to collide, the Athlete launched himself into the air with a mighty leap, ascending to the upper level of the track with remarkable agility. Below him, the rival contender swung the hammer, but the Athlete's lightning-fast reflexes allowed him to evade the strike.

As the Athlete soared above, his rival noticed and continued the weapon's momentum with a backward follow-through, grazing the Athlete's foot with a cruel and venomous touch. The subtle but significant contact from the shock hammer caused the Athlete to take a chaotic trajectory back toward the surface. He tumbled end over end, losing all sense of direction and control. The audience let out a collective shriek as he eventually landed on the ground like a ragdoll.

The Athlete again labored to regain his composure; his energy reserves had already depleted to just over twenty percent. Gasping for air, he lifted his face shield and expelled a mouthful of blood too painful to swallow. It was clear to him that this was far from the promising beginning he planned on.

Pulling down his face shield, the Athlete surveyed the arena, noting that one of his competitors had been eliminated. He felt a flicker of pleasure at the thought of his own survival but knew that he could not let his guard down for a moment—imperative to remain as elusive as possible until he could get his hands on a weapon—no small feat.

As time passed and more contenders were eradicated, the stadium would continuously shift and reduce the amount of surface area, forcing competitors to clash. The heart of the coliseum was now a tiny, secluded island surrounded by water, and it contained the most coveted weapon in the game: the electron gun. With its immense accuracy and ability to fire ten bolts, the weapon was a serious threat to anyone who found themselves in its sights.

Two narrow bridges jutted out from opposite sides of the island, connecting it to the rest of the arena. However, the bridges were only accessible for brief windows of time, triggered by motion sensors on either side of the stadium. Any competitor trying to cross would be completely exposed to danger from all directions, making the risk too great for the Athlete to attempt.

Roaming the tracks with agility and stealth, the Athlete's eyes were fixed on the prize—a baton, a device that would finally grant him a competitive edge. He wasted no time and sprinted toward it, but a cunning hunter spotted his move and stalked him from behind. The Athlete was far slower than the pack, and the predator was effortlessly closing in on its prey, ready to strike with all its might. The Athlete had no plan, no strategy, only instinct and the will to survive.

As the Athlete narrowed in on the baton, he noticed another adversary straight ahead wielding a stun-gun, capable of freezing him in place if struck. Three competitors rapidly converging, each primed to enter a nexus of carnage.

Already positioned at the ready, a charge of electrons exited the firearm, aimed straight at the Athlete. He immediately reacted and shifted his weight backward to descend into a blistering slide. Falling on his back at harrowing speeds, he looked up and witnessed the cluster of electricity narrowly miss and strike the contender behind him, freezing them in place like a statue. Out of nowhere, a newcomer swooped in and delivered a devastating blow to the immobilized combatant, sending them flying off the track and into the unforgiving waters below.

Meanwhile, still sliding forward, the Athlete reached and snagged the baton out of midair; in one fluid motion, he leveraged his momentum and the deft application of his boots to propel himself back into an upright position. As he rose, he spotted the gunman charging his weapon, poised to take another shot. Without hesitation, the Athlete channeled all his strength and skill into a swift, calculated throw of the baton. The weapon flung through the air like an unleashed propeller, striking the shooter square in the chest, with the galvanized impact sending him reeling backward, off the track, and out of the game.

Another duo of contenders engaged in their own battle on an elevated track above the Athlete. As he closed in on them, a shockwave grenade detonated, hurling the duo in opposite directions with explosive force. The blast also dislodged a weapon from its magnetized perch and hurtled it through the air, landing on the lower level just so the Athlete could breeze past and snatch it up with lightning speed.

The sequence of events unfolded swiftly and remarkably. Immediately recognizing the device in his hand, the Athlete deftly placed the palm-sized chip onto a receiver on the back of his helmet. With a click and a hum, the chip sprung to life—activating the suit by using a combination of lasers, electricity, and microwaves to heat the surrounding air, which produced a field of ionized air-plasma around the Athlete, disrupting any shockwave or electrical charge.

As he raced through the arena, his suit crackled with energy. The chip had not only recharged his suit but also sent shockwaves throughout his body—an electrical amplification of intensity and awareness now circulated his systems. The spectators gasped in awe as a radiant blue aura enveloped him, transforming him into a comet streaking across the track.

With each stride, he surged forward; the curve of the track posed no challenge to his superhuman speed. He used the wall as leverage, pushing himself even faster toward the sensor that would grant him access to the island. He had speed. He had the shield. It was time!

Racing along, he waved his hand through the sensor and continued toward the center of the arena. The entirety of the crowd was standing and wholly fixated on the Athlete. Quickly glancing at his display screen, he confirmed four remaining competitors, only one with power above fifty percent. He could not afford to lose focus now. His entire being was attuned to the task at hand, his movements precise and fluid as he made his way to the island. The world around him fell away; his senses sharpened to a razor's edge as he prepared to face inevitable danger.

Charging forward under the blazing sun, the Athlete raced toward the electron gun, impervious to the barrage of enemy fire. With effortless grace, he darted across the bridge with no sign of slowing down. Moving at an unparalleled speed, the crowd held its breath in anticipation as the Athlete easily seized control of the elusive weapon.

Immediately, he zeroed in on his target and unleashed a barrage of electrons, making short work of a formidable foe on a track several layers above. Just as the bridge shifted again, the Athlete arrived on the opposite end, rapidly spinning around and zooming off in pursuit of another opponent. With no escape, the runner was swiftly eliminated with a shot to the back, illuminating the display screen with another player dismissal—only two remained.

In the blink of an eye, two opponents were vanquished, and the arena was thrown into chaos: shifting unexpectedly with mechanical force. The results caused the Athlete to be hurled violently through the air as the ground convulsed beneath him, and his shields were useless as he plummeted to the unforgiving platform with a sickening thud. The crowd's screams echoed across the stadium until his lifeless body came to rest.

A cruel stroke of fate, just as the Athlete's momentum had been building. The jumbotron's flashing lights confirmed his demise, displaying the dreaded words: "zero power."

All eyes were fixed on the Athlete, despite the other two contenders screaming around the arena, locked in combat. His meteoric rise from a place of deficiency had electrified the masses, igniting a fire of hope and inspiration within them. However, agony now consumed the spectators with the Athlete's rapid fall from grace. The influence of athletics showcasing the capricious nature of fate and fortune was on full display, a renowned phenomenon that always left the crowd on edge.

The audience yearned for a comeback, an awakening of the Athlete's spirit. But the Athlete was succumbing to the darkness. As he strained against the immense physical pain, his muscles screamed with exertion, and his vision blurred at the edges. With each labored breath, the world around him seemed to fade into a distant, shadowy realm.

As the seconds ticked by, the Athlete's eyes grew heavy, and he felt as though he were on the verge of slipping into a deep, dreamless slumber. The sound of his heart pounding in his ears became a dull thud, and the roar of the masses seemed to dwindle to a distant hum.

Tabula Rasa

In his last sliver of wakefulness, *something* shot through him with a fierce jolt. With a gasp, the Athlete sucked in a lifesaving lungful of air, his eyes snapping open once more. Coming into focus, his first recognition was that his power bar signaled *on*—at one percent. The display was mirrored on the jumbotron, and the crowd exploded in a thunderous cheer.

His suit was supposed to be accurately synced to his physiological essence, which also indicated his consciousness. But there was *more* inside of him than could be measured, more than could be controlled, even by him. All he understood was that he now had to do whatever he could, no matter the cost, no matter the danger.

The Athlete was awake and analyzing his situation. Since the mechanics of the arena initially signaled that only two competitors remained, the island was now accessible indefinitely unless activated by the sensor; and now contained *another* electron gun. Watching one player chase the other, he realized he had no chance of standing, but then he saw *it*—the baton from the match's opening moments. It lay only a few meters away, a glimmer of hope. He crawled over to the baton, every inch of his body screaming in agony. Removing his helmet, he watched the two contenders heading for the island. Finally reaching the weapon, he placed his helmet precisely on the ground and picked up the baton. The strike would have to be perfect.

Flying across the track, the two contestants approached the bridge. The Athlete contorted his body and struck his helmet with the baton; the electrical current shot his helmet on a line drive, bouncing off the track. On the right trajectory, but the helmet began to slow as it approached the sensor. The Athlete's heart pounded in his chest as he shifted his gaze between the players and the helmet, willing it to keep going.

"Come on. Hit it!"

The helmet's momentum was fading and appeared to fall just short of its target. But the instant the other players arrived at the bridge, his helmet gave one last motion and grazed the sensor sufficiently enough to activate and shift the bridges, sending the shocked contestants to clumsily fall into the water.

Unthinkable. Improbable. The place erupted in a bedlam of noise and color as fireworks illuminated the evening sky in a dazzling display of jubilation. For all but a few, it was a moment of unbridled joy and celebration.

A powerful current of excitement coursed through the air. The Athlete laid on his back and let his head lie motionless on the ground. As he gazed upward at the fiery explosions illuminating the

234

darkness above and the thunderous roar of thousands chanting his name, he knew without a doubt that his fortune had finally turned.

***

Following the game, the athletes and corresponding individuals congregated with a throng of other guests at the post-game event. Each athlete was treated for their wounds, using zinc oxide nanoparticles to handle the severe injuries. Inspired by the regenerative power of starfish and their ability to manipulate the mechanical factors inside stem cells, any human cell could be taken from any part of the body, turned into a stem cell, and then re-differentiated into therapeutic cells. This extraordinary healing method allowed athletes to continuously put immense stress on their physiques with minimal bodily harm. Nevertheless, Sparticon, a brutal sport, has claimed countless lives over the years. Yet, the athletes still managed to emerge from their rugged sportswear, looking refreshed and rejuvenated.

Amidst the buzz of the convention, the Athlete strode confidently, basking in the adulation of his fans. Hands were shaken, smiles were exchanged, and nods of approval followed him wherever he went. But just as he was settling into the rhythm of the praise, he was abruptly snatched away by one of his competitors.

"How, pray tell, did you pull that one off?"

In response to the rival's inquiry, the Athlete allowed a wry smile to grace his lips.

"Mastery of the arts, my dear." With a conspiratorial wink, he concluded his answer. "Truth be told, fortune favored me in those final moments."

His competitor sighed, her eyes rolling skyward with the dissatisfying response. Her dress, constructed from a sleek and lightweight nano-fiber material, seamlessly adjusted its color and pattern in response to her surroundings, blending with the environment like a chameleon.

"Must you be so... sly? And earlier in the match! I am mystified by how you snuck away from me. The impeccable timing with which you dodged that stun... unbelievable!"

"I had a feeling that was *you* chasing me. How did it feel to get hammered into the water, by the way?"

"I'll show you how it feels, buddy."

Their eyes locked as the two athletes grinned at each other, both enjoying the playful exchange. The Athlete respected his fellow opponents, aware that most of his joy came from challenging each other. Yet, in the back of his mind, he was mainly concerned about tracking down his most formidable adversary, hoping that their agreement had not been forgotten.

A chorus of voices soon joined the duo's exchange, recollecting the thrilling contest of prowess. The Athlete, however, was but a spectator within the discourse, his presence fragmented. His gaze swept the expanse, surveying the room for his antagonist's whereabouts. At last, amongst a mob of admirers, he discerned his opulent foe, preening as though victory had already been seized—a common motif of the confident—he knew that this was one round of three, and it would take much more to win it all.

The Athlete and his foe locked eyes from across the room and signaled a breakaway conversation, and the two of them retreated to isolation.

Like déjà vu…

"How did you do that?"

"Oh, you know I planned that the entire time."

"Shut. Your. Mouth."

Emitting a laugh of mild irritation, he grasped the Athlete's hand in a friendly manner while his other arm enveloped the Athlete's shoulder in a congenial embrace.

"That was pretty awesome, man." Tightening his hold and drawing his adversary closer, he leveled an intense, unyielding stare upon the Athlete. "You won't get that lucky at the race."

"Just try and stay dry this time, partner."

"Ha, I'll do my best."

They disengaged the handshake and stood shoulder to shoulder, surveying the spectacle before them. Elegant attendees, adorned in the highest fashions, delicately savored novelty hors d'oeuvres as they sipped top-shelf libations. The gallery was decorated with a tapestry of warriors and Olympian imagery. An event most coveted by the elite. Even with such lavish amenities, the Athlete still had a single thought on his mind.

"Quite the party they throw, huh?"

"You know I couldn't care less about these things, and you also know the only reason I am here is to make sure you don't renege on our arrangement."

"Arrangement? Hmm. I don't think I owe you anything according to the confines of our accord."

"Explain yourself."

"Though you may have earned the coveted points for first place, you did *not* last longer, which I believe was the *actual* agreement. According to the replays, you were "knocked out" and

238

Tabula Rasa

listed as defunct while I was still rolling around. And how they accepted your revival and nonsense after that, I still don't know and won't *personally* accept it."

"You don't have to know anything other than our bet was if I beat you, and undoubtedly, I did, then you would introduce me."

"She's out of your league, you know... even for you."

"With that, I have no doubt."

The Athlete gave him a piercing stare, a silent challenge demanding he fulfills their agreement. With a begrudging nod, he conceded, a testament to the unspoken code of honor between them.

"I suppose you might be right; I must honor my promise. But. I am excited; I am excited because I get to assist in setting you down a path of inevitable failure, precisely what a good foe should do. She has all the ability to rip your heart out and change you entirely. Not maliciously. Only because it won't take long before you start to do everything in your power to make her smile and be ruined when she doesn't accept your love...Of course, I don't know this personally, but I have seen the aftermath of her presence."

"I can't explain it, but I feel like the only reason I pulled that off tonight was because of *her*."

He nodded at the Athlete while taking a deep inhale. Maybe his competitor knows the feeling?

"She's actually *here* tonight."

The Athlete's eyes widened in surprise as his competitor suddenly bolted into the bustling crowd. Without hesitation, he gave chase. As they weaved through the masses, the two men hopped from one group to another, exchanging greetings and idle chatter with effortless charm. Their journey through working the crowd came to a halt as they reached a cluster of people, forcing them to navigate their way through with finesse.

Ahead of him, the Athlete's adversary pulled a young woman into a warm embrace, planting a tender kiss on her cheek before whispering something in her ear. Finally, he turned his gaze toward the Athlete, a cunning smile generating at the corners of his lips.

"I would like to introduce you to…"

"Lazarus!"

"Excuse me?"

The Athlete was caught off guard as the stunning woman extended her hand in greeting, his senses momentarily paralyzed by her magnetic allure. Surely, he thought, someone must have used a stun gun to paralyze his faculties. No training had ever prepared him for the surge of energy passing through him now.

Though she stood among the crowd, there was something noticeably different about her—a confidence and poise that set her apart. His brain finally relayed the message, and he reached for her hand.

"Sorry. That's just what everyone is calling you this evening. You know, due to your ascension from annihilation. That was quite glorious to watch."

The Athlete laughed sheepishly as he made contact with her soft and slender hands that stirred yet another spark of vitality within him.

"That makes sense now. And thank you. I honestly don't know how I was able to pull any of that off."

The Athlete was guarded about his emotions, reserving the details of how he believed that, somehow, *she* was the catalyst that helped him summon the fortitude within to achieve the earlier feats.

As the Athlete and his *muse* locked eyes, the world around them faded away, and the surrounding inhabitants retreated, sensing the depth of their connection.

"I must say, one of the most remarkable aspects of what you athletes do is the speed at which you perform your maneuvers."

"Well, to be honest. We actually have a little secret with regard to that matter."

"A secret? You athletes know how to slow down time?"

"Actually…"

"Oh, stop."

The Athlete snickered—his chuckle was warm but tense.

"I'm just teasing. But we have been trained to slow down how our brains *interpret* information."

"Hmm. Elaborate, please." she asked, looking intrigued.

"So, basically, we have trained our neocortex, which has the job of "predicting" the future, to more accurately gather data and harness that information to make predictions about what will happen next. Through the release of certain neurotransmitters, we have been trained to notice patterns, which then helps the brain notice *more* patterns. This allows us to assimilate and apply incoming information faster and more accurately."

"That is absolutely fascinating. But how do you deal with the fear and nerves when going that fast?"

"Oh, you know we're not allowed to be afraid out there."

With a burst of confidence, the Athlete puffed out his chest following the comment, only to realize too late that that type of bravado would not impress the company he was in. He quickly tried to save himself.

"Um, sorry. Actually, that is a pretty interesting aspect as well. Through training and during matches, a neurotransmitter called anandamide is released, and this helps us to inhibit fear during moments of extreme pressure. I'm not special."

Fortunately, she giggled and slightly turned away, allowing the Athlete to take in every detail of her exquisite face. It was as if time *was* slowing down at that moment. As her mouth opened to release the most pleasant laugh, he noticed each strand of hair obstructing her face along with every pearly white shining back at him. Anandamide must *not* have been currently releasing because the Athlete felt extreme fear of ever losing this feeling.

"That *is* interesting. But while you might be able to eliminate fear in the moment, don't you ever worry about losing something or someone by getting seriously hurt before a match begins? Isn't there anything you're scared of possibly giving up, and does that disrupt actions during play?" She was back to asking questions.

It had been a long time since the Athlete had considered this question.

"Ah, I suppose I don't think of it like that. I've always been so focused on being the best that no other variables were ever allowed to impede that."

The Athlete's rigorous training and intense competition triggered the release of serotonin, which often produced a curious blend of resplendence and confusion in his mind. Fully cognizant of the effects of neurochemistry on his mind and body, the Athlete briefly pondered whether the sensations he was experiencing were simply a result of this phenomenon or was the presence of this young woman before him triggering these feelings.

"So, are you ready for the next stage? The race, I mean."

"Yeah. I usually race well at this track, and due to my outcome earlier, I will be at an advantage starting at the front of the pack. Are you going to watch it?"

"Oh, I don't know."

"Really?"

"Well, now that I have met you, I am going to be worried about you getting hurt out there."

The corners of her mouth rose into a warm smile, and he could not help mirroring the expression. The Athlete felt comfortable in her companionship, and for the first time he could remember, he was nervous about competing—for different reasons.

244

Tabula Rasa

"I will make sure I am *extra* careful while I am out there, just for you, ma'am." he said, bowing slightly as he finished his pledge.

"That is very sweet of you, and I hope you do. Just remember, even if you don't think there is anything to be scared about, I assure you there are people who are terrified of losing you."

***

The Athlete pivoted, surveying his seven opponents behind him, preparing as he was. Upon the speedway's stage, each competitor underwent diagnostics while stretching their muscles. Unlike the battle arena, each contestant claimed their rightful position on the starting line, permitting a glimpse of the imposing raceway. Nestled against the shoreline, a vast majority of the course snaked along the water's edge, featuring hazards, subterranean passages, ramps, and a diverse assortment of treacherous oddities lurking at every bend.

As the Athlete sifted through his mental pre-race checklist, an undercurrent of anxiety churned within; the deafening clamor of the assembly swelled as the clock's relentless march signaled the race's looming onset. His triumph in the battle arena secured his starting place at the head of the group, a vital upper hand; still, the nerves persisted.

For the first time in his recollection, he confronted the sharp edge of fear. "I assure you there are many people who are terrified

245

of losing you." Her words had seeped into his consciousness, stirring an anxious dread of never crossing paths again and a fervent wish that *she* harbored the same emotions.

The colossal digital clock displayed the dwindling seconds before the grand initiation. In poised anticipation, every contender claimed their designated stance, muscles coiled like springs eager to unleash out of the gate. Propelling forth at a velocity of over sixty miles per hour in a mere second, they would jostle for prime placement. The Athlete, graced with an advantaged start, would find himself the prime target, tirelessly fending the relentless pursuits of his rivals.

"Ten seconds until launch!"

The spectators were seething with anticipation as the announcer aroused them. In his head, the Athlete went through the dynamics of the racetrack, preparing his mind to react at each interval. Unquestionably, the adversaries' attacks and the course's fluctuating topography necessitated split-second reactions and improvisation.

"Five seconds!"

His focus now honed on the imminent decisions and the tarmac directly before him—eyes narrowed.

"Four seconds!"

Despite the prevailing intensity, *her* image danced in his thoughts; positive emotions generated peak performance. The cacophony hushed. Time slowed.

"Three... Two... One... GO!"

As the contest started, the Athlete catapulted forward, his boots accelerating him to excessive speeds. With swift and nimble maneuvers, he rounded corners and darted past hurdles in his path. Unpredictable portions of the track sporadically emerged or disappeared, compelling each contender to persistently recalibrate their momentum. As the Athlete dropped his right hip inches from the ground, straightening his left leg for a razor-sharp turn, a gargantuan boulder unexpectedly tumbled into his path. The obstruction forced him to rise and break abruptly. Shifting his mass, he swerved around the sphere, veering to the outer limits of the track. The thwarted momentum facilitated two opponents to grapple for the lead. Head lowered, his eyes scoured the route ahead, seeking an opportune weapon.

Following the curve, a sunlit sand straightaway stretched before them, bordered by the crystalline azure ocean. The sandy terrain allowed their boots to reach higher speeds, though compromising their mastery. The trio of frontrunners jostled for the lead, crouching low to maintain speed, exchanging forceful blows with their neighboring competitors.

They now navigated a narrow, sandy passage framed by water on either side. Vying for the lead, the racers were momentarily captivated by the sight of four colossal blue whales erupting from the waters just offshore with tremendous force. Triggered by pulsating sonar calls, the marine giants erupted from the depths, creating immense splashes and waves that interrupted the race. The harrowing bellow emitted by the massive creatures was as daunting as the surging tide.

Noting the dwindling escape route from the advancing waves, the athletes strained to push forward. The waves seemed to be approaching the shore faster than they could evade them.

Looming before them and slightly to the left, the sandy expanse approached a white limestone cliff face, offering a link to solid ground—a potential refuge. A pair of small openings promised escape from the looming watery threat, but each crevice could only accommodate a solitary figure. Persisting along the sandy track adjacent to the cliff would spell catastrophe.

A single escape route lay at ground level, while another soared two stories high, no larger than a modest window. The impending ramp served as the sole gateway to that elevated sanctuary. With the ramp's proximity granting him the upper hand, the Athlete leaned into his adversaries, their bodies clashing at a staggering hundred miles per hour. As a result of their elite training, the racers sensed time dilating, bestowing upon them the ability to discern the faintest nuances. At the same time, the audience marveled at the thrilling blur of speed.

Propelling himself forward, the Athlete forged a gap, securing a fleeting lead as he compelled the remaining duo to vie for the ground-level passage.

Surveying his environment, the Athlete meticulously calculated the optimal launch point on the ramp, aligning it with the narrow aperture in the cliff face, factoring in the distance, wind, size, et cetera. He assessed the timing of the first wave's assault on the shore and whether his elevation would keep him from harm's reach—fully conscious of these elements and the relentless opponents, he maintained his course at blistering speeds. Perfection was paramount.

The Athlete pitched forward, sprang from the ramp, and instantaneously aligned himself parallel to the ground like a swift arrow cutting through the air. As the water's wall collided with the land, he recognized that his window for escape was scarce. Glancing down, he observed the pair still vying for the final sanctuary. The waves crashed as the Athlete key-holed the tunnel, diving headfirst through the opening, not a moment too soon.

Below, the struggle persisted until the bitter conclusion. Entwined, each racer strained for dominance. A fusion of timing, strength, tenacity, and fortune allowed *one* contender to narrowly skirt catastrophe while the other met the unforgiving surface and was promptly swept away by the ocean's might.

Executing a deft barrel roll upon entry, the Athlete alighted on his feet, maintaining his momentum as he now navigated the shadowy tunnel within the crag. The constricted pathway was riddled with abrupt turns and unexpected impediments, demanding swifter reflexes.

Laser-imaging sensors tracked the racers along the concealed routes, casting live three-dimensional renderings into the sky for the spectators' viewing pleasure. Although the stone muffled the clamor, the cheers from above echoed like a resounding peal of thunder.

The passage eventually opened into a cavernous cathedral—massive in scale. The Athlete observed the track's precipitous rises and falls at acute angles, suspended above an abyss too profound and obscure to fathom.

As the path descended steeply, the Athlete detected an unsettling energy. Suddenly, a competitor plunged from an elevated track, narrowly avoiding a collision. Operating back at peak capacity, the two adversaries thundered down the course.

Up ahead, an opening emerged; the route initially veered away only to curve back inward. A nearby ramp offered the prospect of slicing the corner, which would catapult the Athlete back into the outright lead. However, tumbling into the abyss would render a competitor irretrievable from the contest.

Treacherous, yet the presence of a weapon suspended above the gap convinced the Athlete that the gains outweighed the dangers. Undoubtedly, he and his opponent alone held a significant advantage over the pack, and neutralizing his rival would yield a more manageable race.

The critical juncture approached. His opponent, marginally ahead, displayed no signs of engaging the ramp. As his rival veered into the turn, the Athlete lowered himself and leaned forward with purpose—poised for liftoff. He struck the ramp without losing any speed and catapulted into the air.

Gliding through the skies once more, now crouched, the Athlete locked eyes with the racer beneath him. The Athlete could feel his competitor's wrath, envy, amazement, and trepidation as he seized the weapon mid-flight and initiated his descent back to land.

Instantly upon touching down, the Athlete executed a full rotation and unleashed a single-use pulse wave of energy at his foe. The shockwave hurled the racer wildly through the air, who fortuitously landed on stable terrain. Although, the Athlete was convinced he had banished his opponent to the void below as he swiveled back around.

Once more in the open expanse, the Athlete dashed on the pavement, the beach at his side. His display screen still confirmed the elimination of a single racer. The competitor he had recently encountered must have survived, albeit far behind.

Casting a backward glance, he discerned a small assembly of racers navigating the cliff's perimeter. Seizing his lead would prove formidable. Obstacles and track shifts demanded deft navigation skills as the Athlete accelerated.

Nearly stumbling, the Athlete's pace diminished in an instant. A crucial tool enabled the trailing pack to narrow the chasm as the leaders' abilities temporarily waned. His impaired prowess would let the stragglers close in on his advantage.

Three adversaries advanced rapidly, and the Athlete's need for restored power was paramount. Just as they appeared primed to strike, he surged to full strength, preserving a slender lead.

In the near distance, the track seemed to descend into the terrain, a serpentine obstruction lying unavoidably ahead. The Athlete sank his hips and deftly redistributed his weight, carving through the sinuous path with finesse.

Upon exiting, he surveyed the situation behind him, noting that two of his followers had faltered amidst the twisting—only one remaining close.

The track then abruptly plunged beneath the ground, appearing to merge seamlessly with the ocean's waves. Now encased in a glass tube submerged in water, the racers beheld a mesmerizing marine panorama. The glass's impeccable clarity made them feel as if they were immersed in the depths—coral reefs teeming with a vibrant medley of aquatic life—a segment designed to confuse the senses.

The Athlete shifted his focus from sight to touch, relying on the track's feel beneath his feet to navigate the underwater tunnel. Composure was crucial. Barreling toward the massive tail of a whale shark, he suddenly banked left at a ninety-degree angle, clinging to the walls before leveling out again.

Nipping at the Athlete's heels, his rival carefully strategized their next move. The tube's lower half abruptly sealed, guiding the racers to scale divergent walls where a weapon lay in wait. The Athlete acquired a magnetized stun grenade, capable of immobilizing its target if within close enough distance to attach. Accelerating behind him and closing in quickly, his competitor must have collected numerous speed amplifiers.

Narrowly avoiding being plunged from behind, the Athlete swung his body sideways, rotating around the tube, securing the stun device on the racer's back as he was positioned crown-to-crown directly above them. Knowing the impending doom, the racer attempted to grab the Athlete and disrupt his advances. However, the track violently ascended out of the water, launching the racers into the air above the ocean's waves. Spanning the gap between the tunnel's exit and dry land, the stun device engaged, dooming the challenger to a watery descent. The Athlete could only briefly watch their destruction as he had to calculate his course for the next portion of the track.

Reunited with solid ground, the finish line drew near—glory within grasp. The Athlete darted along the path, nimbly navigating obstacles. Peering behind him, he discerned a pulsating wave aimed at him and swerved just in time. A duo of racers trailed close behind.

The frenetic maelstrom of chaos approached its crescendo. All three racers were within arm's reach of one another now. A perpetual cascade of balloon-sized raindrops began to plummet the players from the sky. They veered and weaved, evading the relentless deluge.

As the rainfall abated, the pavement beneath them morphed into three distinct, slender paths, dividing each racer. The ground below bristled with dangerous impediments, compelling them to remain on their individual tracks that thinned as they sped on. While the paths slimmed to mere shoulder width, gales of wind assaulted them without warning or pattern. The athletes hunkered down, bracing against the invisible assailant. Buffeted by gusts from all angles, they teetered precariously on their lofty balance beams.

The Athlete remained strong as the other racers, no longer able to endure, fell to the waiting ground. Landing safely, they momentarily overtook the Athlete, still perched high above. He knew that by clinging on for a moment longer, he would reap the rewards and vanquish any doubts about his impending win as they all neared the finish line.

With both of his feet linear to the now inches-wide road, the Athlete weathered the accelerating gales, his eyes fixed on the coveted prize just ahead. And as the support beneath his boots disintegrated, the Athlete leaped into the emptiness. Flawless in his timing, he seized the suspended mechanism midair and commenced his earthbound descent.

In his freefall, the Athlete assessed the entirety of his environment, cognizant that seamless execution was critical for victory. Finally touching down, he landed with exultant grace and sprinted ahead. A smooth, unblemished stretch of tarmac marked the final battleground between the racers and their coveted prize.

Travis Lane

Just beyond the finish line was a cul-de-sac of onlookers waiting for the momentous finale—the roaring commotion of the crowd eclipsed all previous decibel levels as the culmination loomed.

Only slightly ahead of the Athlete, his two rivals kept pace, shoulder to shoulder. Patiently, he bid his time to unleash the device, wholly absorbed in precise calculations and timing. If activated imprecisely, failure was guaranteed. He eyed his approach, locked in with unrelenting concentration. The time was now!

The Athlete triggered the mechanism, and a torrent of power surged through his boots, doubling his velocity instantly. Activated precisely, he shot between the two as they separated just enough for him to squeeze through and clinch the victory on a fractional scale.

***

Following the race, the post-match celebrations were regrettably suspended. The contender who struck the wall and was engulfed by the relentless sea failed to persevere. Each racer's suit and helmet were designed to heed such violent lashings, but the inexorable plight of mother nature's influence remains impregnable.

The Athlete wandered down the beach, barefoot and aggrieved. He recognized that previous tragedies in his sport had brought

256

sorrow, yet his self-assurance had obscured the possibility of his own perilous fate. Striving for victory and dominance had been his unrivaled objectives—his only priorities. Now, he felt a pressing need to embrace change and that relinquishing the past was essential for his development as a human. *Unbelievable*, he thought. How could one evening and one human being change so much about him? Logical deduction alone would not unveil the answer to this enigma. He contemplated whether *her* presence might alleviate his sorrowful state. Had he ever welcomed such emotions before, or had destiny unfolded as intended?

He proceeded beside the ocean, listening to the hushed yet formidable pulse of the waves in the calming dusk evening. Studying his footsteps, he sought to clear his mind for a brief respite, but a persistent notion refused to release the Athlete's attention; reluctantly, he found himself compelled to contemplate his immortal imprint. *What truly mattered?* He wondered. *To be remembered?*

For countless years, he had dedicated his essence to the pursuit of immortalization, but a newfound longing stirred within him. He wanted to channel that vitality elsewhere now. Embracing what he had once willfully ignored, he now realized how long he had maintained an unwavering, singular focus for all his energy— arguably wasted.

As if conjured by his very thoughts…

"Hi there."

Disbelief gripped the Athlete. Though his eyes remained fixed on the ground, the voice resonated with undeniable familiarity. Surely, this must be a figment of his imagination, he reasoned.

His face broke into a wide, radiant smile as he prepared to raise his gaze. Halting his movement, the Athlete pivoted toward the girl and gradually met her eyes.

"I was looking for you, and someone said they saw you walk this way."

Rendered speechless, the Athlete maintained his grin. A torrent of emotions far more potent than those from the race cascaded through him.

"I-I am delighted to see you."

The Athlete stammered while attempting poise. She giggled at his nervousness.

"How are you doing? I am not bothering you, am I?"

The Athlete broke from his fog.

"No, no, no. Not at all. I was actually just thinking about you."

"Really?" her eyes widened with disbelief. Or possibly excitement, he was unable to tell.

"Yeah, when you appeared, I ah, felt this sense of…completeness. I had been wandering, and now it seems I don't have to. Sorry, I am not explaining this well. How are you this evening?"

The Athlete shook off the reverie and gestured an invite to resume walking, and the two continued down the shore.

"I'm doing all right, given the circumstances. But seeing you definitely lifts my spirits."

Raising her eyes to his, she offered a warm smile.

"You were amazing out there, though. You really should know that."

"That is very sweet of you to say; I mean that."

"Of course. How are you managing? Do you want to talk about the accident?"

"Thank you for asking." The Athlete could sense the authenticity in her voice and was genuinely grateful for her concern. "The loss obviously saddens me. It is never easy when a competitor goes down. I mean, I understand why they do it because I am out there too, so it's upsetting to lose such a like-minded individual, but you're aware that they wouldn't have wanted to go any other way." As the Athlete spoke, a flicker of introspection crossed his eyes, a hint of something shifting within him. In the face of loss, he seemed on the verge of embracing a new purpose or direction in life, one that had been quietly stirring just beneath the surface. "My aspirations were to risk it all and maintain a legacy at any cost. There was never anything else that overcame me with passion and drive, and I would have been happy to go out in that same fashion. In a sense, I *would* envy them."

"But not anymore?"

Without casting a glance, he extended his hand to grasp hers. A tender smile blossomed at the edge of his lips. Her presence offered comfort beyond his wildest dreams. Walking endlessly along that beach was the most superb reality his mind could generate.

A newfound sense of capability washed over the Athlete, finally enabling him to relinquish old patterns, set aside his pride, and embrace a new perspective in his life. Perfection no longer governed every moment; with her, it was simply about their shared connection. The rest was just noise—no concern for what lies ahead, only that it is experienced together.

Often, a single instant can change everything, but his actions were *not* without basis, ineffable perhaps, but deeply rooted in reason. This realization was evident as a newfound vigor surged through the Athlete, charting a new trajectory in his journey.

Tabula Rasa

The Athlete's gaze shifted out to sea, and he admired the moon's reflection in the water. The waves, fierce and untamed, refused to yield a perfect reflection back at the moon—the ocean mimics life in its ability to hinder clarity. Anticipated yet capricious. Only in the darkest of nights would the waters grow calm enough to reveal the moon's true likeness.

He turned back to face her with a fresh set of eyes.

"No, not anymore."

Part III

"No existence can be validly fulfilled if it is limited to itself."

- **Simone De Beauvoir**

Chapter One

"Prepare to charge!"

The tanks advanced against the line. A barrage of building blocks surrounded the target. It was a warzone. Nothing could escape as the fate of all rested in the hands of *one*. Power and manipulation were his tools.

When the Son asked for a military toy set, his parents laughed it off as a rite of passage. Boys being boys. Days later, he awoke to a 50-piece brand new miniature army equipment set, ranging from little green men in uniform frozen in action poses to an Amtrak train circulating its miniature railway. Now he played happily in his room, feigning sleep when his mother came to check on him before pulling out his trusty, fully charged torch light. With it, "lights out" only temporarily interrupted his wild imagination, which fueled the fantastical scenarios he created during those nocturnal hours.

The screaming was the other interruption, and it was just as predictable as the rest of the evening routine. Without fail, they stirred a profound uneasiness within him. The Son often contemplated whether familial harmony had ever graced a chapter in his brief existence. Surely, there was a moment when their interactions were marked by kindness and unity.

Was the advent of their offspring the catalyst that altered the course of his parents' lives? As the Son emerged into their world, had he unknowingly disrupted their once rhythmic intimacy? And was the turbulence within the household only magnified with each subsequent child? Such burdensome thoughts for a young mind to consider in the preceding hours before sleep.

He dropped the soldiers where they were and scrambled back to his bed. Huddling beneath the covers, he pressed his fingers into his ears and hummed one of his unfinished melodies to drown out the sounds coming from his parents' room. Desperate, he clenched his eyes shut in a futile attempt to block the sound, yet the tears still snaked through, saturating his pillow.

Not only did the abrasive language assault his senses, but the tumultuous clatter of stomping and slamming seemed to shake the walls around him. It was a recurring concern that the thunderous shrieking would eventually be succeeded by lightning strikes of violence.

As usual, his thoughts turned to bitterness and shame. Much of the Son's chagrin came from his inability to understand and alleviate the afflictions that plagued his family. And as the oldest sibling, he felt somewhat responsible for being a guardian of his younger brother and sister.

Why had he not yet grown numb to this relentless barrage? Why did it persist in causing his body to tremble and his heart to race? *Why would they not stop?*

The evenings seemed to stretch till dawn as he pondered in vain, ceaselessly using the blankets to wipe away the beads of cold sweat forming on his forehead and the tears that flowed without restraint.

He considered himself lucky if he got an hour of playful exploits before the muffled voices of his parents arguing took over. Lately, though, that duration had been becoming dangerously limited as the screaming became increasingly aggressive each night.

Sleep eluded him, and playtime ceased until the uproar faded or hopefully concluded altogether. To distract himself, he tallied the woolen creatures, hummed tunes, and imagined distant realms he yearned to visit.

Seeking any means to escape, he ventured into mysterious, uncharted corners of the globe, traversing terrains where only the most intrepid dared to venture; eventually, transported to worlds beyond his own. His fantasies painted him as a symbol of fortitude and guidance; he hoped these traits would spill over into reality if ever faced to defend his siblings.

He spun elaborate narratives about guiding a host of fearless warriors into battle while at other times constructing a tale to merrily bask in the enchantment of an iconic figure, crafting delicate details to effortlessly blend into the stories that completely diverted him from actuality. His mind, yearning for an audience, would often cast him as a gladiator in a sprawling arena, awash in the uproarious adoration of thousands. The *escape* was the catalyst for these inspirational fantasies.

Often, he ended up listening to music. It always calmed him and gave him a brief respite from the shouts, but he never could fall asleep while listening. Nothing assisted in aiding his slumber. This frustrated and angered him. He felt powerless—over his body, his parents, his whole life.

As a result, he tried to regain some of that power by asserting control over his peers. His wrathful disposition painted him as a young terror amongst his classmates. Engaging in relentless mischief against his peers, his seemingly harmless pranks often spiraled into bouts of aggression.

These outbursts concluded with a lack of camaraderie with his peers. His worried teachers lectured and put him in detention, but nothing got through to him. When offered a hand of communication, he would retreat further into his emotional isolation, deaf to their attempts at connection.

His academic performance, too, languished in the depths of mediocrity. In a final desperate bid, they summoned his parents. However, the atmosphere in the room grew tense, and the weight of the situation hung heavily in the air as the educator laid bare the grim reality of their child's plight.

"He is a bright kid, very creative, but he refuses to apply himself. He would rather spend his time harassing the other children."

The principal's gaze bore into the Son as she spoke. Her piercing stare accentuated her exasperated posture. The Son had sat in this chair numerous times, listening to the same frustrations, wondering if sharing his true feelings would help her understand. *Would she be able to empathize and refrain from judgment?* Yet, each time, his voice was held captive by reticence. *What made honesty so daunting?* His eyes sought refuge in his tattered shoes, a sanctuary from the silent war waged between his parents' icy glares.

His parents said nothing on the drive home. His father pressed the gas pedal with an urgency that bordered on recklessness while his mother's eyes mirrored the transient blur of the passing world.

Upon arrival, the Son made a beeline for his room, slamming the door behind him with a satisfying thud of wood. Soon, the silence was shattered by the onset of shrill screams. Did they genuinely believe their bouts were masked by the thin veil of distance and drywall? Were they blissfully ignorant, or was their neglect deliberate? Seething with silent indignation, the Son strained to decipher their verbal volleys, each word heavy with the bitter nectar of resentment.

"You know it is your damn fault. You don't give him any time; this is probably what he thinks being a man is all about! Being a goddamn bully. You only have yourself to thank for setting such a great role model for him!"

His mother screeched.

"Oh, and you do? If you spent more time with the kid instead of spending my money, maybe you would notice something was wrong with him. Do you even check his report cards? Answer me! When was the last time you checked them?"

"Are you serious? I am the only one who checks it; you couldn't care less! And keep your damn voice down; I don't want the kids to hear you shouting obscenities like a wretched ogre."

The arguing did not stop or get any softer. Sometimes he wished they yelled at him instead of each other; at least, that would be easier to process. Perhaps this was the underpinning reason for his recurrent fights at school—simply performing the cyclical flow of rage during human interaction.

Enough is enough, he silently declared, reaching for his headphones and music player. With the press of a button, he surrendered to the masterpiece of a renowned guitarist, an auditory barrier against the outside world.

His parents had bought him a wooden six-string with an electric blue trim a couple of birthdays ago, and it quickly grew into a devoted companion. Even amid the early struggles of learning to play, he connected intimately with the instrument. The moment his fingers began to dance on the six-string, a pause in his cognitive disruption would immediately commence. Slipping into a serene envelope of security allowed the young man to express himself freely. He guarded this gratifying sensation closely, rarely allowing others to enter.

Of course, he could not play it with his fingers in his ears or with the backing vocals of his parents abusing each other. Their constant bickering encroached upon his playtime, but he resolutely carved out time each day to commune with his instrument. He would sling it across his back and carefully squeeze through the fire escape ledge to play there in peace. The simplest haven he could find.

That night, he went to sleep with the usual feelings of dread and inexplicable fear spilling over into his dreams, disrupting any potential for a restful night. The confusion extended into the following day when he went down to the breakfast table to find his mom teasing his dad about the length of his hair by ruffling her fingers through it. A chuckle escaped him as he savored a sip of his coffee, only to catch sight of his son, a silent observer at the kitchen door.

This was their routine, a peculiar rhythm of life—by night, they were adversaries in the theatre of war; come morning, they transformed into lovers from an old age sonnet. This stark contrast unsettled the Son, yanking the security blanket of stability from beneath his feet at a tender age.

These acts of violence seemed so senseless to his youthful sensibilities, only deepening the confusion about the complexities of adulthood. The extreme polarization he routinely witnessed unsettled him, raising questions about his own future and the relationships he would form. A dash of this reality was already manifesting itself in his life, as he was acutely aware of the volatility that marked his relationships with his family and peers.

His dad called him over to come sit down at the table.

"Morning, son. Your mother and I didn't get a chance to speak to you yesterday about what your principal said, but we wanted to discuss the problem together. Here, do you want some pancakes? You know no one makes them like your mom."

He made his remark as he doused his own pancakes with enough maple syrup to drown them. His mother came and sat on the other side of him.

"Your siblings are not up yet, but we thought we could chat, just us."

Her soft voice had increasingly become artificial in these moments. Forking some scrambled eggs onto his plate, she attempted to play the protagonist. The Son reached over her for the salt and pepper but said nothing in response.

"Well, we just want to know why you have been acting this way with your peers at school." His father started while simultaneously putting a big bite of pancakes in his mouth.

"And you are smart as a whip, but your grades just do not make any sense right now." Added his mother.

The Son remained silent. Inhaling the rich aromas of the bountiful breakfast, he merely nudged his food around, fixated on the black specks dotting the yellow landscape of his plate. He wished he could dissolve into it. Like bitter coffee grounds steaming in the water of his mother's French press, he wanted to dematerialize while sitting there—swallowed up by the ground beneath him.

Anything to flee from this conversation. He had no reply, and even if he had, he recognized it was better to hold his tongue. *They would not understand; they would never understand.* How could they empathize with their son's emotions when they were oblivious to their cause? That they were the instigators!

They were as oblivious to the root of their Son's pain as he was to his role in their fights. He felt like he was living in a nightmare where his own captors were blind to the fact that he was their captive. It was a vicious cycle of ignorance. *What point is there in more words?* He pondered before pushing his chair back and retreating into his room.

"What about your breakfast? You have hardly had a bite of food!" His mom called after him.

A door slam was the only response they got.

***

A series of days elapsed similarly, with the Son falling into a deep sadness, languishing over the conversation. He even refused to play guitar for his younger sister, something which had become somewhat of a weekly ritual for them since acquiring the instrument. All his siblings loved to hear him play, but his younger sister held an unmatched appreciation. She used to hum along however much she could, even when he had just begun playing and could not string three chords together.

Despite grappling with his emotional turmoil, the Son still felt an overpowering duty to fulfill the expectations of an elder sibling. He loved them and wanted nothing more than to be a pillar of support, but he was constantly swimming against a powerful current in the river of self-actualization. Unbeknownst to him, the Son lacked the ability to act effectively on their behalf as his own ideological structure cracked at the seams.

"Hey, kids!"

Called out his dad after coming home from work one afternoon. The children left their activities to join him in the living room.

"Who here volunteers to make a playlist for me?"

"A playlist? Make it yourself, dad; I was just about to start my paper mâché collage for school."

"Well, I guess that means we will have to listen to my old-timey music on repeat for the whole road trip."

Which was followed by an unconvincing rendition of an old classic.

"ROAD TRIP!"

Squealed the Son's younger siblings in unison while commencing with a little dance around the sofas.

"We are going to drive up to the same canyon that grandpa proposed to grandma at, for a family camping adventure. To top it off, we are going to stop at all the famous local eating joints on the way."

Their father started dancing with the two kids, and he quickly focused his gaze on his one child, *not* in motion.

"We will be camping at a place specifically designed for rock climbing as well, bud. You and I can descend a few *real* crags. And maybe you could even play us some tunes by a bonfire?" he said, trying to include his son.

Dread instantly started welling up inside the Son. He understood that the prolonged confinement with his family was a recipe for more fights. Except on a trip, there would be no escape. His liberation from homestead disarray was achieved with school and absconding to his room. Deprived of these outlets, the prospect of slipping away seemed bleak.

Would some sort of explosion between his parents occur within the confining quarters that neither he nor his siblings could avoid? Could the wrath be directed toward them? The thought of darting into the dark and treacherous wilderness just to break free oddly brought comfort. He exhaled slowly, trying to dispel his nervousness.

Since climbing had been a childhood endeavor that was now growing into a gratifying passion, the idea of shutting out the *noise* and focusing on his immediate surroundings would qualify as organic therapy. There were few opportunities to let the mind drift into life's uncertainties as maximum cognitive effort was required during an ascent. And the Son seldom had the chance to navigate a bona fide rock face. *Maybe this trip won't be so bad after all*, he momentarily considered.

"I suppose you told them about the trip?"

His mother remarked, grinning as she walked in and saw all the commotion.

"We are going camping! Come dance with us, mom!"

His younger brother grabbed her hand and ushered her behind the sofa. Their mother somehow lured the Son into the dance as well, and for a brief interlude, they all skipped around in delight, moving to the tune of the father's off-pitch crooning. Then, just when he realized he had a massive grin on his face, he also remembered the screams from last night.

His anxiety from a moment ago resurfaced with vengeance. The Son began to sense an eerie detachment from his legs as if they were not his own. Composed of inorganic material, unnaturally heavy and almost alien. They felt fake—a sudden disruption in communication between his cerebellum and the rest of his body without warning. Much like the disjointed reality he frequently found himself submerged in, a reality that paralleled the one where his "loving" parents harbored intense loathing for one another and wished for the other's demise. At least, that is what they said. At least, that is what he heard.

***

Vacations were *not* uncommon in their family, with trips planned each summer and every winter. Sometimes even during fall break, they made quick trips to nearby family members. Most views from the outside looking in showed a healthy household where the children were also indulged with the latest toys and gadgets. There was nothing the children were left wanting. Every one of their interests or hobbies was encouraged, no matter how fleeting.

This trip was different from their usual excursions, however. A tour designed for the Son to bond and reconnect with the family. Both his parents agreed it was essential for them to surround their eldest child with love and remind him that having fun is what being a kid is about. They hoped they could get closer to him and understand his erratic, withdrawn behavior with greater clarity over this road trip.

As the days passed, the Son found himself ensnared in the vibrant energy that had filled their home. Discussions were brimming with anticipation for their upcoming trip—the essentials to pack, the local delicacies they had to try en route. Even his parents seemed to be in a good mood, and for the first time in a very long time, there was no yelling to interrupt his playtime or guitar practice. He even made a special tune just for his little sister and let her name the melody.

He and his siblings had created a "secret language," which was mainly merging words together in multiple languages, a fun puzzle they would each abide in to trick one another. One would mention a phrase, while the others would have to decipher the meaning somehow. "Iris Rêves" was the name of the new song he was to master for his young sister. Decoding the meaning behind her song titles was hardly a challenge, as they mostly revolved around the wholesome pleasures of a little girl's life.

As dawn broke on the day of the trip, the Son rose from a deep sleep; the room tinged with wary anticipation. His sister peeped her head in the room and, upon seeing he was awake, carefully made her way to his bed, tiptoeing around the scattered toys and music sheets that were strewn about the floor.

She was equally attentive to gauge her brother's mood. Unaware of their parents' conflicts, his siblings bore the brunt of the emotional fallout through his mood and actions, which served as a painful conduit of the unseen parental discord. Yet, when she saw him beaming at her graceful maneuvering, she sprung onto his bed with delight.

"Please play me a song before we go, please."

She implored him, putting her hands together and pouting her lips. He had meticulously prepared his guitar for travel the night before, should he opt to bring it along. Despite his lingering uncertainty, he decided to prepare it for the journey, nonetheless.

As time passed in recent weeks, an overwhelming wave of lethargy had seized a part of his mind, turning even his most cherished rituals into burdensome baggage. Reflecting the prevailing mood, the guitar now weighed heavily in his hands. Aware that his guitar could offer him solace and limit his exposure to family disturbances, he solidified his resolve to bring it along.

"It's all packed away; I don't want to open it back up."

He gestured to the locked case in the corner. She volleyed her head back and forth from a glance at the guitar case and a disgruntled glare back at her brother.

"Am I *not* special enough for you to open it up for me? ... Hmm?"

His grin extended to the limits *right* before the lips parted and broke into a genuine smile to reveal those elusive ivories. She had a way with him.

"All right, fiiiine."

Conceding to swift and absolute defeat by her big doe eyes, he finally unwrapped the case, took the guitar out, and sat back down on the bed, resting it on his crossed leg. He started singing random thoughts and added intricate new notes as he went along. He weaved patterns with the chords, losing himself in the gentle melody he was spinning. It sounded like magic, something almost spiritual in nature. He felt an ineffable joy when his two hands worked perfectly in unison, and each note arrived as intended. As he concluded, he released a deep breath and shifted his attention to his sister, who stared wide-eyed, thoroughly entranced.

"You have to play this for me every single day on our trip. Every day!"

She stated matter-of-factly before jumping off the bed, only to quickly return and deliver a kiss on his cheek before finally leaving his room.

Released from restraints, his smile finally broke free. His closest kinship lay with his young sister. Detached and distant within a crowd, he found solace in holding her close, creating an intimate world of their own. They candidly shared their thoughts and secrets, confident in the solidity of their trust. He wished he could be better—for her.

The Son finished repacking the guitar and lugged it along with his duffle bag downstairs. He placed it next to the neat line of bags all arranged by the door, ready for adventure. His siblings were already seated at the table, engaged in a spirited debate about who would claim the coveted window seat, the duration of their occupancy, the selection of songs, and the destination of their first stop.

Unbeknownst to them, their parents were locked in a tense standoff, their interaction marked by rigidness and stiffness. His father sat in silence; his face contorted in a grimace as he turned the pages of the newspaper while his mother washed the dishes with unnecessary force.

Both were still heated from an earlier exchange that had not concluded of its own volition. They were prize fighters waiting for the bell to be rung to commence the next round. His father would occasionally glance up from his paper to glare at his wife but only to roll his eyes at her perceived ignorance while she prepared her next exchange of words through mumbles and muffled jabs.

Exasperated, she stalked off, muttering something about getting ready to leave.

Frustration coursed through him as he wished he was like his blissfully unaware siblings. His heart then filled with trepidation, knowing he would, once again, stand alone to bear witness to the unsettling developments between his parents. The imminent storm, a familiar and dreaded presence, loomed ominously on the horizon.

***

The family piled into the car, the kids pausing to figure out who was sitting where. Once a harmonious resolution over seat switching was reached, their adventure commenced. Over the loud singing and general excitement of his two younger siblings, the Son noticed that his parents barely said a word to each other. His father's forehead creased in deep thought, stealing glances between the map and the winding road. After a couple of hours on the road, they pulled into the parking lot of a local deli known for its exceptional burgers.

"We're here."

They all rushed out after their father's announcement, eager to eat and take a bathroom break. Once inside the underwhelming, ordinary roadside diner, he and his brother settled into a booth beside the window while their mother and sister made their way to the ladies' room. It was relatively empty given the time, but they chalked that up to them being on the later side of lunch hours.

Finally, his father entered the restaurant and anxiously approached their table.

"Where is your mother?"

Tension in his voice was evident.

"She has gone to the bathroom. Is everything okay, daddy?"

The Son's younger brother showed genuine concern.

281

"Yeah, no worries, my little dude; just tell her to meet me by the car when she comes out."

Shortly after his father left, his sister ran up to the table and started going through the menu. As soon as their mother joined them, the Son's younger brother turned to her.

"Daddy wants you to meet him by the car."

While snatching the menu out of his little sister's hand and whining, he continued.

"You cannot even read properly. Let me see it; I'm starving!"

"Go ahead and order, kids. I am going to see what the problem is. Make sure they don't just order ice cream and milkshakes, sweetie."

His mother smiled at her eldest son before getting up and going out. Often bequeathed the responsibility of an impromptu parent, the Son struggled with the burdens of growing up faster than he desired or was supposed to.

A few minutes passed, and the children still could not make up their minds about what to order. That is when they heard the muffled sounds; their mother's voice was yelling at someone.

"How could you forget! It was on the top of the counter. I literally reminded you before we walked out. How... how can anyone be so stupid? I only have twenty bucks on me, you have all the credit cards, and the kids are hungry. What are we going to do?"

They could not make out what their father said in response, but the arguing continued back and forth. It was no surprise that the Son resorted to bullying his classmates, given the consistent and toxic example set by his parents. His parents had no consequences other than their self-inflicted carousel of manic-depressive mood swings. The Son felt his love for his parents dissipate with each argument since they both clearly indicated to one another that there was nothing to be loved.

A waitress eventually came to their table to ask them if they were ready to order, along with an inquiry about the whereabouts of their parents.

"They are coming."

The Son managed to finally utter a response just as the waitress was about to depart, assuring her that she could return in a few minutes for their order.

The arguing got louder and louder until the Son was certain everyone in the restaurant could hear. His siblings cast nervous glances in his direction, their eyes beseeching him for answers, though he consistently found himself unable to provide any.

Once again, the unsolicited task of presiding over the air of trepidation fell on him. He slouched in embarrassment, hoping to melt into the cheap diner upholstery. Ultimately realizing no other solution would materialize, he finally acquiesced.

"It's fine; you guys stay here. I'll go see if they're coming inside."

The Son calmly rose and started walking to the door. The amorphous legs were back. He did not want to go see what was wrong, but his legs were carrying him with a strength entirely of their own. His heartbeat got louder, partially drowning out every other sound around him. The familiar cold sweat started trickling down his back as he stood behind the corner, summoning the will to go up to them. He was terrified, rooted in that moment with fear—it felt like quicksand.

Outside the customary sanctuaries provided by school, work, and hobbies that usually assisted in circumnavigating their persistent conflicts, the family's retreat now funneled them into an inescapable torment. Fearful that a dispute could devolve into physical harm, the Son preferred to be the only target of any such assault. His main concern was his inadequacy to manage these situations, given that his siblings' safety was possibly at risk.

His mother spotted him from the corner of her eye, motioned to his father, and the yelling abruptly stopped. She said a few clipped words to him before beckoning their child over. Sheepishly, he walked toward them, heart still playing out a deafening drum solo that he could feel in his spine with each step he took.

"Honey, we were just sorting out some details about the trip. Don't you worry; I will just come sit with you guys. Your dad has to go back and grab the wallet from home before joining us."

Her voice was soft and falsely reassuring. Each bore a defensive posture, arms folded, back foot rooted in anticipation of a strike. Their eyes blazed, mouths watering with the primal urge to sink their teeth into the other. Two bullies in a face-off, etching their spectacle into the minds of their audience.

The Son offered a mere nod, pivoted on his heel, and began his retreat toward the deli. As soon as he reached the door, he could hear his father's voice bellow.

"Are you happy now? Thanks to your loud ass yelling, he probably heard everything that came out of your vile mouth."

"Well, if you had not forgotten the wallet, that I reminded you of, might I add, then maybe we would all be sitting inside eating right now instead of pillaging through the car for change to pay for lunch! Now we have to sit at this fucking deli for three hours waiting for you to bring your wallet. Can you not see how messed up that is?"

285

The last few words rang out in the Son's ears before he closed the restaurant door behind him and sat back down at the table, older than he was a minute ago in a way that had nothing to do with time. As the oldest sibling, he was thrust out of childhood and summoned into the ranks of maturity. Indeed, he could grasp the magnitude of the disarray.

He sunk into the plush lining, dropping his gaze as he struggled to hold back his tears.

Could they not keep it together for one trip? Could they at least try not to be such terrible people to each other, he thought bitterly. What he overlooked was the extent of their efforts—failing to see how much they *were* trying. Trying to be involved parents for their kids, nurture their creativity, give them the best life possible, and try to find the love in each other through the love they share for their children.

But it takes time and maturity to recognize these things. A veil often hangs between children and the realization that their parents are more than just providers but separate entities with their own identities. The Son failed to perceive his parents in this light, which stoked his bitterness—practically hated them for it. They were two tyrants maneuvering and manipulating their environment to attain a brief and pointless triumph. Blinded by the strain this growing animosity was placing on

286

their marriage, the Son viciously blamed them for robbing him of innocence he did not even realize he was clinging onto.

A few moments later, his mother sat down wearing a clown-like grin. The Son could no longer tell which façade his parents presented was a mask or their true self. Perhaps long ago, they both abandoned their genuine personas and merely attempted to mimic their surroundings. Was the human mind so susceptible that situations could shape sociopathic conduct? A condition always on edge, simply awaiting the appropriate push.

Unable to conceal the tenseness in her voice, their mother addressed her children.

"Have you kids ordered yet? Get whatever you want; your dad forgot the wallet at home, so it will be a while before he is back. That leaves us with a bunch of time to kill and a whole menu to explore, so treats all around! I think I am going to get waffles, a banana-split sundae, and a big old bacon burger."

***

The course of the expedition unfolded with minimal incident, mostly devoid of the usual parental confrontations. Along the way, the family patronized several restaurants, each famous for its own unique offerings, from hotdogs on a stick to bacon draped in chocolate, but the Son only consumed little and participated even less. His appetite, along with residual excitement for the excursion, had all but faded away.

Despite a handful of navigational errors, they managed to establish their camp within the canyon. His parents played happy family, and no more screaming matches took place. The Son was torn, unable to determine which situation was more nauseating: the spectacle of them jovially engaging the children in play; or the fact that they were so good at acting pleased with each other, holding hands and teasing one another.

The Son brooded over the twisted charade they were staging. He found that he was retreating deeper into his own world, isolating himself from them and spending more time playing his guitar. He liked having it close. It endowed him with an inexplicable sense of safety. Like an instrument of escape; it became a means to immerse himself in the melody while simultaneously offering protection in times of strife.

Fortunately, their campsite was situated in a desirable area for numerous gradations of rock climbing. This also allowed a bit of retrieval for the Son. Although he and his father never progressed beyond climbing jargon, it allowed both of them a momentary escape from the family while honing their internal focus.

He craved the freedom to dash away and navigate the rocks alone, but safety precautions were drilled into him, and the children were instructed not to venture far from view due to the abundance of dangerous terrain and steep slopes surrounding the campsite.

288

Coming into the lofty tent after a climb, he saw his sister playing with his guitar case and aggressively snatched it away from her, immediately rendering tears.

"You know you do not always have to be such a bully. She just wants you to play for her."

His little brother muttered as he walked over to their sister to console her.

"I can do whatever I please."

The Son asserted his dominance and pushed his brother onto the sleeping bag. Every time he attempted to rise, he was shoved back down.

"Stop it! Leave me alone!"

Cries of help beckoned from his younger brother, yet he showed no signs of relenting. Could his brother not comprehend that his guitar playing was dictated by his own whims, not by the directives of others? Who was he to call him a bully when he was content with being ignorant of his parents' victimization? Why should he alone suffer the truth? The Son felt just like his parents at that moment—meting out senseless acts of aggression. He maintained his dominant stance, pushing back until his brother's shrieks summoned their parents.

"What are you doing?"

His father angrily seized him by the shoulders while his mother rushed over to the younger brother. The Son just looked down, face hot with anger.

"I don't know what to do anymore; I just don't know!"

As his mother struggled to keep her tears at bay, his father could only express his disappointment with a frustrated shake of his head. His mother and brother were both visibly shaken, possibly stirred by the intimidating presence of the older son. Was it feasible that the Son's parents had, at last, acknowledged their role as the primary instigators of his behavior? Had things finally gone too far?

They appeared ready to throw in the towel as the look on their faces reflected the hopelessness in their eldest son's eyes. They felt completely at a loss, convinced that no effective actions were within their grasp.

***

The Son did not say or do much after that evening. His siblings stayed clear out of his way, and he skulked off alone at every opportunity he got.

On the final evening, his father rallied the young ones to construct a bonfire as his mother prepared the s'mores. They all laughed along and sang camp songs while putting the wood in a pile, except the Son, who mindlessly went through the motions of collecting driftwood from around the site. As the fire roared to life, they nestled around its warmth, marshmallows and chocolate melting on sticks over the flames.

The Son, an observer on the fringes, peered into the tableau of a "loving" family, contemplating his place within. Each painted smile, and each rehearsed laugh only deepened the chasm of his solitude. A heap of grievances had fueled the Son's frustration, bringing him to a critical boiling point in recent days.

At last, his mother extended a marshmallow-laden stick toward the Son, her voice a gentle tone urging him to grasp it.

"Come now. You'll turn into a stick yourself if you barely keep eating the way you have been."

She said while squishing down her graham crackers.

"Isn't that a requirement to be a rock star, though?"

His father added with a broad smile on his face.

"I don't want to be a rock star, and I don't want your damn s'mores!"

The exclamation point came when the Son hurled his stick into the fire and stomped off to his tent.

***

After they had put his younger siblings to sleep, his parents thought it was time they re-attempted to have a proper one-on-one with their child. They realized they had to try and level with him to figure out what was going on. They felt like they were losing him.

"Son?"

Was the only warning before his parents entered the roomy, custom-made tent. Inside, it comfortably housed an inflatable mattress, a seating arrangement, and a compact table that could be unfolded to one side. The olive-drab print of the tent painted a warm, earthy scene inside, while the solid fiberglass frame stood tall against the gentle wind, firmly securing the bedding in its place. A small transparent panel on the tent's side functioned as a window, which was fitted with a roll-down fabric for moments of desired seclusion—a frequent want.

The Son sat on the bed, headphones in, with his music blaring loud enough to permeate an eight-foot radius around him. His father signaled him to silence the music.

"We need to talk. Please just listen." His father wasted no time. "We love you very much. Your siblings do too. We know there's a sweet, caring boy in there who loves playing music for his sister. We know there is good in you, and we just can't understand why you are acting like you are not any of those things."

Were they playing dumb, or did they actually have no clue? He mused in silence. For the first time, it occurred to him that perhaps they were sincerely ignorant of their contribution to his actions. Their feeble efforts to veil their nocturnal disputes were, in essence, impotent—he caught every word. It was an ugly specter that unfailingly surfaced, and the charade they then staged the following morning stirred a wave of nausea within him.

His mom tucked a lock of hair that covered the kids' eyes behind his ear. He *also* failed to notice his role in the disequilibrium of the familial relationship.

"You make us so proud with your music. The way you look out for your younger brother and sister. You're my baby, and seeing you smile is all I want. What's the problem? Let us in. Please."

She was practically begging now. Her anguish was heavy on his heart, and he needed to flee.

"I don't sleep well anymore! Every night, I hear… everything. Stuff I don't want to." The Son's voice escalated beyond a whisper now.

"It scares me." He added, his face now flamed a vivid crimson as he confessed what he had been evading all along. His mother enveloped him in her arms while his father, drawing closer, placed a hand on his shoulder, squeezing it firmly.

293

Neither of them said anything, as the shame was apparent on their faces. It was possible they did not trust themselves to speak at that time, *blame* on the tips of both his parents' tongues. His mother's face glistened with fresh tears, suppressing any forthcoming words of regret.

A swift and nearly silent retreat from the tent ensued as the adults restrained their emotional display. Both of them clung to the hope that their affectionate embrace would suffice to ease his tender heart.

The Son remained seated, each blink an attempt to dissipate his tears. He languished there, his body caught in a cycle of restless motion, the passage of time becoming an unrecognizable blur of minutes and hours. The words of his confession to his parents reverberated in his mind until new tears traced their wet paths down his face.

All the Son could hear were the sounds of nature easing into the embrace of the moonlit hours. He sat up and rubbed his eyes before looking over at his guitar. He would probably wake everyone up if he started playing now. As he weighed his options, the distant murmur of his father's voice reached his ears.

"You know this is because of you. He's messed up because of *you*."

With equal tenor, his mother retorted.

"I used to think you were at least a good father, but now I realize even that was just me fooling myself. Look what you have turned him into. He is a mess, and you only have yourself to thank. Why are we even together, huh? I should take the kids and go, for their own sake. To save them from you, you bastard!"

Jamming his headphones into his ears, the Son dialed the volume up to its deafening limits. *Why are they still yelling?* It seemed their voices were always raised in anger after speaking to him. The Son thought he should have chosen to remain silent and scolded himself, his body trembling with unchecked rage. *Why did they even bother asking if they were going to do exactly that?* He longed for invisibility, to vanish unnoticed into the surrounding woods, forever hidden from sight.

The sound of his little sister's tears seeped in from the neighboring tent, no doubt startled by the uproar. This was too much; his vision started to blur. Everything was falling apart. *He* was falling apart.

He catapulted from his bed as if fired from a cannon. His heart hammered with such ferocity that his rib cage strained to contain it. Surrendering control, he allowed raw emotion to commandeer his actions as rationality receded. A pent-up, vehement shriek escaped him as he seized his guitar, turning it into a tool of destruction against his surroundings. The onslaught was brief but violent. A chaotic whirlwind of rage was replaced with grief when he saw his broken case and guitar, remnants scattered around the tent.

The Son took to his heels, darting out of the tent into the cloak of the night. One of his parent's voices rang out after him as he sprinted away from the campsite. Ignoring the call, his sprint was haphazard and aimless. The only objective was to get away.

Racing through the forest, he was pelted by branches and leaves, but the onslaught did little to hinder his pace. While the evening air held cool, his blood surged hot within him, provoking a torrent of perspiration. His face was a river of sweat and tears, the mingling fluids blurring his vision, but his arms continued their relentless rhythm.

Now entirely removed from the campsite, the moon, and stars served as his only light source, with the potent pine aroma invading his senses. The awareness of seclusion sent a momentary jolt of fear up his spine, but he countered it, quickening his stride further into the thicket.

His singular perception of adulthood was awash in ceaseless confrontations and the search for verbal ammunition to target those supposedly loved. An unending flight into the night's darkness appeared far more enticing.

He felt broken and beyond repair, knowing he closed a door he ensured would be too heavy to open again as his trust in people evaporated. Evaporated, vanished—vanished as the ground beneath his feet had suddenly.

It all unfolded too quickly for comprehension, and a whirlwind of thoughts barred any possibility of adjustments. His body flung forward as the energy from his stride no longer landed on solid ground. Cartwheeling down the steep incline, his extremities flailed for a piece of good fortune—anything to halt or curb his violent descent. No part of his body was exempt as he was hurled into turmoil down the serrated face of the cliff.

The ominous crunch and snaps reverberating into the night were the grim symphony of the young bones and flesh plummeting downwards. He found an *escape*, albeit an unfortunate one.

As the shroud of unconsciousness and the finality of death loomed closer, the Son's hand blindly seized upon a firm root jutting from the precipice. The heavenly outgrowth bound to his palm, but the force of his fall was so powerful that his weight ruptured his arm's muscular and skeletal configurations.

His body ceased its descent on the steep incline; however, the boy's arm only remained marginally sutured by fragments of tissue. His bloody and battered body lay motionless, his existence barely hanging on by a literal human thread.

As the edges of wakefulness began to blur, a pulse of gratitude shot through him, swiftly followed by a pang of sorrow as he realized that his severed fingers would never again respond to his commands. The notes of a guitar would never be created by him. The embrace of another individual would always be half complete.

With consciousness beginning its swift retreat, he resigned himself to the whims of destiny, relinquishing a fragment of his self.

Chapter Two

The stretch of road seemingly invited the mind to unfurl its stresses. The smooth, desolate path in front needed only the most rudimentary of senses to navigate. Framing the road, the austere landscape unfolded like an alien terrain in a far-off solar system. The ground itself seemed to reject the notion of life, its cracked and arid surface an unwelcoming canvas of rocky outcrops and shifting dust. Aside from the occasional turn indicator, the vehicle remained silent during this particularly exhausting straightaway.

Conversations transpired, and momentarily, the necessity of words evaporated. Gripping the steering wheel with *one* hand, his mind drifted away from driving but far from languid.

The Mentee deliberated over prior exchanges and future objectives. Several of these dialogues and schemes had recently been the topic of shared scrutiny amongst the trio of companions journeying with him.

A fragrance, only possible from a perpetually transient vehicle, penetrated the nostrils with every inhale. Lingering odors expelled from innumerable occupants blended with the masking deodorants, orchestrating an agonizing tension headache.

It was the moment during a road trip when his body offered to surrender. All his senses were extra responsive, and each sensory

299

input crammed neural fodder in the already cramped void behind his eyes. In certain moments, he felt a force that seemed capable of ejecting his eyeballs onto the vehicle's dash.

Regardless, the Mentee maintained his focus. His concentration was spurred by raw excitement. Over the ensuing days, the Mentee had the opportunity to fast-track his career if his wisdom and tireless labor were showcased aptly. At last, his endeavors would bear fruit.

"Does anyone want any snacks?"

A question wafted forward from the confines of the backseat as a colleague reached into his bag, unveiling a plethora of expedition refreshments.

In the Mentee's mind, memories began to unfurl, reminiscent of traded treats between him and his siblings on their family outings. His calf muscle tensed as his foot depressed the accelerator, an attempt to repel archaic thoughts.

A collection of courteous independent declines followed the appetizing offer from the colleague in the back.

"Everyone sure about that? I have beef jerky with flavors to satisfy any tastebud."

Another appeal from the backseat was countered with a familiar refrain of cordial refusals.

The once intriguing topography that encircled them on the drive had now lost its charm, surrendering their view to relentless monotony. Persistent glimpses at the clock led the Mentee to an unnerving perception of time, each minute seeming to stretch beyond its traditional sixty-second lifespan.

Four full-grown men crammed into the confines of a modest rental radiated an air of constraint, rarely finding a moment when comfort was a shared experience. The Mentee despised being on the road and kept the speedometer near the fringe of infractions.

The second companion sharing the backseat cast an interested gaze into the bag of treats, its mouth brimming with an array of glossy wrappers. It was a convenience store on wheels—an arrangement of treats, including chocolates, chips, salted meats, and cookies, nestled within.

"I could have sworn I saw you put your suitcase in the trunk. Is this little bag only dedicated to snacks?"

"Absolutely! Snacks are an important part of a road trip, *arguably* the most essential part!"

The Mentee's associate tore into his jerky, drawing a deep breath as he halted momentarily, poised on the precipice of a tale, even as he continued to chew.

"Yeah, my old man used to make a big deal of stopping at practically every beef jerky cart we passed along the way. Me and my siblings have probably tried every flavor of jerky this side of the country. It's still a thing with him, actually. When he visited last year, he made me drive him to six different stands, all because they were supposed to be the "best." Anyone's guess on where he got that notion. I put on a whole bunch of weight that summer, actually." After another pause to gnaw at the salted, dried meat, he continued. "Some of the fondest memories I have from my childhood are of those road trips…"

While his colleague continued his narrative, the Mentee erected a wall of silence around his atmosphere. The road down memory lane was one he seldom traveled, preferring instead to remain focused on his professional obligations and the pavement stretched before him— aware that navigating into the realm of the past often birthed discomfort and regret, he made a habit of concentrating on the *now*— a practice that necessitated continuous reinforcement.

As he was subtly drowning out the chatter around him, engaging only when prompted by social cues, his mind began to dissect the agenda for the coming days, practicing the events where his expertise would be in the spotlight. Reflections on the work he and his team achieved together served to elevate his pride and bolster his confidence. Although, as the newest member of the team, he felt extra pressure on his ability to perform.

His boss, seated next to him, and his two senior colleagues in the back, continued their exchange of mental souvenirs. Being well-seasoned professionals, none of them harbored a flicker of personal doubt, and the Mentee deemed himself lucky to merely accompany them. Even though their self-assuredness kindled a flame of optimism in him, the Mentee could not evade the nervous tremors that accompanied the fear of failure.

A discomforting lull in the conversation nudged his attention back to his immediate surroundings. It finally dawned upon him that his three colleagues had concluded their tales of road trips shared with friends and family, subtly bequeathing the podium to the Mentee. In the wake of his coworkers' nostalgic narratives about their families and childhoods, a sting of jealousy involuntarily pierced the Mentee's ego.

As if to dissipate the brewing tension, the Mentee attempted to launch a lighthearted jest.

"Without a doubt, gentlemen, this is by faarrr the most invigorating and memorable road trip I have ever been on."

His protracted "far" and the grin at the corner of his mouth were enough flare to erupt the vehicle in laughter. Cue the applause.

Before the exuberant mirth had a chance to subside and any prying questions about his childhood could arise, the Mentee addressed his colleagues in the back.

"I was just going over some details in my head while driving, and I was wondering if you could explain, *real quick*, to me again the specific reasons and significance of why we are using silver."

The Mentee looked through the rearview mirror as he announced his inquiry. His focus was fixed on both, confident that either could respond proficiently. In truth, he was already well-versed in the properties of silver and the rationale for its utilization. His question was merely a vehicle to redirect the dialogue in a different direction. Employing the tactic of diverting attention from the past to the present, he sought to stifle the painful emotions that followed in their footprints.

"Well, we need to think about the hindrances first. Why *don't* these 'things' typically work? Hmm? Moving through the air decreases its strength is an obvious problem. But of course, the main dilemma is energy usage. So, let's assume we need a conservative amount of power. We need an energy transfer of around, let's say, twenty-five kilojoules, which would require a *whole* lot of energy coming from our lithium-cobalt batteries. And on top of that—needing to recharge after each expulsion would be extensive."

Even though he was familiar with his colleague's discourse and trajectory, the Mentee lent an attentive ear. With deep respect for his team members, he found himself ceaselessly soaking up knowledge from their collective wisdom, nurturing the dream of someday acquiring the expertise and boldness required to lead a team of his own.

Amid his colleague's exposition on silver, he had somehow procured a snack and was munching between phrases. Remarkably, his consumption did not dampen the enthusiasm of his audience.

"So, since tungsten has a melting point of six thousand, one hundred-and-seventy-seven-degrees Fahrenheit, or three thousand, four-hundred-and-fourteen-degrees Celsius, oooorrrr three thousand, six-hundred-and-eighty-seven Kelvin, and silver has a melting point of…"

"Just Fahrenheit is fine!"

"Ha, sorry. One thousand, seven-hundred-and-sixty-three degrees… ah, Fahrenheit. We have to actually encourage the electrons to get through the work-function of the silver filament at a *lower* temperature. Silver is obviously the best conductor of electricity due to the high number of free electrons. As the fuel electrons escape the silver, like a stream escaping a fast-moving current of a river, the Wehnelt cylinder collects these, in a sort of way, and are transferred back to the power source. Okay, damn, I have to say. This beef jerky *is* incredible."

"Would I steer you wrong?"

"What other flavors do you have in here?"

As the duo in the rear seats delved into their stash of dried meats, the Mentee refocused on the road ahead. He held scant concern for whether the conversation would resume; he was merely relieved to have evaded the topic of family matters. Lacking recollections, or perhaps just failing to summon any, he had no tales or beloved travel treats from youthful trips to contribute to the conversation anyways.

Nonetheless, he cherished his independence and the tranquil solitude his solitary life offered, but these ruminations stirred by those around him churned up a confusing emotional whirlpool. As the miles rolled by, the Mentee was confronted with the unsettling possibility that his intense desire to depart from his family and live alone was a mechanism of evasion. He recognized that he still harbored feelings of bitterness toward his parents and, to a lesser degree, his siblings—feelings that continued to gnaw at his conscience. Yet, in that fleeting instant, a hint of longing for them permeated his mind, and his propensity to lay his personal misfortunes at their doorstep seemed to lessen.

However, the impending opportunity to drop in on his sister during the trip ignited a glimmer of excitement within him. Among his entire family, he shared the strongest bond with her, maintaining more frequent contact, genuinely investing effort, and having a particular fondness for her child. His visits to her and her family were infrequent, and this work trip provided the Mentee with an opportunity to fulfill his role as a brother and uncle, particularly as his reservoir of excuses was nearing depletion.

Although younger than him, she had entered matrimony early and had branched away from the family at a young age while only his brother continued to reside with their parents.

"Ok, sorry. So, basically, we are using silver because of its unbelievable ability to conduct electricity, and if we keep the current at a certain level to avoid reaching its melting point, the energy being recycled will continue to be powered without necessary and exhaustingly long charges."

"Thank you, professor," his colleague next to him said with a teasing smile.

"You're welcome, ass."

The energy within the vehicle was spirited. Among them, there existed an agreeable balance between hard work and leisure. They relished each other's company while maintaining a deep-seated respect for their professional accomplishments.

Their supervisor glanced at the Mentee but addressed everyone.

"We mustn't forget priority numero uno. The bigwigs will only keep funneling us money if we prove that we can work with the magnetics department. Their systems must align with ours, and of course, they must also be willing. Any updates from your pen pal?"

Without the support of his team members, the Mentee drowned in fear at the thought of presenting in front of strangers. However, when the phrase 'pen pal' escaped the boss's lips, the Mentee's faculties were instantly aroused.

"Ah, not really. The last message on the share drive was actually just a little joke about this company retreat."

"What did they say?"

"It was actually, um, a backend coding platform joke."

"A what?"

Over the course of several weeks, the Mentee found himself engaged in correspondence with the company's magnetics department, situated at a different location. Utilizing a shared corporate server, they began exchanging computer coding intended to enable the Mentee's team to run simulations with their internal operations. Following numerous back-and-forths with the magnetics team, the Mentee felt a sense of camaraderie, as though he had forged an intellectual bond with a friend or friends.

To the Mentee, the arcane coding began to take on the shape of musical notation, understandable with a certain mastery. It enabled the embedding of clandestine messages discernible only to those with an eye to identify them. This gave rise to an influx of playful and subtly coded messages within their professional exchanges. The Mentee found himself enthralled by the prospect of finally meeting the recipients on the other end of the complex communication chain.

"Not trying to sound pretentious, but it is extremely hard to explain if you aren't familiar with that type of coding."

"Who is this person?"

"That's the thing, actually. I have no idea if it's one person, several, a man, a woman. Maybe just a clever computer program—probably not that, though. The only account identity is convoluted and misleading. Probably intentional."

"Weird. Well, we will meet them soon enough. If we can prove our systems work and they have mastered controlling the nanoscale air gap, we could all be on the verge of something pretty groundbreaking."

***

At last, the Mentee and his associates found themselves at their intended destination, their mutual sigh of relief mirroring the car's restful hum as it nestled into a spot outside their accommodations.

As they each checked into their rooms and settled in, the Mentee was denied a chance to unwind, with an evening rendezvous at his sister's demanding his attention. Even though fatigue clawed at him, this was the solitary evening he could spare. Thus, he chose to suppress his exhaustion, readying himself for the night's commitment.

"Hey! You made it!"

His sister exclaimed as he walked in the door, wrapping her arms around him in a big hug. She was still clad in her apron; auburn hair deftly knotted into a neat bun. He returned the embrace with one arm as the *remainder* stayed motionless by his side. The moment he crossed the threshold, tantalizing aromas wafting from the kitchen greeted him, instantly filling his nostrils with a comforting familiarity.

"I'm just putting the finishing touches on dinner; take a seat."

"What are you cooking?" With that, the Mentee lifted the lid on one of the pots and took in a deep whiff.

"Oh, you know, this and that, a little bit of everything, I suppose."

His gaze surveyed the butternut squash lasagna with a look of appreciation before it got arrested by the bone broth stew simmering on the stove. Beside it, an array of diced vegetables stood ready, anticipating a hearty sprinkle of carefully chosen herbs and spices. In the oven, a chicken roasted to a perfect golden-brown, while a tray of creamy potato and cheese dip baked on a level above, subtly absorbing the smokey essence—an impressive display.

They chatted and caught up while she cooked; before long, dinner was ready. He helped her set the table, placing the last spoon down just as his brother-in-law came home.

"Hey, how have you been? So good to have you visit."

Depositing his briefcase on the coffee table, he then raised his voice to summon his son for dinner. The Mentee harbored the hope of engaging minimally with his brother-in-law, whose persistent display of disinterest in his own family was palpable. Maybe he reminded him of his own father too much.

Shortly after, his nephew's sullen shuffle down the staircase echoed throughout the house. Embodying the quintessential adolescent male, he was attired haphazardly, his eyes sagging from sleep deprivation and excessive screen exposure. But upon

311

catching sight of his uncle, a spark ignited his eyes, casting off the gloom.

"Hey, champ, how've you been?"

"Good. I'm happy you're here."

They ate their meal in relative silence, except for small talk or when his brother-in-law would curtly ask the Mentee's sister to pass him a dish—she would wordlessly hand it over to him, avoiding any eye contact. The undercurrent of tension was not lost on the Mentee; however, given his prolonged absence, he opted for silence, deeming it inappropriate and unappealing to pry. In truth, he realized he was too fearful to venture an interjection.

As the meal drew to an end, the brother-in-law grumbled something about a shower and swiftly excused himself from the table. His nephew, too, claimed the need to attend to homework and retreated to the sanctuary of his room upstairs, stranding the Mentee and his sister in an atmosphere thick with unease.

With a weary sigh, the Mentee's sister rose and set about the task of cleaning up the remnants of the meal.

"Here, let me help you."

The Mentee started gathering dishes and quietly eased them into the sink to be washed.

"No, no. I will take care of it; please sit. You have been driving all day, just sit back and relax." She said, quickly taking the glasses from his hand.

"I insist, sis. That was a lovely meal; the least I can do is help you clean up afterward. If I am being completely honest, the only time I have a home-cooked meal is when I come to visit you. I rarely cook for myself. And by rarely, I mean never."

He made sure his sister saw his grin as his only move was to attempt to lighten the mood.

"So, what do you eat? Please tell me it is not a whole bunch of take-out and protein bars."

"No, don't be silly! Sometimes I throw instant noodles into the mix, just to spice things up."

"I mean, the last time I saw you this skinny, you were—"

"I don't do that stuff anymore!"

"I know, I'm sorry. I was just saying. And you're not seeing anyone either?"

Casting a "spare me" glance toward his sister, the Mentee persisted in his silent dishwashing. Frequently grilled about these subjects and perennially annoyed by them, he promptly redirected the conversation in his sister's direction.

"What's been keeping you busy in your world lately?"

"It has actually been really tough around here lately."

His sister nearly burst as she inundated him with repressed thoughts, seeming to have waited endlessly for a chance to share.

"My son hasn't been doing too great. His grade point average has fallen dramatically; he is barely scraping by in his classes. He has stopped socializing with all his old friends and just locks himself away in his room all day. He was such a happy, energetic kid, always laughing and making other people laugh. Not only that, but he used to be part of a whole bunch of after-school activities, all of which he has dropped now. He doesn't even go rock climbing anymore, and that was something he would make time for practically every week."

Tears were now spilling down her cheeks. She sniffed and dabbed a tissue under her eyes before continuing.

"He has always been so fond of you. When he saw you today, he smiled for the first time in weeks it seems like! I was wondering if you could have a word with him and see what is bothering him and what kind of headspace he's in." His sister paused to catch her breath from the exhaustion of hysterical tears. "For the life of me, I have tried everything to get him to talk, even bribed him with toys, ha, and still nothing. He has totally shut himself off from us, and I am afraid I can no longer reach him. He is still in there, somewhere; I just know it."

Shifting uneasily in his spot, the Mentee's eyes were skittish, continuously straying, a silent testament to his determination to sidestep the situation. Yet, confronted with his sister's raw emotional state and brutal honesty, a wellspring of empathy swelled up within him.

Usually, a victim of rash decisions, he found himself holding pause, musing over the fondness he held for his nephew and the unwavering reciprocity he knew his sister would show if their roles were reversed. His deliberation soon bore fruit, convincing him that he had a duty to intervene, even if it was limited to a heart-to-heart with the young man.

"Okay, let me try and level with him. No promises, though; it is a tough age for a kid."

"Yeah, I remember what you were like at that age. Easy is not the word I would use to describe you."

His sister's final words, despite their flippant nature, struck deeper than intended. He acknowledged them with a subtle nod, ensuring his pain remained unseen. Though he worked tirelessly to erase his childhood trials from memory, he recognized their undeniable impact on his personality and yearned to steer his nephew toward a less tumultuous route.

With a turn, he commenced his ascent up the stairs, leaving his sister to the solitude of the kitchen. Treading lightly to evade his brother-in-law's attention, he arrived at his nephew's door and rapped gently. When there was no response, he cracked the door and poked his head in.

Merely stepping into his nephew's room unleashed a jarring sense of déjà vu that was potent enough to anchor him in place. Frozen in position, he blinked rapidly in an attempt to ward off the unanticipated surge of emotions that struck him with relentless force. He could hardly bring his focus back to the present. When he finally managed to regain his composure, he noticed the boy sitting at his desk with headphones on. The whole scene was eerily reminiscent.

The Mentee regularly entertained the fantasy of imparting all the necessary wisdom about life with his younger self—bequeathing a blueprint representing the fabric of cognitive development. Though an impossible feat, he found himself with a chance to engage with a reflection of his youthful self. He wondered why he should squander his wisdom on impractical daydreams of rewriting his own past when a tangible opportunity for personal growth stared him in the face.

He approached his nephew, tapping his shoulder gently as a cue to remove his headphones.

***

"Hey, kid, I came to check up on you; you disappeared so quickly after dinner."

The Mentee positioned himself on the edge of his nephew's bed.

"Sorry, I did not see you there," He claimed, turning in his chair now to face his uncle.

"That's okay. How is school going, buddy? Any cute girls in your class?"

"Not really. School kind of sucks."

"Oh really? And why is that?"

"I don't know. It just does."

"What about rock climbing? Your school has such a good wall. And when we went out to the park last time, I could barely keep up with you, and that was only the second time you were lead."

"Don't know." The Mentee had to make do with a mere shrug as an answer to his persistent inquiries. There was a long silence for a while. Sensing the boy's unwillingness, he questioned the purpose of this seemingly fruitless conversation. He got up, ready to walk out the door, when his nephew exclaimed.

"Can you please help me?" His voice came out in a whisper and the Mentee stopped in his tracks.

Rooted in fear, the Mentee's gaze was fixed on his worn-out shoes, leaving him unable to face the situation head-on. A complete exhalation through his nostrils cleared his head and heart. Gathering his courage, he redirected his stance, facing the red-eyed carbon copy of himself. The anguish so starkly mirrored his own, making it impossible for him to ignore the plea for help. The earlier reticence to talk now made sense, as it mirrored the turbulent emotions, he himself had experienced as a young man. His love for his nephew was boundless, and he prayed earnestly that he could offer sound guidance.

"Of course, I can! What is it?" the Mentee asked, walking back to settle on the bed.

"Did my mom tell you they might send me to this youth military school?"

"No. This is complete news to me."

"Yeah. They are having a few people over tomorrow night. My principal, a few teachers. They will all make a decision about it, I guess."

"I can't believe your mom never mentioned this. I know she is upset right now, but."

"I don't blame her. She doesn't want me to go, but she will basically say whatever my dad wants her to say. That's why I *need* you."

"I don't understand."

"Can you come back over tomorrow for dinner? I just know that if you are here, my mom will be brave enough to say how she really feels."

A surge of disbelief swept through him, anchoring the Mentee in his tracks. The prospect of his nephew being thrust into such a perilous existence made his heart lurch. In his mind, he could already see the young man, fragile and innocent, tossed into situations of peril and ambiguity. The terrifying thought gripped him, giving birth to momentary, overwhelming sensations as his mind became a theatre for a grim panorama of worst-case scenarios; no, he could not conceive the idea of such a young child being thrown into the jaws of danger.

He was no oracle, but deep within, he knew that his nephew deserved more time to savor childhood and be allowed to make these life decisions at a more suitable age. His sister's lack of protest on the matter was equally jarring, a silence that left him unnerved. He understood that simply stopping the boy from leaving was *not* a solution; he needed to go beyond that to be of any real help.

"Buddy, I will talk to your mom and dad tonight before I leave about keeping you here, but I can't come tomorrow. I am so sorry, but I have an important work meeting in the evening and just simply cannot miss it. Hey, but I promise that I can convince them to at least hold off on this meeting until I can be a part of it. Okay?"

The Mentee got nothing more than a frail validation, a threadbare response, but he was yet to possess the strength and ability to delve deeper. He offered his nephew a reassuring smile before pulling away to address his sister and brother-in-law.

When he saw his sister again, her intuitive stare landed on him, deciphering his newfound awareness of her son's situation.

"Military school, sis?"

"I just don't know what else to do. Well, I guess *we* don't know what else to do. *He* thinks it's the best thing for him right now."

Referring to the father of her son, that was also now conveniently gone, visiting friends. Exasperated and confused, the Mentee attempted to pry further.

"He is still so young and impressionable. Aren't you afraid of resentment from a decision like this? I think both of you really need to consider this decision a lot more."

She concurred with every objection he raised to the idea of

sending the young boy away, a compliance he interpreted as a reflection of her submissiveness toward her husband. He sought a promise from his sister to reschedule the upcoming meeting, urging her to inform him before tomorrow evening. The Mentee, in turn, pledged to make a greater effort to stay in touch and create more opportunities to see her and his nephew. He sensed her wish for his continued presence and a few more shared moments, but a compelling impulse to withdraw into seclusion took the upper hand.

The final moments at his sister's and the journey back to his hotel were nothing but a blur as his consciousness refused to settle on any particular thought. His mind was in a frenzy, whirling in an unending loop—sleep was a futile wish.

***

His thoughts wandered afar as dawn unfolded, setting his course through the workday with a sense of detachment. The Mentee's mind was increasingly drawn to his sister and nephew, their silence amplifying his concern as the hands of the clock swung past noon. His mental meandering had so far remained unnoticed, shielded by the day's simple rhythm of social interplay with other divisions and immersions in an array of presentations.

The main conference room was oriented like a job fair. Different departments erected kiosks to demonstrate their expertise and technicalities. Visitors flowed through the exhibits;

their dialogues wrapped around the presented elements like tendrils of curiosity.

Much like his companions, the Mentee drifted aimlessly, engaging in idle chatter; all the while, his mind was lost in a tangle of its own thoughts. The moment his boss hinted at a shift toward the magnetics department, the Mentee's fingers found their way back to his phone, seeking the reassurance of a message from his sister—nothing.

The magnetics department was set to unveil their new advancements to the firm before entering a strategic discourse with his team and the executives, aiming to chart a course for future collaborations.

Upon arrival at the lecture hall, every available seat was claimed, forcing them to pivot and establish a comfortable standing area near the back. A stage of moderate capacity, the auditorium welcomed a torrent of employees to gather and watch the spectacle. The presentations had already sprung into motion, capturing the audience's undivided attention toward the speaker on stage.

"Does anyone in the audience know how most birds migrate and, without fail, arrive at their intended location?"

As the orator began his introduction, equipment on the platform continued to be shuffled around with calculated precision.

"Good travel agent?"

The lecturer retorted a friendly chuckle before continuing.

"For the wealthy ones, maybe… and penguins. What's more intriguing, in fact, is that the eyes of most birds house a natural compass. Fascinating, isn't it? This function is made possible because their retinas are endowed with a protein known as cryptochrome. This protein, in fact, is remarkably attuned to Earth's magnetic fields. Thus, considering the unique mechanism of a bird's vision, it might just be possible that they can actually perceive these fields. And this extraordinary characteristic enables them to maintain their course accurately."

The orator seized momentarily, allowing the audience to marinate in the mirth of the anecdote that was sure to herald the next demonstration. Overhead, a large projector spilled light onto a split screen—one side showcased a tableau reminiscent of a home computer screen, its counterpart a vacant slate. With the scene thus set, the presentation continued.

"I sense your curiosity. Fine for these feathered creatures, but what's next? Well, it's *not* just birds that maintain this protein. Numerous creatures, ourselves included, make use of these proteins to preserve the delicate balance of homeostasis. Naturally, our navigational acumen has veered from those primitive, intrinsic capabilities such as birds continue to possess. Consequently, our ability to discern magnetic fields has all but vanished."

With every practiced footstep, the presenter paced methodically while pausing on each about-face to study his audience.

"Our team is just on the precipice of the capabilities and possibilities that cryptochrome might yield if adeptly managed and delivered. Today, we shall exhibit a fairly rudimentary application that we're refining, involving the use of enhanced cryptochrome introduced to the human retina. If you turn your attention to the screen suspended above me to your left, its display will mirror that of your typical computer home screen. The computer is *this* very one that shares the stage with me, its monitor linked to the projector for the benefit of your collective viewing." He gestured to the equipment on stage. "The basic components of a standard processor are still obtained, but we manipulated silicon and other semiconductors in the monitor to basically react more *magnetically...* And now, please welcome one of our coders on stage to help demonstrate the functionalities."

A young, confident woman marched on stage. Her attire and posture conveyed that of an educated professional. Still, the

Mentee and his colleagues were too far back to observe any other specific details of *either* of the demonstrators. She sat down, facing the computer as the instructor continued.

"A camera is strategically positioned to ensure everyone can simultaneously observe her eye movements and the ensuing actions on the screen. To begin with, our operator will merely be shifting objects, catching hold of each item with *only* her eyes and dragging it to a new spot. Following that, she will adorn an electroencephalography device, essentially a system that monitors brain activity via electrodes. And with this device in place, coupled with the integrated cryptochrome, she'll gain the ability to interact with the screen with much, much greater precision." Pausing briefly for a choreographed moment of tension. "All right. Shall we begin?"

His knees buckled, causing him to falter, but his teammate intercepted his descent, deftly repositioning the Mentee before he could hit the floor. As he found his bearings again, he grappled with the indescribable shock that rippled through his body. Refocusing, he saw the large screen on his right depicting a pair of commanding eyes, the perpetrators of his brief paralysis.

The demonstration validated to the audience how the cryptochrome in the eyes could manipulate items on the monitor. As the spectators watched the screens in unison, the orator was compelled to assure them, dispelling any skepticism and confirming her eyes' authentic influence over the sequences displayed above.

The Mentee found himself entranced. The actual exhibition faded into the periphery of his consciousness, his entire being irresistibly drawn to those *eyes*—seductive and fiery, the energy was powerful but ethereal. He observed her eyes, bewitched by their magnetic allure and the immobilizing effect they wielded over him. Held captive at the moment, possibly by choice or perhaps out of necessity, the feelings were just too potent to brush aside.

His trance was broken as he finally registered his colleague's faint nudge on his arm.

"Hey bud, you okay there? You look dizzy. Do you need to go back to your room?"

"No no, sorry. I'm fine—just a little lightheaded. I think all I need is some water."

"Hope so. Let any of us know if you aren't feeling well and need to go, okay?"

"No, really. I'm fine, thanks."

"Okay. Well, they seem to be wrapping up, so we can visit with them backstage now."

Lost in his reverie, the Mentee failed to notice the presentation's conclusion and the onset of the crowd's departure. Immersed in his daze, the Mentee was immune to the relentless march of time.

He redirected his focus back to the stage, hoping to find the young woman still there, but she was nowhere to be seen. Then, a memory surfaced—she was introduced as a coder. With this, he was assured of the possibility of meeting her backstage, igniting a newfound fervor within him.

"I'm ready! Let's go back and meet them."

***

Backstage a customary assembly of work associates commenced. As familiar faces gravitated toward each other, conversations swirled around the currents of business inquiries. Swiftly taking in the room's details, the Mentee struggled to discern the bearer of the eyes that pierced his senses as her other traits remained a vague silhouette in his perception.

He meandered alone through the reception area, striving to lock eyes with anyone who might be a potential match. His forehead was beginning to glimmer with perspiration as he feared that his sought-after encounter might have slipped away.

A restless energy overtook the Mentee as he traversed the room with growing anxiety. Yearning for a spark of passion and ambition in his existence beyond work, he found an unexpected trigger. Even this untamed motivation was unexplainable to him. *Where is she? How on earth did she manage to disappear,* he pondered. Seldom engaging in affairs of the heart had bred an environment of indifference, surrendering to the belief that an intimate connection was, perhaps, an elusive dream. Could it be that his enduring beliefs had performed an abrupt about-face?

As he made his way across the room, the Mentee was repeatedly lured into conversational clusters by his colleagues. Forcing a smile onto his face and nodding politely to avoid causing offense only served to exacerbate his growing unease.

Meanwhile, concerns for his nephew gnawed at the edges of his consciousness, adding another layer of distraction. The mounting tide of emotions nearly provoked him to disgorge his dinner for all to witness. His anxiety was scaling daunting heights, compelling him to consider abandoning his quest and retreating into solitude.

"Here we go! This is the person I wanted you to meet."

He heard the familiar voice of his boss behind him and begrudgingly pivoted toward the commentary.

"I figured you coding pen pals needed to finally meet in perso..."

The words faded, blending seamlessly with the other ambient sounds. His awareness constricted, his vision focusing like a spotlight on the celestial beauty standing before him. A completely new set of nerves now struck him. The familiar, ineffable feelings returned, causing his knees to wobble under the intensity. Battling the rising tide of unsteadiness, he mustered scattered fragments of his composure, desperate to maintain an appearance of normalcy.

Hastily, the Mentee placed his arms behind him, a subtle maneuver to mask his flaws, while attempting to sculpt what he imagined to be a congenial grin. All the while, he was oblivious as to whether the entire episode had occurred in a split second or if seasons had transitioned in the interim. Regardless, he was cognizant of one irrefutable fact—he was no longer the same.

"Ah, so this is the one I have been sharing messages with."

Her voice resonated like a familiar song that once held a cherished place in his heart. Held rapt in the indelible moment, his nerves were held hostage by its powerful allure. Mustering coherent speech felt like scaling an insurmountable peak.

"Ya...ah...I...ah...well...um..."

Losing complete composure, he desperately searched for a lifeline—an internal nudge for redemption.

"I...ah...I...imaaagine an imaginary menagerie manager imagining managing an imaginary menagerie...whoo...okay, now I'm warmed up!"

He punctuated with an extravagant smile. He clung to the hope that the random idiom, a relic from actors' diction drills he had somehow retained, would serve as his much-needed rescue.

Luckily, her laugh burst forth with a joyous clamor, its melody attracting the attention of many as it gracefully swept through the room, capable of spreading an infectious cheer throughout. Casting her gaze down, she tried to stifle her giggles with a slender hand, her laughter still entirely audible. The momentary diversion offered the Mentee his first opportunity to observe her with undisturbed clarity. While studying every nuance of hers, he questioned whether she was even aware of her own radiant charm.

Her demeanor suggested a hesitation to fully reveal herself as if attempting to conceal a magnificent gem in plain sight. Her perceived flaws were, in his eyes, the quintessence of beauty. Her stance was confident but reserved. She seemed poised, capable of seizing the moment with fervor, yet her innate nature appeared to be gentle and harmonious—a lioness in her element, always on standby to bare her fangs.

The young woman gracefully concluded her laughter, shifting her gaze back toward the Mentee. Usually, maintaining eye contact with others necessitated a deliberate effort, but with her, it was as natural as breathing—complementary forces balancing each other—the inaugural enduring gaze between two souls ordained by fate.

The conventional concept of time lost all relevance again, becoming an inconsequential form of measurement during their encounter. As the surrounding environment disintegrated and collapsed into obscurity, their moment, in contrast, was a snapshot frozen in time, untouched even as the Earth continued its steadfast orbit.

"Okay, people! We are moving to the adjacent conference room for some refreshments and then breaking off into our smaller groups!"

With a sudden shift in their environment, they were shook back to reality. The announcement disconnected the fusion of nuclei as the binding energy was only momentarily disrupted. Resurfacing for a breath of air, they each rid themselves of any lingering avoirdupois from the moment. Simultaneously, they became aware of his boss's presence, a silent spectator in the mold of Nick Carraway. He lobbed a frothy smile at them before pivoting to depart for the conference room. Retiring, he left them in their own world, just as the universe had designed.

The Mentee proceeded awkwardly.

"You know, ah, we both have something in common."

"Oh yeah?" she raised an eyebrow, intrigued by his statement.

"Yeah! You have no idea what I am about to say… and neither do I."

The resounding notes of her laughter rang out again, filling him with the extraordinary satisfaction that he could be unapologetically himself and still provoke such joy in her. Having long held the belief that his peculiar antics were best kept private, the walls of self-consciousness started to crumble.

It became clear to him then and there that his life's mission was to keep her in a constant state of bliss—joy discovered in another demands amplified reciprocation. The sensation was beyond words, indescribable from every corner of his consciousness, yet he was certain that her laughter and smile were now his lifeblood; sustenance to maintain homeostasis.

As one, they rotated and navigated their way through the crowd of coworkers, their eyes remaining inseparably linked. On their journey toward the conference room, they exchanged the necessary courtesies that formed the foundation of a new relationship.

Engrossed in their conversation, the Mentee realized he had unconsciously started to use his arms for emphasis, a gesture unfamiliar to his usually reserved self; the abrupt realization halted his movements. She caught onto his temporary pause and the subtle blush coloring his face. Responding with a comforting smile, she sent a silent message to him that his vulnerability was embraced. With her subtle assurance, he felt his true self begin to emerge from the shadows, transforming lingering shame into rising self-belief. Her presence sent a powerful current through the Mentee, a force impossible to dismiss. His behavior felt endearingly dorky, and he harbored a silent prayer for a semblance of reciprocation in her feelings.

As the conference room filled with the hustle of employees, the Mentee and the young woman slipped away into a private corner, maintaining the flow of their conversation. Both engrossed in the realm of computer programming, they shared and compared their knowledge, excitedly bouncing ideas off each other. They further explored the possibilities of groundbreaking technological advancements, envisioning the potential that could spring from the prospective collaboration between their two divisions.

While the Mentee was captivated by their discourse and her mesmerizing presence, the thought of his nephew and his sister's silence gnawed at his consciousness. Corridors of his mind echoed reminders of the familial crisis that demanded his attention. The Mentee's heart and mind were awash with warmth, yet a gut-wrenching ache coursed through him as he thought of his nephew's distress and his own perceived inaction.

"Is everything okay?"

The Mentee was blindsided by her question, a radical shift from the trajectory of their dialogue. Though, he found himself drawn to complete transparency, unable to offer anything less than his genuine thoughts. The peacefulness that had washed over him since their meeting was relentless, giving him no cause for reticence.

"Ah, how can you tell something is bothering me?"

"To be honest, I don't know. I suppose I just feel a shift in your energy... like there's something bothering you. If there is, we can talk about that if you think it might help," she offered generously.

With an expanding smile, the Mentee felt a warmth spread within him, the kindling stoked by the empathy she exhibited. Another sense of delight quickly enveloped him as she voiced recognition of the unique, indefinable energy between them. He found a sense of ease in her company that gradually stripped away his cautious restraint, urging him to abandon his guarded persona.

"Well, I really do not want to interrupt our conversation. I am enjoying getting to know you, and I also don't want to burden you with personal issues."

He yearned to share his thoughts, but a sense of politeness held him back, mingled with the apprehension of making mistakes or jeopardizing his connection with this remarkable individual.

A significant moment unfolded as she extended her hand, firmly holding his and the artificial appendage of his other arm, their eyes locked in a shared gaze of unwavering truth. She, too, exhibited raw authenticity.

"Nothing would make me happier than to help you right now."

Tears welled in his eyes, and he strained to hold them back, but their insistence only magnified his emotions. Gratitude etched across his face, he reciprocated her gesture with a warm smile, venturing to share the depth of his feelings.

He opened up to her, discussing the complexities surrounding his sister and nephew, unearthing every detail and highlighting the significance of the evening while also expressing his ongoing concern over the lack of communication.

"Do you think you should be at that meeting tonight for your nephew?"

"I don't know. I want to help, truly. But I just, ugh. I don't know." Genuine uncertainty filled his admission as he acknowledged, with a touch of vulnerability, that he honestly had no answers. "Plus, this meeting tonight is *really* important. I honestly just don't know."

"What is it, exactly? You can tell me what you are thinking."

"In recent years, I've become adept at keeping people at arm's length. To be honest, my interactions with others haven't been the most uplifting. It's not just the pain my heart has endured; I also find myself doubting the positivity I can bring into others' lives, hence my restraint to even try and help."

She observed the Mentee's discomfort. A sense of a compassionate individual stood before her, delicately balanced on the precipice of a transformation—a soul scorched, battered, and bruised. Ignorant of the cause yet finding solace in the belief that *suffering* was unwittingly embraced. She knew what to do.

"Do you know why I believe Beethoven was so influential?"

The inquiry struck the Mentee with surprise, yet he sensed the substance behind the question.

"Um, perhaps his deafness?"

"Of course, right? That is *precisely* what I believe. The man loved music; it was nearly everything about him. While he was already a success, his *deafness* arguably compounded his greatness. You can't have one without the other."

The Mentee leaned forward, imploring her to elucidate on the emerging narrative.

"What do you mean by that?"

"The universe continually displays polarity, and I don't think humans are exempt from that. We can't experience joy and happiness until we know what it's like to feel pain. Heartache can only exist when there is love. Life is beautiful in this way. We navigate through our existence with constant influxes of positives and negatives, which are absolutely mandatory to take in stride. Both are lessons, though. Good and bad are subservient to each other, reminding us of each moment's importance and what can be learned. Without appreciating and living with each, one can easily just… drift away."

In that slice of time, the pair remained still; their words muted and bodies motionless. With an impression of fresh air, the Mentee sensed his bitterness fading, replaced by the sensation of new beginnings. Through her warmth and empathy, she unlocked a door once held shut by relentless despair. She offered the words that had been lingering, unspoken, at the edge of his consciousness. She had been his compass, guiding him through the now-illuminated path that lay ahead.

It became clear to him that his role was to support his nephew, and the Mentee's suffering was a lens revealing the love available to those bold enough to accept. Filled with the drive to champion his nephew, he sensed he was beginning to comprehend the fundamental fabric of his essence. The vision of his future, radiant in the glow of newfound clarity, set aflame a surge of fervor, momentum, and thrill.

Guided by instinct, the Mentee wrapped his arms around the woman before him. Her reciprocal embrace cradled him, a sanctuary that welcomed a cascade of tears. He desired to lose himself in the soft labyrinth of her curls, but the call of responsibility pulled him back. He eased away from her, his eyes locking with hers, reflecting an unexpected comfort found in his exposed vulnerability. Words were rendered redundant, their shared realization affirming the course he was set to tread.

Making a beeline for the exit, the Mentee paused momentarily to catch a final glimpse of her.

"Thank you."

"You will never need to thank me."

With a warm smile, the Mentee promised to correspond with her. He darted toward the door, ignoring the trailing call of a colleague; nothing could deter his course. Like a flash of lightning, he was already seated behind the wheel, miles down the road, before his tears had a chance to dry. Clutching the steering wheel, laughter and tears intertwining, he found a sense of purpose—

giving meaning to his existence. The Mentee's *role* was about to change.

Chapter Three

With a velocity that outpaced reason, he contemplated a detour to procure some sweet confections on his return home—his last forty-eight hours had been saturated with consecutive seminars on the topic of Childhood Emotional Development, allowing him scarce moments at home, reserved only for the necessities of personal care. While one more lecture awaited his attendance tomorrow, today's session concluded ahead of schedule, and the prospect of a quiet evening meal with his wife and son was an inviting thought.

The Father had committed much of his life to the dual purpose of learning and educating others about troubled youths, acquiring a wealth of accolades and recognition. Yet, these tributes paled in significance to the lives he had positively influenced; the individual cases where he played a pivotal role in helping a child reclaim their life from emotional hurdles mattered most. This fulfilling experience of bringing about transformation was among the core reasons his zeal for his vocation continued to burn so intensely.

He pulled the vehicle into a spot before making his way into the warmly illuminated bakery, his eyes taking in the assortment of donuts showcased behind the pane. For his own indulgence, he chose two glossy glazed ones, a duo of vanilla delights for his wife, and a pair of chocolate-infused donuts for his young son. He hoped coming home with a small treat would serve as an apology for not being around much for the last couple of days. With the box stowed on the front seat, he set off for home base.

As his vehicle eased into the driveway, it felt as though the hands of time had exaggerated the length of his departure. With one hand navigating the door and the other securely holding the box of donuts, he stepped into the dining room.

"Oh hey, love, you made it just in time."

As he entered, the familiar comfort of his wife's voice filled the room. She transferred a steaming dish of potatoes from the stovetop to the table before gracing him with a kiss on his cheek. He halted her movement back to the kitchen, spun her in a fluid whirl, then guided her into a dramatic fall.

"Time to tango, my darling." He spoke in an indiscernible accent as he grinned and kissed her before she giggled away.

"Would you guys get a room?" His son breezed into the room, a playful note of sarcasm hanging in his words. His parents' adoration for one another was an unending display, unabashed and as natural as the tides. Both born of homes where love was faint, they resolved to charter a different course for their son.

"Maybe not a room, but definitely dance lessons at the very least." His mother quipped at her dance partner as she narrowly dodged the Father from stepping on her foot as he spun her around.

"Son, help me with the potatoes before you sit down, please."

"Sure; what would you like me to do?"

"Just mash them up, please; I have already peeled and salted them. Maybe your father could set the table while I transfer the gravy into a pouring dish?"

Acknowledging her with an affectionate salute, the Father started arranging the dishes and cutlery around the herb-encrusted baked salmon. Once the table was neatly set and the food was arranged with care, they readied themselves for the evening meal, seating themselves, eager to enjoy the food before them.

"How are the talks going, love?"

She supplied a generous helping of salmon onto her son's plate as she inquired about her husband's work.

"So far, so good. Two down, one to go. I'm glad we wrapped up a little earlier today." The Father answered as he took a bite out of the soft, buttery mashed potatoes.

"These potatoes are goooood! What's different about them today?"

"I added some garlic to them." His son answered so softly that the Father was unable to catch what he said.

"Sorry, what was that?"

Unchanging in volume, the child reiterated his statement, each syllable carrying the weight of the first. His gaze remained anchored to his meal, shoulders drooping like an elderly man succumbing to slumber in his armchair—he ached for different surroundings.

"Son, if you want me to hear what you have to say, I will need you to speak up. No one is going to be able to understand you if you mumble to yourself like that."

Undeniably irked by the day's initial interaction with his son, the Father watched the boy push his half-consumed meal away with a roll of his eyes before standing to exit.

"What? That was quick! What did I say?" He said, throwing his hands in the air as an expression of his confusion. He often needed his wife to mediate their communication as of late.

"You know what you said, Mr. Tango."

"What? That he should speak up? I am just trying to make him a more confident speaker; there is no reason for him to whisper to himself when asked something. And I was only asking him what he added to make the potatoes better, not grilling him about why his grades have been slipping for the past month."

Flustered, the Father shoveled another bite of salmon into his mouth.

"You could have said it more encouragingly than that, I feel. I am glad you got off work a little early today so you could join us for dinner but do try and make it on time for his guitar recital tomorrow. They have been practicing in school the whole term for it."

His wife sat up and added a bit more fish to her son's plate as she wryly reprimanded her husband. Taking a breather, the Father realized his poor approach. He expected so much from his young son that he sometimes forgot he was still a child.

"Why are you putting more food on his plate?"

"I am going to take it up to him. I don't want him to go to bed hungry, and I know he is too stubborn to come down to get the plate. Salmon is his favorite."

"You really spoil that kid; you know that? When was the last time I got breakfast in bed, even?" A remark delivered in mock hurt while the Father made dramatic puppy dog eyes at her.

"You will get breakfast in bed when you finish learning how to dance without stepping on my feet."

"Wait!"

"What is it?"

"Take these up for him as well. They are chocolate, his favorite."

The Father opened the box of donuts and placed two, one on top of the other, on the edge of the plate. Then, sinking into his chair with a resigned sigh, he shook his head before continuing his meal while his wife, armed with a warm smile, exited the room. Despite their differences, it was clear that the Father harbored immense love for his son.

The evening's task included refining his notes for tomorrow, yet the part of the guest speaker sparked greater anticipation in him. His guest of honor was someone he had once worked with, a young man who had faced considerable challenges as an adolescent. This once-troubled youth had shown the Father that for all his familiarity with his work, there was always room to navigate problems from a new perspective.

Currently, he was a prosperous young adult, commanding a flourishing start-up. His success was a mirror to the Father's past, a vivid illustration of the motivations that had drawn him to his profession.

***

The next day passed rather quickly for the Father, who was totally consumed by the lectures and talks. The speaker's narrative gripped the audience, eliciting a wave of emotion that culminated in tears. The tale of the Father's involvement in his life stirred the listeners, igniting a flurry of questions and a desire to delve deeper into their history.

With the question-and-answer session spilling over its allotted time, the Father suddenly found himself behind schedule for his son's recital. After muttering some quick farewells, he dashed toward his car, ringing up his wife as he set off toward the school.

"Hey, honey, I am running a bit late. I just left the talks."

"If you just left, I don't think you will have enough time to get me and make it to school for the recital."

"Oh, damn. You're right. I'm sorry."

"Why don't you go straight to the school, and I'll call a cab to meet you there directly? Then we can all go home together after it's over."

"Okay, that sounds good. Let's do that, then."

The Father responded apprehensively, sensing his wife's tone, and could now hear her gathering her things in preparation to leave.

"Yes, I suppose we will have to. Why are you running so late, though? I reminded you of the time yesterday."

"You see, the thing is, my secret dance class ran late because I was learning an incredibly complex Salsa move, so really, it simply could not be helped, baby girl."

He was not able to audibly discern her laugh, but he could practically feel the curve of a smile shaping her face. Together, they possessed the knack to mend any ripples that disturbed their collective chi.

"Very funny. I am serious, though; I'm sure your talks ran a bit over, and I am forever proud of what you do, but you need to be a little more aware of things that have to do with your son. You know how stressed he is about today's recital and how much hard work he has put into it."

Her words resonated with him, always carrying undeniable importance. They often served as a counterbalance, bringing him back into equilibrium. Her solemn tone was a signal, urging him to direct his undivided attention.

"I know, you're right. I will see you soon, babe. Save me a spot in case you get there before me."

"Will do. Bye, baby."

With each passing mile that brought him closer to the school, the Father's forehead creased with worry. A mere ten minutes after the commencement of the program, he arrived, eyes roving among the spectators for his wife. It was nearly time for the son's solo when he finally spotted her.

As his son stepped forward, the rest of the students remained in the background. The performance was slated to be a fresh spin on classic melodies, but suddenly a barrage of unexpected notes erupting from the amplifiers disrupted the plan. A collective convulsion from the audience occurred as he began playing a deafening guitar solo from a popular metal song.

The unauthorized musical detour drew startled, wide-eyed stares from the audience. His head thrown back in musical ecstasy; he sent the strings into a frenzy under the watchful eyes of the crowd. Even those discomforted by the surprising performance could not deny the apparent harmony between him and his instrument.

Shock rippled through the onlookers, but none more so than the school's music teacher, who appeared on the verge of collapse. A few youthful voices broke into cheers from the crowd, and a sporadic hooting ensued. The music teacher quickly restored order, ushering the rest of the students back to their planned performance as he dashed to unplug the guitar from the amplifier.

It took a moment for the crowd to gain their composure as the event came to its conclusion. Once the drama on the stage had ebbed, some of the children offered a modest bow. Amidst the dissipating applause, snippets of laughter and jest rippled throughout. However, the young man's actions left the Father with a knot of puzzlement and dismay.

Once the show was over, their son sheepishly approached his parents. Without a word, the Father pivoted, steering his wife and son toward their waiting car. His face remained stern, while his wife's features were clearly a display of concern. She recognized the situation for what it was—less a rebellious act, more a "silent" plea for help.

After a span of resounding stillness on the drive home, the Father finally broke the silence.

"Can you explain why you chose to do that *tonight*?"

Despite the Father's attempt to soften his probing, the son offered no response, his vacant stare locked onto the world outside the window. His patience wavering, the Father restated his question, his voice gaining amplitude.

"Because I wanted to."

"Did you do it merely because you felt like it? Or was this an indirect appeal for attention?"

"No, I just wanted to play what I wanted to play. I am sick of the annoying music teacher always forcing me to play what he likes."

"And you thought the best time to play what you wanted was during a recital everyone worked very hard to put together. The music teacher is *not* making you play what he likes to listen to; he is training you to play different things, even things you may not like, in order to increase the scope at which you play."

The Father felt the soft touch of his wife's hand on his thigh— a silent signal urging caution in his approach.

"I don't want to learn how to do all that. I know what I like, and I am going to drop out of the band to focus on my own music anyways, whatever I want that to be."

His son's sharp rhetoric was painful to hear, the chill and detachment in his manner evident as he defensively crossed his arms over his chest. Though he had set the stage for controversy with his audacious act, his naïve mind failed to anticipate this level of confrontation, leading him to retreat behind a curtain of indifference.

"You need proper training first. Trust me. Also, you should just be lucky that you even have the ability to play. Not everyone is so fortunate. Music is not something to be taken lightly if it is something you really do care about. And if you want to continue making music, I suggest you pick up your grades. I know they have been slipping over the last month; you cannot ignore your studies, bud. This is your future we are talking about. I wish you just cared more about it."

His son responded with a dismissive roll of his eyes, refocusing on the contents outside the window. His mother adjusted herself in her seat, recognizing the emotional undercurrent that, when stirred within her husband, often clouded his ability to apply his known wisdom when engaging their son.

Upon reaching home and no sooner had the Father maneuvered the car into the garage than the son shot out, letting the car door slam in his wake before storming up to his room.

"Hey! It is not okay to slam doors in this house, young man!"

The Father called out to him in a combination of bewilderment and irritation as he began to follow bchind his son. His wife halted his progress, ensnaring his attention by locking eyes with him.

"It's okay, love, let this one go. We need to talk. Let's go upstairs and unwind first; you have had a long day. Did you even eat anything after the talks?"

Her voice was soft and comforting, and as she spoke to him, she gently pushed some hair out of his face, her eyes holding an unwavering focus on his. The Father let out a long sigh, shaking his head before tenderly grasping her hand and pressing a soft kiss to it. Occasionally, he was struck by the notion that she understood him more deeply than he understood himself. With a soft smile, she gestured subtly, directing him with a nod.

"Okay, why don't you go to our room? I'll make a quick sandwich and bring it up for you."

His gaze was filled with unspoken gratitude. She was his anchor in the turbulence, a guiding sound in the mist when the path was unclear. Every day, he felt a need to show his worth to her, knowing that his inner conflicts would become unmanageable in her absence.

"Thank you." A warm smile and loving kiss were shared before the Father ascended the stairs, and she redirected her steps toward the kitchen.

***

Selecting two slices of bread, she dotted the pan with butter, set the flame to a low simmer, and lathered each slice with another coat of butter. Next, she selected deli ham and turkey, along with all the accouterments that unite to produce a hearty sandwich. She ensured a generous addition of cheese for that perfect melt, just as she had during their dating years. Then she proceeded to spread a hint of baked garlic confit on the outer faces of the bread before introducing it to the now-melted butter on the stove.

The sandwich's readiness was announced, with the cheese bubbling and oozing over. She swiftly transferred the sandwich to a plate, cut it in half, and arranged it on a tray with a frosty beer before making her way to the bedroom. On her way, she passed the closed door of her son's room, the space behind it pulsating with the echo of blaring music. She released a soft sigh before entering their room, where she discovered her husband settled comfortably in a chair by the window.

"Here you go, love."

"You're extraordinary; my love for you is boundless. Tomorrow, I am cooking dinner, and I'll do all the dishes for a week, I promise."

"You better. I felt like I was walking out of a 1950s infomercial the way I was bringing in a sandwich and a beer."

His wife's quip nearly triggered a spray of beer from the Father's mouth. They laughed and smiled, their eyes revealing a mutual, unspoken affection.

"Okay, look, there is something I want to say, so let me just tell it to you like it is, the way I see it."

Her husband chewed slowly with eyes wide open, emphatically waiting to hear her advice.

"I know you love our son. It is clear as day that he means the world to you, and you want the best for him. But I wish you extended the same courtesy to your son as you do to all those youths you work with and whose lives you have changed."

353

Travis Lane

"What do you mean, same courtesy?"

"I mean, the main thing that your work focuses and centralizes on is communication—the importance of having a safe space and a chance to talk. How many times have I heard you say to the people you work with that if a child does *not* feel safe, they will not talk? There is a reason he did that solo in the middle of the recital, a reason why he slams doors and mumbles to himself. It's because he doesn't feel safe."

"But I *have* provided a safe space for him! He has everything he wants. When he wanted to get into music, we encouraged him. We take him on trips and always try and have dinner together. You and I never fight, knock on wood. What more safety could he want when he has two loving parents who not only love him but each other?"

The Father now stood up and began pacing around the room.

"My darling, having safety does not mean a safe space. Do you really think you have been encouraging about his music? Encouraging in the way you think is right or in the way he needs? Think about what he actually needs, empathize with where he stands, and let him open up to you without the fear of you telling him how he could be better. Wanting your child to be better is part of being a parent, but I think our son needs you to just let him be the way he is as opposed to the way *you* want him to be. His best

354

version may not be the one you envisioned, but it may be what is best for him."

As his wife concluded her thoughts, the Father resettled himself on the bed, nodding in measured agreement. It was at that moment that a sudden realization crashed over him. His endeavors to improve his son were inadvertently exacerbating their situation while shutting more channels of communication. He had, unknowingly, become a mirror of his parents. While lacking their knack for theatrical intensity, he remained oblivious to his son's growing independence.

How did I not see this? He buried his face in his hands; the anguish of understanding that he had driven his son to seclusion mirrored his own youthful experiences too closely. Almost too much for him to bear as he was beginning to feel wracked with guilt. His wife saw his expression and sat down next to him, taking his hand in hers. Her embrace never failed to have the same effect. He felt a tide of comfort envelope him like a calming infusion seeping into his veins. Were he to be ensnared by any addiction, her touch would rank supreme—a cure as potent as any nature could bestow.

"Don't blame yourself. You *love* him. You have been too close to the situation to see it objectively, perhaps I have, too, which is why it took me so long to say anything, but you can still remedy

355

this. It is never too late. You must establish that open chain of communication between you two again."

Before finding the right words, the Father eased his head into his wife's lap—his preferred retreat during times of internal strife. A meditative calm set in as she sifted her fingers through his hair and worked her soothing touch down his neck.

"I thought... because I knew so much about troubled youths, I was giving our son exactly what he needed." His words carrying an air of self-rebuke. "My expectations for him and his needs are two completely different things. I just assumed that I was giving him all he needed because I let myself believe that I knew so much about troubled youths that I was automatically doing the right thing."

His wife gently rubbed his neck, her voice full of understanding as she retorted.

"Being an expert on troubled youths doesn't necessarily mean you have all the answers as a father. Every child is unique, even ours. But remember, love is our strongest guide. That is what truly matters, and I will always be here to help you navigate these waters."

"This whole music thing was just him trying to express himself, and, in turn, I tried stifling and telling him the right way of expression. I've been trying to apply my professional knowledge to a deeply personal matter. I need to separate the two. I need to be his father first, before anything else."

"We'll figure this out—together."

"His music, his passions, they should be *his* choice. I should be nurturing them, regardless of what form they take on. Oh, but what if it's too late?"

His own question shook him to his core as he prophesied his son being subject to the same relationship he had with his parents.

"Remember one thing, when love is there, it is *never* too late."

Her arms held him close, their shared silence carrying a language of its own. Each moment lingered, a testament to their enduring connection. He straightened up slowly, meeting the steady gaze of his soulmate, a daily reminder of his unwarranted stroke of luck. Women of her kind have monuments raised in their names.

"Thank you. Èvā a môr, baby."

"Èvā a môr. And you know that you don't ever need to thank me."

Long ago, they both agreed that saying "I love you" was insufficient and too diminutive to how they really felt. Love was overused, antiquated, and ephemeral on the cosmic scale, while they believed their union was forged at the dawn of existence and now situated firmly on the path of eternity.

His parents had professed their love for one another, yet their actions had painted a starkly contrasting image, leaving the phrase bereft of its essence. When the Father shared with his wife how he and his siblings would create linguistic blends from various languages, she found it endearing. So much so that she suggested they coin their own idiom to articulate the timeless love they had for each other.

Was it possible that the hands of destiny had intertwined their paths eons ago? Was their journey one of shared influence and near misses, now reaping the rewards at this intersection of time? Regardless, their feelings were far too vast and intangible to define or explain. Long ago, they had abandoned the pursuit of understanding, choosing instead to bask in its unexplainable beauty.

Anticipating the moment, the Father cleared his throat, exhaling a breath that felt heavy with unexpressed sentiments.

"I need to speak to him and tell him I'm sorry."

Standing tall, the Father wiped away the tear marking its passage down his cheek before he moved and departed the room in search of his son.

***

The robust music seeping through the door prompted him to knock with amplified force—no response. The familiar vibrations of music pouring from the room sparked a laugh in the Father; he could easily have been the one in there, lost in the rhythm. He echoed his first knock with a more forceful one. Yet, the music persisted, and the door showed no inclination to open.

He sighed and conceded defeat, knowing the only way to get through to someone his age these days was through their cell phone. He pulled his mobile from his back pocket and dialed his son's number. After two rings, the music turned off, and his son answered.

"Yes, Dad?"

"Could you open the door, please? I'd like to talk to you."

The boy walked over and opened the door before returning to settle into his desk chair. The Father sat at the foot of the bed while his son shifted to face him. A slight chill of déjà vu ran down the man's spine, which he quickly brushed off to focus on the matter at hand.

"Do you want to go get some ice cream from the drive-through like when you were younger? Just you and me?"

An edge of hope in his voice as he spoke. He hoped to retreat to the days when he was superhuman to his son, and every action was powerful, and every joke landed accordingly.

"Didn't that place shut down like five years ago?"

"No, it's still open. I passed it the other day on the way back from a conference and thought it would be nice if we could check it out together."

"I mean, sure, if you really want to. I remember the brownie fudge was good. But I do have a decent amount of homework to do."

"You know, my teachers used to say that I will never amount to anything because I procrastinated too much. You know what I told them?"

"What?"

"*Just you wait…*"

His son could not help the upward pull at the corners of his mouth while still rolling his eyes at the absurd quip. The Father was grateful that his charm's effectiveness was passed down from his mother.

The son hopped off his chair, and they both went down to the car, passing his wife in the kitchen.

"Where are you guys going?"

"Just to get some ice cream. We will be back soon. And you know I'm picking you up a few scoops of your favorite. Don't you fret, doll face."

The Father smiled and winked as he grabbed the car keys off the mantle before getting into the car with his son.

After driving for a while and listening to the radio's typical tunes, the Father finally broke the silence.

"I don't think I am inaccurate in saying that between school, music, and your other extracurriculars, you may be a bit more stressed than normal."

"And how could you know? You are hardly ever there; all you do is work."

His voice was sharp and defensive, alerting the Father that the idea of the ice cream trip had not lowered his son's guard. The boy's eyes shifted toward the passenger window; his sight not drawn by the outside view but seeking an escape to any world that was not this current conversation.

"That's not fair. I *have* been there. Guiding you and pushing you on to be the best you can be, but I also am aware now that I *haven't* been the best listener."

361

"That is definitely true, and, well, sometimes you push too hard, Dad. It's just exhausting."

"I may sometimes be a little tough, but that is only because I see your true potential. What you are capable of if you only applied yourself. When you get bad grades or pull stunts like you did on stage today, you take away from all that potential that I want you to tap into."

The Father's desperation was palpable, aching to help his son uncover the meaning laced in his words. Once soothing, the radio's background music was now an irritating distraction, disrupting his flow of thoughts. It astounded him that, despite dedicating his career to counseling young people, he was inept when it came to reaching out to his own son. His hand clenched the steering wheel, the other hidden, discreetly concealing his artificial appendage—a reflexive gesture borne out of mounting unease.

"What about what I want, Dad? What about the potential I see in myself for my music? I know I should have talked to you and Mom before playing that song at the recital. But it felt so good while I was up there, letting the music I wanted to play flow through me. That moment, the moment where I was doing just what I wanted to do, gave me more confidence than I have ever felt before."

Looking back toward his father now, his son's eyes lit up as he spoke, and it was apparent the joy that radiated from him even when just talking about playing the guitar the way he wanted.

"Look, for a huge part of my life, I didn't know what I wanted to do. I tried doing a bit of everything until I was lucky enough to figure it out. It seems you know what you want to do, but it's still a bit early for you to narrow your choices this way. I want you to focus on all your strengths because, believe me, kid, there are a bunch you've got there. Also, what is wrong with expanding your catalog of expertise while learning and mastering as much as life can possibly throw at you? A modern-day Renaissance man."

"I want music to be my main focus. Nothing feels close to as good as when I am playing. I just wish you would support me."

"I do support you, Son. I really do! But I need you to understand that without a well-balanced education to guide you, music alone won't take you very far." A momentary pause gripped the Father—a testament to the difficult topic.

"I certainly remember the days when I lost myself in the music. Trust me, I truly do. Being able to escape from the noise and disruptions that seem unavoidable as we go through life. It pains me that I cannot experience those sensations again, but you have to know that you could be missing out on other opportunities that could change your life for the better."

363

"You're just saying this because you must not believe my music is good enough to carry me through whatever I want to do."

"It is the exact opposite! I just think you should have as much in your arsenal as possible, and with that big brain of yours, you have a lot more room for ammunition. Playing music, however, makes you happy; I will not try and tell you there is a right way or a wrong way. I will ask, though, that you talk to me more. Speak to me. No matter what you say, I promise we will tackle any problems—together. Talking about it will never make it worse. Does that make sense, my man? And please don't ever forget that I love you."

Turning his gaze to the boy, the Father found himself confronting a youthful manhood he had previously failed to acknowledge—not necessarily his appearance, but an aura that the young man exuded. The bond he felt with his son was more profound than mere fatherhood, entering the realm of a shared brotherhood. More parallels existed between them than either would confess, another testament to their striking resemblance.

"I hear you, Dad. And I love you too. I will also try and communicate better."

"Thank you. And yeah, of course, dude, you were pretty good up on that stage tonight. I must admit, it gave me chills—in a good way. And look, if you are having problems in school with your homework, you know your mom and I are here to help. We don't judge; we are simply your number one advocates. If there is something you want to do, experience, or achieve, let me in. I will listen even if you don't want me to help. Even if I am at work, I am always a phone call away. I want you to know that you come first, son. I am sorry I haven't been around so much; it's just so rewarding to do something you are so passionate about, and I want that for you too. If you say music makes you feel that way, then go for it. Just don't let anything else slide along the way. I will always be pushing you to be the best you can be. That's my job, kid."

A pivotal moment was upon them, marking a profound shift in their relationship—ushered in by simple dialogue. The Father swelled with pride at his son's ability to express himself so well, a contrast to his own youthful inclination toward isolation. As a father, he felt pride and relief that he had managed to avoid the pitfalls that plagued his own elders. No ice cream on Earth would taste sweeter than this evening's. He gave his son's hand a reassuring squeeze as they both set their sights on the path before them.

Chapter Four

Even without being able to see, he could sense which road they were on by the unmistakable pothole that they had hit during the previous right turn. An adversary he often tangoed with. He laughed to himself, knowing he submitted defeat to such a mundane obstacle as he recognized it delivered the final blow.

He found himself engrossed in the sparse cluster of stars visible through the small overhead window; he felt the lines etched by laughter and worry on his face tighten as thoughts of an uncertain future loomed.

Briefly, his attention wavered when the first responder, lifting his head adorned with thinning hair of once-raven darkness, gracefully adjusted the oxygen mask upon his face.

Just as the Husband's eyes were settling on the comparative fastidiousness of his surroundings, his wife inched closer to his head on the small seat next to the stretcher. As she leaned in, her crystalline eyes, speckled with hints of spring, met the Husband's gaze, their depths reflecting the tranquil cerulean waters of the sea. Her slender fingers gently brushed against his temple; her touch as delicate as the strands of chestnut hair that framed her face. *What is a sky full of stars when I have her to look at?* he wondered.

His pupils dilated, and a small, tired smile mechanically spread across his face, but his eyes expressed worry. She took his hand in hers, resting them both on the edge of the stretcher as the first responder on his other side checked his vitals and administered an IV drip with skilled, deft movements. His wife returned his smile, but he could see the mirroring of his own concern in her expression. Swallowing became a challenge as tears welled up effortlessly, pooling before making their way down his cheeks, moistening the disposable linen.

Turning his attention to the window on the adjacent wall, the Husband observed the flurry of trees and undergrowth passing by. The vegetation whizzing past seemed to hold an intensity of color he had never noticed before. A peculiar current running through the dusk air pulled him into an acute consciousness of his surroundings and circumstances—his life was ebbing away in an ambulance, journeying toward the hospital, his wife at his side, in what could very likely be his last few breaths.

He found himself questioning why his senses, despite his deteriorating health, were operating with such acute intensity. His surroundings became starkly vivid, the air thickening as though submerged underwater. Each drip of the saline solution was perceptible as the cocktail entered his veins with authority. Corners were smooth as he traced a medley of equipment surrounding him. But nothing pierced his senses more than the siren's provoking oscillation.

He wondered if this peculiar cradle of space and time he found himself in was his mind and body's desperate bid to drink deeply from the fading world around him in these waning moments—procrastinator. His heartbeat quickened, an echoing drum in his chest, as the realization dawned: every sight, sound, scent, and touch might be his final encounter with existence.

"I think this is it. Feels different this time." The Husband's voice trembled as his muffled words barely penetrated the mask.

"Don't say that, baby. It's just a hiccup. We will be home tomorrow morning. Okay? Just a hiccup."

His most cherished comforts were the familiarity of her presence and the soothing sound of her voice. Yet, the looming dread of losing that solace was stoking the fires of his panic. All the unanswered questions, the risks left untaken, and the words unsaid or misspoken began to spill forth in his mind. He chastised himself for his vulnerability and the unwelcome intrusion of *regret* in these fleeting moments.

The Husband's breathing grew more rigorous, the mounting anxiety pressing in on him like an impending storm. His gaze turned to her, a silent plea for salvation.

"Did I live a good life? I was a good person, right?" He asked, desperation evident in his voice—he needed confirmation. Regardless of one's spirituality, when faced with the end, time becomes the overarching concern. In his quest to absolve himself from the gravest transgression, he needed to know that his time alive had *not* been squandered.

"Baby, of course! You are the most fantastic person I have ever met. You have no idea how lucky I am that I got to spend my life with you." Her tears now streamed uncontrollably, dousing a floor already accustomed to trauma. While the situation was familiar to the paramedic, palpable reverberations were emitted from the binding energy of the two lovers. His posture remained professional and stoic, but his eyes reflected an awareness of the intensity of his surroundings.

"W-what if I had more time?"

"What, baby?"

The Husband's speech was becoming desultory, exacerbating his wife's plight of futility. She squeezed his hand harder, anything to be a beacon of support for him.

"What do you mean, dear? Had more time for what?"

"I have no masterpiece. I'm no hero. My name will... my name will be forgotten. Forever."

Noticeably trembling, the Husband ached for just one more day. *Please, I can do so much in a day!* He prayed. Even with a lifetime of so much joy, he was penetrated by the inevitable curse of dying regret. The thought of his name never being spoken again and ultimately eradicating even from his loved one's memory frightened him more than his impending demise.

His wife leaned in, her voice a hushed whisper that breathed warmth against his cheek.

"My love, you don't need a monument, and you don't need any sort of legacy. To our son and me, you were the star and the champion of our lives. Because of you, our lives were the best they possibly could have been. Every day, you went out and conquered the world for *us*. Being able to experience life with you has brought me more joy than I once couldn't even imagine. And don't you always tell me your *only* job is to make me happy?"

A momentary ripple of laughter broke the monotony of their relentless sobbing. As she pressed her lips to his cheek, she tasted the tributaries of salty discharge. And just like that, the Husband's breathing began to regulate as the aquifers beneath his eyes dried up. Even amidst the harsh reality of their inevitable farewell, she stood as his guiding light. Clarity rushed in as quickly as the compressed oxygen from his mask.

Tabula Rasa

Since their paths first crossed, his primary motivation was to better himself each day—simply to be deserving of her presence. If she was happy and enjoying life, then everything around him seemed to be running accordingly. The frightening circumstances for the old man had disrupted his spiritual doctrine, but the comfort of her idyllic words and warm embrace cleared his vision once again.

The ambulance came to a stop, and his wife stepped out of the vehicle as more first responders came to assist the paramedic in wheeling the Husband's stretcher into the building. *Had the journey finally come to an end?* A fierce tension between his eyes seemed to paralyze every muscle. The piercing white lights of the hospital ceiling flew past him, merging into a singular trail of illumination across his sight before finally surrendering to the darkness.

***

Emerging from the depths of unconsciousness, the Husband cautiously opened his eyes. He let his eyelashes flutter lightly, acclimating his vision to the sterile radiance of the hospital room.

Enveloping his bed stood the reassuring presence of his siblings, wife, and son. They were all talking amongst themselves in hushed tones, all except his wife, who was seated on a vinyl

371

chair next to his bed, her eyes intently focused on her love. Once they all noticed he was awake, they concentrated their emotions on him, soliciting all their available goodwill to enhance his comfort.

Guided by his wife's reassuring whispers in his contemplation of mortality, his lapse into unconsciousness served as a cleansing reset—a reawakening. In the midst, he was swept into the embrace of a dream. It was a dream devoid of imagery but rich with an array of sensations. A sanguine energy that offered assurance, poetically voicing to him to accept passage and recognize that *this is not the end.*

As he lay suspended in that space, he seized a fleeting second to soak in the gravity of his situation. Every corner of the world appeared to be drenched in a soothing calm, and he started to wonder if, since his diagnosis, he had ever felt such peace. Feeling blessed to have his dear ones within arm's reach, he recognized the privilege of his circumstances.

Turning to his beloved ones, he found his voice.

"If I didn't know any better, I'd say you all had just seen my hospital bill."

Persistent in always trying to lift his loved one's spirits, the Husband seldom strayed from optimism, even when darkness hovered and all else seemed engulfed in it. As the grim revelation of his illness surfaced, he gathered the strength to stifle his inward lament; his former self would not have demonstrated such elegance in adversity. He would have succumbed to victimhood, perpetually cloaked in a nebulous of cynicism. Rejecting the descent into despair, he chose to treasure each day a little more than the last. Night after night, he stole a few more precious moments from sleep just to observe his goddess softly breathing in her slumber. As he looked at her, he found his mind perplexed that she had decided to spend her precious earthly moments with him. Time, that elusive element—it was what he yearned for the most. Given scant time remaining, he was not afforded the luxury of dwelling in melancholy.

The Husband attempted to sustain his stoic demeanor for his family.

"We were always aware that this journey would lead us here. We've spent a year and a half trying to dodge this, but it seems to have finally found us, just as they said it eventually would. So, why don't we all try to make the best of this time we have together and keep those frowns at a minimum?"

The wound created by the loss would never fully mend, but the Husband schooled his kin on the power of unremitting energy. As he prepared for his inevitable departure, he insisted that no one be burdened by unending grief. Parents never truly fade away if the values they embed in their children take root, hopefully yielding virtue that amplifies over generations. The Husband harbored a deep conviction that, alongside his wife, they had instilled principles of righteousness. His son, surpassing his and his wife's every aspiration, bore their legacy, easing the Husband's heart with the knowledge of his preparedness for any life challenges.

Yet, the Husband was persistently touched by a sense of duty to rectify any inadvertent lapses in attention toward his son over the years. His bond with his son was strong and deep, but it was often overshadowed by his profound sentiments for his wife. His wife knew him in his full complexity and authenticity, while he occasionally masked himself under the guise of "the parent." A love that defied words, indeed, yet tinged with a slight regret for perhaps not exhibiting the same degree of affection and attention he bestowed on his wife. Despite his lingering wish to have expressed more warmth and love, he found solace in knowing his son would be well provided for in his absence.

A courteous knock prefaced the doctor's entrance, a woman with sharp eyes keenly peering from behind sophisticated spectacles, her gait steady and resolute, the embodiment of unspoken experience.

"Hi, everybody; nice to see all of you here."

The room's grieving visitors delivered a flat, communal greeting. The doctor directed her gaze solely on the Husband now as she pursued his chart.

"And *you*, how are you feeling?"

"Look around, doc. I am surrounded by the most wonderful people ever to exist—I'm cool."

"Your outlook is a true gem. I hope you know that."

Halting her movements momentarily, the doctor offered the Husband a smile of authenticity, bearing the unwelcome responsibilities that came with her position.

"As discussed previously, you're familiar with the protocol now. All necessities have been readied and are in place. There's no need for concern—just cherish your time with your family. Should you require anything, simply press the button. Rest assured, I'll be the only one to respond. Does that suit you?"

"Of course, doc. As long as you do me one favor."

"What is that?"

"Have yourself a wonderful day. You make people's lives possible and worthwhile up until the very end. And I thank you for that."

"I wish we could have done more."

"Oh, I know. We fought like hell, and that's all that matters."

It was a heavy moment as they finally relinquished their weapons and surrendered, yielding to the unconquerable foes of time and nature.

"You enjoy yourself as much as you can and stay comfortable. Goodbye, everyone."

By that point, the entire room had lost its bearings, and the wife was constantly brushing away the teardrops from her cheeks with a damp tissue—mainlining grief. Leaning in, she brushed her lips against his cheek, granting him a lungful of her presence. Her scent, intoxicating from their initial encounter, remained undiminished. A mere inhale transported him into an impenetrable calmness. Her traits bore the power to mesmerize each of his senses. He was aware the profoundness of this moment owed much to his circumstances, but the sight of his beloved in such agony truly yearned for sedation.

The Husband coughed, and his whole body creaked and ached in protest. The disease had become the occupying force within his body. The pain associated with Stage 4 of the illness was more than any textbook or doctor's lecture could have prepared him for. Although he took a fist full of prescribed pills every couple of hours, some of them being painkillers, none managed to completely get rid of the dull ache that had been with him for a year and a half now.

Every attempt at a full breath was a struggle. As months slipped away post-diagnosis at an incurable stage, the days seemed to blend together. Steadily, the affliction pervaded his body, seizing both its functional capabilities and autonomy. The scope of palliative care was limited in tempering his anguish as his organs gradually surrendered, one after another.

His siblings drew nearer, and he placed a kiss on his sister's hand while his brother gently squeezed his arm. The Husband let his eyes drift shut, wandering into the realms of his earlier memories. A phase of his life never escaped his mind, a time where he felt destined for failure, merely drifting through life, always in a state of preparation for the coup de grâce. Navigating to dark corners of his mind, he had once lost faith in his capacity for future dreams and aspirations. Memories that he eventually turned into weapons to overcome the myriad of other turbulent situations encountered in life.

Earlier, the notion of mortality disturbed him, but with his life's reflections passing by, he felt a sense of gratitude for his pursuits. He had an emblematic wall of accomplishments that anyone with his aspirations could be proud of.

Foremost among his achievements were his positions as a husband and a father. The sum of his accomplishments was only made possible through *her* unwavering support. Her faith in his potential spurred him on, tested him, and catalyzed his self-improvement, guiding him to become a better man.

***

His wife came closer to him and clutched his hand in hers, holding it tightly while continuing her steadfast gaze into his eyes. The room's atmosphere, thick and quiet, hinted at the brevity of time he had left. She managed to voice a decree from behind a veil of tears that fell onto his chest, dampening his gown.

"I will find you again, in any life, in every universe; we *will* be together again. I am yours, and you are mine. We... we are *one*."

Their very essences, interwoven into a dance only they could comprehend, defiantly surpassed the constraints of space and time—a connection of cosmic proportions. For ages, he bore his traumas solo, without aid, to the point where he had dismissed the prospect of another easing his load. Not only had she freed him from the shadows of his negativity, but she also guided him toward a life of hope and fulfillment, revealing the true allure of existence.

The Husband blinked, resisting the welling tears, determined to maintain his composure for the sake of everyone—one last time. Gone were the spurts of panic, replaced instead by a troubling path of introspection that aimed to humble him.

From the outset of their relationship, an unspoken understanding enveloped him and his wife, setting them apart from the rest, that they carried an innate awareness of their uniqueness. At no point had they encountered a couple who could articulate parallel feelings, and the multitude of love stories that spanned the ages seemed to also pale in comparison.

Prior to the intrusion of his illness, they embraced the conviction that their love eclipsed the fundamental realities they understood. However, uncertainty crept into his thoughts, raising questions about the substance of their being. Despite his resolute faith in their love, *was it enough?*

He immersed himself in a profound inquiry, seeking to unravel the truth. Was finding that love and cherishing each moment the only test to achieve salvation? Or was he moored to illusions of fairytales and scriptures delivered by cultural naiveté? From their subjective measures, they were the epitome of eternal love, but he could not free himself from the thought regarding *who* or *what* passes final judgment.

Seized by a profound ache surpassing all previous torments, the Husband hovered in the delicate space between morphine drips. A novel desire for a swift transcendence possessed his weary soul. With unwavering certainty, he recognized that his battle had drawn to a close, the final act poised for its definitive conclusion—this was the undeniable curtain call. In the absence of subsequent scenes to unfold in the theater of life, the Husband now longed for that last exhale, the ultimate emancipation.

A deluge of intrusive thoughts inundated his mind, unsettling his peace and threatening to fracture his delicate equilibrium. If only the torrent of racing thoughts could abate, he could embrace the gentle closure of his eyes, relinquishing himself to the soothing calmness that awaited.

Even with a lifetime largely devoid of religious dogma, he found himself contemplating the possibility of an encounter with the Almighty, an ethereal rendezvous that beckoned from realms unknown. *Had the final account been settled, summoning him to a divine audience?* The day of reckoning—an encounter he perceived himself woefully unprepared for.

In his current prone state, he contemplated—just as he had done countless times before—whether he had lived up to the standards of virtue. And in the vast expanse of the universe, *who* held the scales of judgment? His sole certitude rested in the realization that his wife served as the driving force behind his relentless pursuit of moral growth, urging him to surpass the man he was the day before. She embodied the catalyst that breathed purpose into each new morning, infusing every dwindling moment of this fleeting life with profound meaning.

Tabula Rasa

What better reality could I have hoped for? His mind wondered.

For him, the opportunity to earn each passing second with her was only attainable through the pursuit of righteousness. Maybe he had already spent time in Heaven, and each subsequent reality was certainly Hell if it was void of her. Her presence reverberated through every fiber of his being, adding meaning to each moment.

With a gentle movement, the dying man adjusted his head, longing for the intimate exchange that awaited in the depths of his wife's eyes. Despite the gnawing uncertainties that tugged at his consciousness, her presence had an inexplicable power to soothe his troubled soul. Casting a glance upon her remarkable allure shattered any lingering sorrows, allowing a ray of hope and serenity to permeate the depths of the Husband's essence.

His lips quivered as he struggled to speak, initially mumbling to gain momentum before each sentence came to fruition.

"I-I'm *not* afraid."

Once more, tears found their passage down his face, but this time, they revealed a luminous flow emanating from the origins of gratitude. His existence was graced with joys that soared beyond the realm of expected, their radiant echoes defying the very constraints of imagination; each one was a note in the captivating melody of his existence. Concurrently, his communion with nature

381

remained wild, unfettered, and pure—a symphony forever in harmony with the planet's rhythm.

He now stood ready to pay his respects, offering them to whom they were rightly owed.

"T-thank you. Thank you for giving m-my life purpose and every day making me feel comfortable about who I am. Èvā a môr, baby. Forever and always."

"Oh, èvā a môr, my love. Èvā a môr."

the end

Epilogue

I am… I am…

Dead…

Physical sensory functions remained unavailable, but the Sentient was familiar with the conscious void he occupied, including complete memory of his life and afterlife voyage. While supremely aware of his existence, the Sentient felt orbital to a grander collective nucleus—diminutive esse within the crucible of the universe. It was evocative of sitting at an abated train station, aware of the presence of others but situated contently, comfortably descending into his own mental and emotional processes.

What happens next?

He asked himself, aware that an introspective discussion would ensue.

What do you want to happen?

I don't know… I just miss Her.

Amen.

His collection of thoughts and emotions were interrupted when the authoritative presence emerged once again.

Tabula Rasa

Presumably, your journey was enlightening. Dematerializing your body and orienting within this mindful void facilitates a genuine connection with yourself—essential to gain an undeniable understanding of the dichotomy within your consciousness.

The Rhetorician paused briefly. The Sentient was able to interject but remained silent, absorbing the details while feeling confused, but clarity was presque vu.

As one engages in inner dialogue, a sense of familiarity undeniably arises from those exchanges. Although this phenomenon is a common human experience, its remarkable nature often goes unnoticed; the act of introspection can be a crushing endeavor. Even more demanding is the task of delving deeply into one's inner self, remaining entirely present while suppressing all discourse, only then to achieve an authentic connection with cognition.

Expanding further, the Rhetorician continued.

The perception of one's reality is shaped by the complexities of consciousness and external stimuli, invariably leading to continuous dissonance in judgment. At times, an instinctual sense pulls one toward a specific path; on other occasions, the mind processes data to yield deductive conclusions—enigmatic forces vying for navigation rights and coercing influence. Human consciousness is never completely exclusive.

Slowly, the information began to coalesce in the Sentient's mind as it illuminated his awareness. Throughout his life, he often sensed intense polarity within his thoughts, where two distinct parts worked independently, yet, ostensibly toward the same purpose. Despite this unification, the Sentient could not comprehend the underlying motivation behind this duality.

Why are things this way?

The concept of a soul most accurately describes these circumstances. In a manner akin to the formation of a conscious entity, a soul is crafted with the primary aim of binding an untapped spirit to a newborn earthling. The soul plays a role in consciousness; one does not work without the other, similar to a crab and its shell—the soul and its carrier. Together, each entity creates the amalgamation of perception. The genesis of creativity is just one sublime example of the forces working together with human beings. Therefore, your afterlife journey had details idiosyncratic to your intrinsic nature as well as actual experiences specific to your soul's many odysseys on Earth. Invariably, humans have a penchant for drama. Even the most mundane scenarios emerge as embellished visualizations. Comparable to dreaming, allowing the mind to be wholly unfettered during a postmortem journey provides the subject with intense personal insight in conjunction with phantasmic scenarios. While one's odyssey may exemplify remarkableness, it is the integrity and character that make the individual extraordinary.

Throughout the Sentient's life, he was incessantly conscious of this "presence." Always accompanied, and yet despairingly unable to escape from; producing collaborative triumphs while also periodically confronting the terrors within—persistent discord over "living with himself." Voices competing for deliberation, a constant, tumultuous debate that fosters potent self-doubt; at times, so overwhelming that it creates desires to seek liberation from life's constraints, viewing escape as a more enticing option than the strenuous task of pushing onward in the face of adversity.

The Rhetorician continued.

As an individual's earthly life ceases, thus begins the assessment of their soul. Should it be concluded that the soul fell short in establishing a harmonious connection with others, it is then allocated to a new vessel. The influence that gives the carrier its vitality dematerializes into concentrated energy and then disperses throughout the universe. Fundamentally, the objective is the union of one soul and carrier—to fruition. A clean slate for every individual to embark on their existence in the world and cohabitate with the surrounding environment.

What happens if the objective is not met?

Travis Lane

A soul's essence is granted but a finite span of "time" on Earth to attain its salvation. Admittedly, the system has no control over the exploits of human nature. Existence on Earth is constantly amplifying its complexities in the pursuit of these objectives. Unquestionably, this escalation augments the challenge for the soul to maintain harmony; as it inhabits more carriers, its moral compass grows increasingly disrupted. Some souls, so deeply distress, burden and torment every vessel they come to occupy— propagating self-loathing, pity, pain, and hatred until exhausted to a state of visceral numbness.

The Sentient had experienced all the cynicisms of life. Navigating to the best of his abilities with the tools provided, he stumbled relentlessly. Paying heed to internal dialogue is a turbulent procession. But his equilibrium was achieved from an external voice of reason. *Was it enough to reach salvation?*

Though the soul's essence is frequently relayed to a new carrier, it does not assure emphatic intervention. Every carrier, irrespective of its predecessors, is blessed with renewed opportunities. A fresh start. There is an opportunity to position oneself within a nurturing environment and among individuals committed to encouraging growth and aiding in self-actualization. Indeed, each new dawn brings with it the chance to rewrite one's story, to alter one's course, and to manifest a change that can steer one's journey toward their truest potential.

The Sentient recognized the importance of the impact others had on his life. So easily could the toxicity of people lead one down the paths of personal destruction and communal affliction. Conversely, the necessary antagonists that promote competition and the advocates who render support, pave the way for betterment. The obstacle is recognizing judicious judgment.

Echoes from previous carriers remain constant throughout a soul's journey—discreetly orbiting in the nearly indiscernible atmosphere. These residual resonances held significant sway in the journey you undertook. You designed scenarios and worlds with immense detail by unconsciously designing an intricate web of history, imagination, and the realities your most recent carrier experienced. Life on Earth sees its inhabitants ebbing and flowing through a series of roles they choose to engage in, and benevolence is, by no means, universal and is as susceptible to fractures and misinterpretations as any other characteristic. At disparate coordinates on the timeline, your essence may not have been graced with the optimal influences to behave prudently. However, during your temporal existence, you harbored something distinct.

A whirlwind of thoughts and emotions struck him in a kaleidoscopic convulsion. This emotional maelstrom flung wide the doors of enlightenment. Acknowledging the entwined relationship between his life and the contours of his journey, the Sentient questioned the degree of authenticity of his experiences and how much was the spawn of his imagination. Were his aspirations to become a leader and a luminary unique to him, or merely echoes of his predecessors?

He then contemplated his choices during his "time" on Earth and questioned the magnitude of impact each minute decision had. The gravity of every decision and interaction manifested themselves to him in a haunting, yet enlightening manner. Yet, amidst the turmoil, he possessed something unique.

The beings with whom you surrounded yourself with either aided, wounded, tested, and molded your essence. Yet, it was Her influence that was the most profound on your existence. In your previous life and throughout your quest for salvation, you sought Her guidance to lead you on a virtuous path. Even during your bleakest moments, you always discovered the righteous route with Her assistance. In the end, your achievement of salvation would have been unattainable without Her guiding hand.

With no meaning, his life felt lost—near "visceral numbness." Devoid of purpose, he acted indifferently to his surroundings—a state of unworthiness, nudging him toward poor judgments. His world came into focus when she graced his life. Every facet of his decency was a reflection of her influence.

He realized he had never matched the radiant goodness she brought into his life, and it tormented him to contemplate the challenges her soul must have faced. He consistently reminded her that she had always been his savior, but would she ever truly comprehend the magnitude of her love's accomplishments?

Why are humans given the ability to comprehend so much about their life, love, past, present, future and beyond, but we are still so frail?

Humanity, in concert with its surrounding ecosystem, is gifted with all the essential elements required to fashion a utopia; everything necessary to construct an existence so filled with abundance and virtue that the idea of an afterlife would be arbitrary. A reality that has been spoiled. What you unearthed in your most recent life is evidence of the perpetual forces at work within the universe. Bonds that invariably find their way back to each other, no matter the distances traversed in the realms of existence. Yet, comprehension of this remains largely limited. The energy that fuels all existence is not bound by the constructs of time. It courses unpredictably along a continuum composed of space and time, aiming to achieve sentience. This same energy is what brought you and Her together on Earth. A force that remains elusive to human understanding, but one that was momentarily, but undoubtedly, glimpsed and experienced in Her gaze. This power has safeguarded the core of your consciousness through countless circumstances.

The Rhetorician paused, letting the words settle, but the Sentient's yearning for understanding remained, pleading for further elucidation. While he had attained "deliverance," his heart remained ensnared by the overwhelming need for Her happiness and liberation. His existence, his very essence, was intertwined so profoundly with Her that his life held meaning only in the lift of her presence. Salvation was a barren concept, a hollow victory, if Her serene rhythm did not beat alongside his.

Before he could marshal his thoughts into a coherent inquiry, the Rhetorician broke the silence.

Thy soul, having journeyed through the cosmos, shall finally be granted respite. No longer will it be cast adrift, haphazardly navigating the expanses of the universe. Instead, it will be anchored to its counterpart, forging an eternal, unbreakable bond.

For the Sentient, his counterpart, his soul's mirror was *Her*. In other spans of existence, she appeared differently. Sometimes as a guiding light, sometimes as a resonating echo, but always a meaningful presence shaping his journey in unseen ways. He felt immersed in the reverberations of gratitude from the many avenues of his consciousness for having discovered this ethereal bond.

He had danced in a terrestrial paradise, his footprints marking a Heaven on Earth that was entirely sculpted by Her. He, in his wholeness, was fated for tranquility, destined for an eternity of peace. Everything that came to be, every bit of him that evolved and grew, bore the indelible mark of Her sculpting hands, shaping him meticulously and relentlessly. As the resonance of his past quieted, he nurtured one final thought.

I am… I am…

*I am, because **we** are.*

Made in the USA
Las Vegas, NV
28 January 2024